**Praise for Benny and the Bank Robber:**

"Looked like a kid's book. It really surprised me with a lot of interesting twists and being deeply spiritual."

"... Heart wrenching to imagine what Benny was going through, but uplifting to watch the way he grew into his faith."

"Emotionally charged front to back!"

"It deserves a ten star and recommend to everyone. Lots of valuable lessons."

"Story that readers of any age can enjoy. The adventure and excitement will keep a reader engrossed."

# Doctor Dad
# Benny and the Bank Robber 2

**by**

**Mary C. Findley**

*Doctor Dad:Benny and the Bank Robber 2*







Findley Family Video Publications

"Speaking the truth in love."

## Table of Contents

## If you haven't read *Benny and the Bank Robber ...*

Benny Richardson found the drunken hit-and run cart driver who killed his father in Philadelphia, but Benny's mother still said they must move to frontier Missouri. From active church services, classical concerts and university lectures, ten-year-old Benny began the bleak trip to a life on a frontier farm with his Uncle Tom and Aunt Caroline. Slow trains, slower barges and rain, filled Benny's days with misery and his heart with anger against God.

A mudslide smashed their barge and left Benny alone with his injured mother. Benny's first impulse was still to pray. Did God send fellow traveler John Clancy to get a doctor for Benny's mother? As grateful as Benny might be, the man was a mystery he couldn't begin to solve. A hidden bag of disguises, laughing ways that vanished in a heartbeat along with painted freckles and a disappearing Irish accent were bad enough. A hardened contempt for the Bible made Mr. Clancy exactly the kind of person Benny wanted to avoid. His mother needed surgery and a long recovery. She begged Mr. Clancy to take Benny to Missouri.

Benny started to discover more frightening things about Mr. Clancy. Suddenly became a prisoner of a card-playing, knife-throwing bank robber with a savage black stallion and a grudge of his own against God for letting his $10,000 in stolen gold sink in the Conemaugh River.

Jeremy Carlisle knew how to survive, on flatboats, at backwoods farms, in the woods where no one could help Benny escape. Finding the lost gold almost cost Jeremy his life, but he ignored Benny's insistence that God wanted Jeremy to live to accept Jesus Christ. Jeremy taunted Benny about how no one would believe the "bank robber" story. He also reminded Benny of how far away God seemed and how little the boy knew about His Word. By the time they crossed the Mississippi River his faith was failing fast. He liked and admired the bank robber, enjoying his wonderful songs and comic acting bits. Jeremy's invitation to keep traveling with him grew more and more tempting.

A "Cougar Evangelist" forced Jeremy and Benny to stop and listen to God's Word as they stayed with Doc Daniel, a solitary scholar with a deep knowledge of the Scriptures and infinite patience to care for physical and spiritual hurts. Jeremy finally found Christ and surrendered. A trial for kidnapping with Benny's mother as the star witness almost destroyed any hope Jeremy might have for the future. Benny reunited with his mother and his aunt and uncle and took up farm life with more peace and joy than he could have imagined, until the news of Jeremy's ten-year prison sentence set him to questioning God all over again.

Still, Benny found an unlikely new friend in Jason Owens, son of a Philadelphia brick maker, and an astounding legacy of his dead father on a birthday never to be forgotten. A new school in Osage brought the new trial of a relentless bully. When Caleb Sutter, the violent son of a drunken thief, lost his family, Benny found God prompting him to ask his mother to adopt his persecutor. God had other plans for Caleb, to Benny's relief, and his life went on with an exciting horse race and a nagging surprise Jeremy would only hint about in his cryptic letter.

(But, there's much more to the story than this brief summary!)

## Chapter One -- Something's Wrong

Benny Richardson followed his friend Jeremy out of the farmhouse where he and his mother lived with Benny's Uncle Tom and Aunt Caroline in southern Missouri near the town of Osage. They had just come home from Jefferson City, where they had met their friends Daniel Connors, Junior, and his wife Elizabeth. Dan, who was a lawyer in Virginia, had given them the biggest surprise of their lives.

Jeremy Carlisle, who had become a Christian after a series of adventures traveling with Benny, had been pardoned and released after serving only two years of his ten-year prison sentence in Philadelphia. Jeremy had confessed to stealing from the bank where he had worked. Benny and his mother had found Jeremy waiting at the rented house in Jefferson City where Dan and Elizabeth were staying, and now after a week they had brought him home to the farm with them.

Doc Daniel, Dan Connors' father, had made the trip back to Osage with them also, but he had already left them to ride home, another twenty miles distant. They had finished unhitching the cart and unloading their bags and the supplies Uncle Tom had picked up in Jefferson City. Uncle Tom led the horses away to the pasture. Benny's mother and Aunt Caroline shooed them outside so they could start dinner preparations. Benny's best friend Jason Owens and his father Carl drove up at that moment. The wagon stopped dead in the barnyard. Father and son looked down at Benny and Jeremy. Jason's eyes got wider and wider under his mop of red hair. His freckles stood out as his face got whiter and whiter. Carl Owens quickly got down and came up to Jeremy, hand outstretched. He was shorter than Jeremy but he didn't hesitate to look him straight in the face.

"You must be the famous Jeremy Carlisle," he said. "Welcome. I'm Carl Owens. That's my son Jason. We heard everybody was back. The wife wanted me to send over a couple of pies and say welcome home."

"Thanks, Mr. Owens," Benny said. "Yep, this is Jeremy. Hi, Jason." He quickly carried the basket with the pies into the house and set them on the kitchen table.

When Benny came back outside, Jason had not moved from the wagon seat. He simply stared. His father walked around and said something to him. Jason tried to look somewhere else, but his eyes kept coming back to Jeremy's face. His father slapped him between the shoulderblades like he had when Jason had come to Benny's birthday party. Jason almost fell off the wagon seat, but it made no difference. He didn't even try to get down to talk to Benny. He just sat and stared at Jeremy's face.

Carl Owens made some small talk to Jeremy and Ben. When Uncle Tom returned he shook hands with him and chatted a little longer. Jason never moved or said a word. Benny knew he was going to get a licking when he got home. Carl Owens said his good-byes and they left. Uncle Tom went off to the barn pshawing and waving Benny away when he asked if there was anything Uncle Tom needed help with. Jeremy sank down on the porch and rested his forearms on his knees, covering his face up.

"Jeremy, Jason just needs to get used to it," Benny whispered. "Don't be mad."

"Mad!" Jeremy raised his head just a little. "I'm not mad, Ben. I just sort of forgot about it. But it's going to keep happening everywhere I go. How can I be a doctor or a preacher -- traveling, meeting people all the time ..."

"'Be not afraid of their faces,'" Benny quoted, "'for I have overcome them.'"

"It's more likely they'll be afraid of my face," Jeremy grunted.

“I found some other verses.” Benny dug in his pocket and pulled out his father’s Bible. “‘His visage was so marred, more than any man, and his form more than the sons of man ... he was despised and rejected of men, a man of sorrows, and acquainted with grief, and we hid as it were our faces from him; he was despised and we esteemed him not.’”

“Ben ... Ben, why are you reading that? There isn’t much comparison between the Lord Jesus Christ and me.”

“Let me finish and I’ll tell you. ‘He was wounded for our transgressions, he was bruised for our iniquities: the chastisement of our peace was upon Him, and with His stripes we are healed.’

“Jeremy, I know you’re not Jesus and you didn’t die for my sins, but I can’t stop thinking it was my fault the cougar attacked you. I think about how I was rebelling against going to Uncle Tom’s, and how much trouble I caused because I couldn’t accept God’s will. And you got in the cougar’s way and made him attack you instead of me.”

Jeremy put an arm around Benny and hugged him tightly. “The Lord God of Heaven sent that cougar. He is perfect in wisdom. Maybe it came after both of us. But since we both know God forgives sins, we’d just better stop beating ourselves up over the consequences that don’t go away.”

*****

Jeremy sprang up off the porch. He leaped over the pasture fence and ran across the field to where Black Switch grazed near the apple orchard. The horse perked up and watched him approach. He took a few dainty steps, trotted, then broke into a gallop.

Jeremy halted, but the stallion didn’t even slow down. He piled into Jeremy and knocked him flat. Even then he surged forward, pushing Jeremy with his head, snorting, whinnying, dancing around him.

Jeremy rolled away, all the way back down the slope, with Black Switch cantering after him. At the bottom Switch lay down and had a good roll himself. Jeremy draped himself across the horse as he lay belly-up on the grass and laughed himself to exhaustion.

"I thought maybe he'd forget you," Benny panted as he ran up and dropped on the grass beside them. "Guess he didn't."

Black Switch snorted, waved his hooves, then rolled onto his feet. Jeremy still lay on the ground. Switch prodded him with his nose until he got up, then sidled up to him until his hands rested on the horse's back.

"He wants you to go for a ride," Benny prompted.

"I haven't been on a horse in two years," Jeremy murmured. He ran his hands over Black Switch's glossy coat. "I'd forgotten how beautiful you are, old man. The first time I saw this horse, Ben, I knew I had to have him. I changed my whole plan. I risked everything to get him. Yes, my beauty, I did, didn't I?"

Jeremy grabbed a hank of shoulder mane and swung up onto Switch bareback. The horse burst into a gallop and they were out of sight in a moment. Benny loped back across the pasture and found that Uncle Tom was suddenly agreeable to some help with the chores, after all.

*****

"Uncle Tom, did you see how well Black Switch remembered Jeremy?" Benny laughed as he helped him transfer feedbags from where they had placed them just inside the barn door to the storage room. "He knows him even with a different face, and he loves him!"

"Bah!" growled Uncle Tom. "A horse knows somebody by his smell, not how he looks. And as for loving, well, a horse just needs grass' and brushin'. Lovin' a person, now that takes some work, and not everybody's ready to take on that work, no matter what they might feel like they want."

Benny finished helping Uncle Tom in silence, wondering what that outburst meant. Something funny had been going on all week, with whispered conferences between the adults. They had all been so happy to learn Jeremy was free, but something had happened that very first day, and although his mother, Jeremy, and all the

Connors had continued to be cheerful around Benny there were many sad and even angry looks passing between people when Uncle Tom and Aunt Caroline were around. Benny had never seen either of them do anything but be kind and hospitable, except for Uncle Tom's occasional fits of gruffness now and then. Aunt Caroline, in fact, seemed more anxious to hug Benny and his mother than ever before. She was doing it really often, and seeming like she was trying not to cry. Benny's mother seemed to be trying not to cry, too, but whenever Benny asked what was wrong Jeremy or Dan or Doc Daniel would pull him away to the study to look at more maps of the way west.

Benny had been through enough times of trouble and heartache to know it when he saw it tumbling into his life yet again. He was sure nobody had died. Nobody had even been hurt, except that Dan Connors had pinched his fingers when the piano lid had crashed down on them while he played a rollicking song for Jeremy and Benny's mother the night after their arrival. Everyone had been crowded around the instrument enjoying the performance, Jeremy and his mother standing close together and blending their voices so nicely.

But all of a sudden Uncle Tom had banged on the piano and stalked away, which was what had made the lid drop on Dan's fingers. Uncle Tom had hardly even apologized, but Aunt Caroline had, over and over, nursing Dan's fingers with cold water and vinegar and trying not to cry again. Whatever it was, it had something to do with Uncle Tom, and, Benny had to admit, something to do with Jeremy.

*****

When the barn chores were done, Benny saw that Jeremy had returned in time to give Black Switch his food and water and a good currying before supper.

"Ma'am, this food is wonderful," Jeremy said to Aunt Caroline as they sat down to fried chicken and mashed potatoes. He turned to Uncle Tom. "I noticed you had Switch bled."

"Err ... he was ailing a bit," Uncle Tom admitted. "He's fine now, though."

"I can see that he is. I plan to pay you back for his keep. I can't tell you how grateful I am for your trouble."

"He's a good horse," Uncle Tom said, embarrassed. "I'm afraid you'll find he's ... developed a sweet tooth, though. Ben must have been sneaking it to him."

Benny hadn't told Jeremy about Switch's illness or Uncle Tom's "sugar therapy." He'd have to explain it later.

Jeremy was silent a few minutes. Benny could see that he was troubled once again by Uncle Tom and Aunt Caroline's efforts to keep their eyes away from his face.

"I found a cabin back over the hill past the orchard," Jeremy said finally. "Is that where you lived when you first came out, sir?"

"Ah, my bachelor digs," Uncle Tom chuckled. "It's rough, but it's solid."

"I was wondering if I might stay there while I'm visiting," Jeremy suggested. "Your house is crowded enough with family."

"Well, now, as a matter of fact, I was going to say we've been out to clean and fix it up. Stocked up some provisions -- flour, salt, a little bacon and beans. There's wood to split. You'd even have the lean-to to keep your horse nearby, if you like. There's a well, and everything you need." Uncle Tom and Aunt Caroline both looked very relieved.

"Sounds first-rate," Jeremy smiled. "I figure I can do my own cooking over there so I won't be in the way."

"You're -- you're welcome at our table anytime, Mr. Carlisle," Aunt Caroline stammered. "We don't mean to drive you out. Truly we don't. Thomas, tell him --!"

"Ma'am, there's no need." Jeremy pushed back from the table. "You folks have been kinder to me than anyone on Earth has ever been. I think I'll retire now."

## Chapter Two – My Best Man's Mother

"Mother, I want to know what wedding Jeremy was talking about back in Jefferson City," Benny finally said to his mother about midmorning the next day, after the chores and breakfast and washing up were finished until lunch preparations began. Benny's mother had just put some dough at the back of the stove to rise. "I've been asking people all week, and they always found something else to talk about."

"Oh, yes, darling, let's take a walk and we will talk about that wedding." Benny's mother led him off across the meadow behind the house. They walked arm in arm in the spring sunshine. "I've never walked down this path," his mother said. "Isn't this a pretty little wood?"

Benny wondered why his mother was acting so funny. He wanted to ask again about this wedding. He'd already been waiting a whole week, though the time had gone by fast, with Jeremy free and back with them and so much to catch up on. The subject had come up in Benny's mind a few times but somehow both Jeremy and his mother had managed to change the subject and make Benny forget about it when he asked.

Like now, for example. His mother was too busy acting like a schoolgirl, skipping through the trees, picking flowers, crossing a stream on stepping-stones. Benny hadn't gone this far into the woods before in this direction, either. They stopped above a kind of gorge with a fast-flowing river below. A waterfall cascaded over the rocks and sprayed the trees.

"Oh, Benny, look how beautiful it is down there," his mother said. "I think we could climb down, don't you?"

Before Benny could answer, his mother slipped and tumbled down the slope.

"Mother!" Benny cried. He couldn't even see where she had gone, and started to move forward.

"Benny, stop," His mother's voice ordered. "Stop. Listen to me." Benny leaned out a little. He saw the edge of his mother's dress trailing in the rushing stream. "Don't come down here," she said calmly. "I can't move, and there's no place for you to even stand. You'll have to get help. There must be another way to get down here. Go and find help."

"Mother, I can't leave you."

"Benny, I'm just barely hanging on. There's something wrong with my arm. You have to hurry."

Benny turned and ran. He had lost his sense of direction and realized he wasn't even heading back toward Uncle Tom's farm.

*****

He stumbled through the trees and burst out on the hillside above Osage. Looking wildly around, he spotted a tall figure crossing the street.

"Caleb! Caleb Prentice!" Benny shouted. Caleb looked up and saw Benny. He started to turn away. "Caleb, please. My mother's in the river gorge over the hill," Benny breathed, chasing after Caleb and grabbing hold of him. Caleb shook him off.

"Get away from me, Richardson." Benny had feared and avoided Caleb ever since they had first met, when Caleb had tried to force Benny to pay to enter the schoolhouse. Caleb had caught Benny and beaten him badly once, a thing Benny had managed to keep hidden from almost everyone. He couldn't forget how much Caleb had always hated him, and Benny avoided him as much as he could, but he had no choice this time.

"Caleb. Listen to me. My mother will die if you don't help her. Is there another way to get down to the river?"

Caleb seemed to actually hear him at last. "Your mother? What's she doing in the gorge?"

"She fell off the path behind Uncle Tom's farm. Please, help me!"

“Come on,” Caleb loped off across the slope. They came into the tree line almost a half-mile below where Benny thought he had left his mother. Benny was having trouble keeping up with Caleb. His long legs ate up the ground. Benny followed as best he could.

They splashed along the edge of the river and started upstream. It was shallow and rocky where they got in, but farther up it became almost like rapids.

“I see her.” Caleb breathed.

“Where?” Benny strained to look. Caleb stepped out farther and almost lost his footing.

“There. She must’ve slipped down from where you left her. It was just below the waterfall, right?”

“How’d you know?”

“It’s such a pretty spot. You’d want to get down, and think you could make it.” Benny saw his mother huddled under an outcropping of rock, clinging with one hand to a dead tree below the waterfall.

“Mrs. Richardson!” Caleb pulled off the jacket he wore and threw it onto the bank. He shouted over the rush of water. “Mrs. Richardson!” Benny’s mother turned her head and saw them.

“Listen to me,” Caleb said calmly. He unfastened his belt and pulled it out. “I’ll need yours too,” he told Benny. Benny quickly gave it to him. Caleb fastened them together. “Can you grab hold of this belt?” He asked Benny’s mother, swinging it toward her.

“I’m sorry ... I’ve hurt my arm. If I let go, I’ll fall.”

Caleb felt his way forward a few steps. Benny followed. Caleb slipped the end of one of the belts around a stout young tree and made a slipknot with the other buckle.

“Here’s what you have to do,” he said, speaking to Benny without looking at him. “Grab hold of the belt and swing yourself over to that rock. It’s going to be slick, so watch it. Get her up somehow, and try to pass her down to me. Use the belt as a safety line. Don’t let go of it. The river will suck you down in two seconds. Here.”

Caleb shrugged out of his shirt like lightning. “Tie this under her arms and onto the end of the belt. That should keep her from going in.”

Benny waded forward. Caleb grabbed him by the shoulder as he slid and went under. Choking, Benny felt himself being set on his feet again. "No time to go swimming, Richardson. Get moving." Benny crept over to the rock where his mother lay. She made only a little whimpering noise when he passed the shirt under her arms. He had already tied one sleeve to the belt, and he knotted the other in place a moment later.

"Pray, mother," Benny whispered, and pulled her up. His feet almost went out from under him again, but he stayed up and swung his mother over to where Caleb stood poised in the fastest part of the stream. Benny could never have kept his feet and caught the full weight of his mother in that current. For once he was glad for Caleb's strength.

Caleb struggled to the little strip of bank, dragging Benny's mother. Her skirts were heavy with water and Caleb shivered in the icy spray. Benny stumbled after him and they unfastened the belts and set off downstream, supporting his mother between them. "Tell your mother to try a few less petticoats," Caleb grunted as they lurched and staggered along.

*****

Doctor Shepherd opened his door to them and Benny thought he was going to fall down dead right in front of them.

"What's happened?" he asked feebly.

"My arm -- I can't move it," Benny's mother said weakly. They laid her on the couch in the doctor's sitting room. He took one look and then stared at the two boys.

"Her shoulder's been dislocated. It must be put back into place. I -- don't have the strength," he faltered.

"Caleb?" Benny asked. The older boy paled.

"No, no, it takes knowledge of how to do it, too." Dr. Shepherd shook his head.

"Maybe Jeremy could do it, Doctor Shepherd," Benny said. "You know -- the man Doc Daniel told you about. We brought him home with us. He's at my uncle's house."

"Perhaps. Perhaps he could. I'll need Sally Grimsby as well."

"Caleb, I have to go to my Uncle Tom's. Please, can you stay here with Dr. Shepherd in case he needs help before I get back?" Benny hurried out into the entryway, then realized that Caleb had followed him.

Benny stared up at him. Caleb was a head taller than Benny. Without his shirt Benny could see his heavily muscled arms and shoulders. Benny tried to go out the door but Caleb stopped him.

"You are pushing me 'way past what I ever thought I would take from you, Richardson," Caleb said. "I'm catching a ride to go to Ohio for school at three o'clock. I can't miss it." Benny looked at the stained, soggy clothing Caleb wore and realized it had been a fine traveling suit.

"Caleb, I'm sorry," Benny said. "I really am. I don't know what else to do. I'll hurry as fast as I can."

*****

Benny took Dr. Shepherd's old horse and pushed the animal as fast as he dared. He sped off to the farm. Uncle Tom, Aunt Caroline, and Jeremy were shocked when Benny rode up on the doctor's old horse, soaked and exhausted.

"Jeremy, Doctor Shepherd needs help. You've got to come right away."

"Ben, where's your mother?"

"She's there. Hurry, Jeremy!"

"Show me the way, Ben," Jeremy urged when he had jumped on Black Switch and they had turned back toward Osage. "Can't that old nag go any faster?"

Benny was finally able to point out Dr. Shepherd's place to Jeremy. Black Switch tore out ahead. Benny stopped at the house of Mrs. Grimsby, the town midwife, and told her what had happened. When Benny finally got off at the doctor's horse, Caleb was hurrying down the front steps.

"Thank you, Caleb," Benny said. "You saved my mother's life." He held out a hand.

Caleb turned away, gripping his ruined clothes. "If it had been you, Richardson, I'd've let you drown. Get out of my way."

*****

Jeremy was kneeling beside Benny's mother as she lay on Dr. Shepherd's sitting room couch wrapped in a blanket. Dr. Shepherd came out of his examining room. He looked so old and frail.

"Ben," Jeremy whispered. "What happened?"

"She fell," Benny said simply.

"Let's talk later," Dr. Shepherd said, rallying the little strength he had.

"What -- what's wrong --?"Jeremy persisted.

"Dislocation of the shoulder. Come, now, my boy. It shouldn't be that difficult."

"Doctor Shepherd, this lady -- I -- can't do this."

"Just as Daniel said. Too softhearted. Young man, a doctor can't always just give a dose of sugar and make everything all right. Sometimes you must cause pain to help. Make up your mind if you really mean to be a doctor."

"I'd do it -- I'd do it for anyone else -- but her --"

"There isn't any time for this," snapped Doctor Shepherd. "I had to tend my own wife as she lay dying. I couldn't make her well, and I caused her pain every day. Mrs. Richardson isn't going to die, and you can help her. Get on with it."

Jeremy took a deep breath. He knelt beside Benny's mother and picked a dead leaf gently out of her hair. She stirred and opened her eyes. "Mrs. Richardson, what have you done to yourself?" Jeremy asked.

"I've caused such a lot of trouble," she said. "Look at Benny. He'll have pneumonia."

"Dear lady, do you ever think about yourself at all? Where do you want to put her, Doctor Shepherd?"

"In my consulting room," the doctor gestured. Jeremy lifted Benny's mother from the couch and bore her into the next room. He placed her on the high table. Benny tried not to listen to her small cries of pain.

"Now what?" Jeremy asked.

"I've sent for Sally Grimsby," the doctor said. "There has to be a woman present. She must be undressed, of course."

Jeremy swallowed hard. Benny heard a sharp knock and let in Sally Grimsby. She followed Benny into the consulting room, looked around, and gaped in horror when she saw Jeremy's face. But when she saw Benny's mother, she suddenly became all business.

"Draw these curtains," she ordered, and then did it herself before anyone could react, grabbing the drapes that hung on a runner and could be pulled around the table. "All you men, eyes around."

Sally disappeared behind the curtain and they heard Benny's mother cry out.

"So sorry, dear heart," Sally soothed. "There's a lot more hurt to go through, I'm afraid. You try to be strong for your boy out there."

She poked her head out and glared at the men. "Who's to come in?" She demanded. "Doctor, I know you must. What about him?" She jerked her head at Jeremy.

"My -- uh -- my new assistant, Sally," the doctor explained.

"Such goings on!" Sally said. "Here." She opened the curtains partway. Benny's mother lay wrapped in a sheet, only her head and injured arm exposed. "Get on with it, then."

Benny saw the look on Jeremy's face and was sure he had never seen him so white. He stepped forward with the doctor without hesitating, though. Dr. Shepherd administered a dose of laudanum.

"That seems like a lot," Jeremy said.

"Second dose," Dr. Shepherd muttered. "I gave her some when they first brought her in," he explained. "She has an unusually strong will, though, and I don't think I can put her under completely. We shall have to try to distract her."

Jeremy put out a hand and touched Benny's mother on the shoulder. She moaned. He pulled his hand back, but glanced at the doctor and reached forward again.

"Abigail, sing with me," Jeremy said softly.

Benny's mother opened listless eyes. "What shall we sing?" she asked dreamily.

"I Sing the Mighty Power of God. All the verses."

Dr. Shepherd's directions were calm and quiet. Jeremy picked up Benny's mother's arm and braced himself, and Sally took up a position on the opposite side of the bed. Benny's mother began to sing and Jeremy joined in.

*****

By the time it was over, Benny found himself weeping in Mrs. Grimsby's arms. He looked up and saw tears in the stout, hard-faced woman's eyes too. Sally pushed him gently away and drew the curtains shut as the three of them left the table.

"Sally will stay?" Jeremy asked the doctor. "I've got to go get her brother and sister-in-law. They don't even know what's happened."

"As long as I'm needed," the grim-faced woman said. "You're quite a fellow. Must be the one she's been sweet on so long. Couldn't figure an angel like that lovin' a convict. Specially lookin' like you. But I guess I see what she sees in you now."

Jeremy hugged Benny and they walked out to Black Switch. "We can't take that poor old fellow back," Jeremy said, patting the doctor's horse. "Put him away, Ben, and we'll ride double on Switch. I think he can handle it that far."

After the horse was taken care of, Jeremy socked Benny in the arm. "You didn't tell me it was your mother Dr. Shepherd needed help with," Jeremy exclaimed. "You saved your mother's life, boy," he said, rumpling Benny's still-mud-caked hair. "You know that, don't you?"

"It was Caleb Prentice," Benny said. "He knew the way to get her. He helped me all the way."

"Caleb," Jeremy laughed. Benny had shared the story of his struggles with the town bully in his letters to Jeremy in prison. "Who would've thought it? God does work in mysterious ways, doesn't he?"

Benny stopped in the act of getting on Black Switch.

“Jeremy, what did you mean about attending a wedding soon?” Benny asked. “Mother was finally going to tell me, but she didn’t get a chance.”

“Why, it’s my wedding, Ben. Want to be my best man?” Jeremy grinned.

“Who are you gonna marry, Jeremy?”

“My best man’s mother,” replied Jeremy.

“You’re going to marry mother?” Benny exclaimed. “And we can all go west together?”

“If that’s all right with you.”

Benny hugged Jeremy. “It’s all right with me, sure!”

## Chapter Three – "I Make All Things New"

Uncle Tom and Aunt Caroline had come into Osage with the wagon to bring Benny's mother home. They put her quickly to bed. She slept through the whole next day.

"Shouldn't we get Doc Shepherd over here to check on her?" Uncle Tom fretted.

"She's all right, Mr. Laughlin. Really she is," Jeremy assured him. "I know I'm not a doctor, but she just needs rest and time to recover. Dr. Shepherd will be by in a day or two, and we can get him here sooner if she changes. Come on, Ben. Let's get out from underfoot."

"So, you asked mother about getting married and she said yes?" Benny asked excitedly. Jeremy nodded, but he didn't seem all that happy now. They wandered around in the yard. "Well then, when are you and mother going to get married?" Benny asked. The front porch was becoming their regular "talking place," so they sat down on the steps together again.

"Ah, Ben, it seemed so easy in my nice, safe prison cell to fall in love with your beautiful mother, and the first time I saw her again to ask her to marry me. But your good Uncle Tom has given me a little advice on that subject which I can't ignore."

He glanced up at the porch door and saw that no one seemed likely to come out immediately. He removed a folded paper from his pocket.

"Tom apparently wasn't aware your mother would agree to marry me, and this morning he handed me this letter."

*My sister is a sweet-natured, unselfish woman,* Jeremy read aloud. *She would give her whole heart to anything she made up her mind to do. She'd kill herself trying to do a thing before she'd give up.*

*Here's what you're offering my sister with marriage to you: A life of endless hard work, clearing land, building, digging a well; and she'll work right beside you.*

*Then you'll travel to preach or tend sick folks and she'll be alone for days or weeks. That's how Daniel Connors did it. He had a beautiful young wife once. She loved him, worked with him, waited for him, and buried four children alone because he couldn't even make it home to preach at their gravesides. He did manage to be around to bury her, though.*

*'I believe men are supposed to protect women, especially if they love them. My Caroline stayed safe in Pennsylvania while I cleared our land and lived in a little shack of a cabin until I had a proper home and a producing farm to bring her to.*

*Abigail used to have comforts and security while she was growing up in our family. She struggled all through that marriage to a poor teacher. She had to clean other peoples' houses to make the rent on that tiny apartment they had. I had to learn from my nephew what they went through after Jonathan Richardson died. I swore she'd never want or suffer like that again.*

*I must stand opposed to this marriage, and I will do everything in my power to prevent it.*

Jeremy took a deep breath after he had finished reading Uncle Tom's letter to Benny.

"He's right, of course. I haven't really got a thing to offer your mother. A prison record, a face to frighten children, no property, no money – and there's every hardship facing your mother and you that your uncle says here besides. I have nothing much to look forward to at all."

*****

He jumped up and went to chop some more wood, although it seemed to Benny that they already had a month's supply. Benny got up to follow him, but then saw that his mother stood looking out the porch door, her arm in a sling.

"Does he miss having all that hard work to do like when he was in prison?" Benny asked. "Why does he keep chopping so much wood?"

"Sometimes when something's troubling you, the best way to get your mind off it is to sweat it away," Benny's mother sighed, coming out and sitting on the porch swing. Benny sat beside her.

"Mother, Uncle Tom doesn't want you to marry Jeremy," Benny said. "Are you going to marry him anyway? Jeremy said we could go west with him. Jeremy and I will make sure you don't have to work too hard. He read me that mean letter Uncle Tom wrote, and he was so sad."

"Darling, I think Uncle Tom really expected me to stay on the farm and let him take care of me for the rest of my life. We've had several talks. I've told him that only God knows what's best for me. He's made me stronger, I think, through all these hard times we've had. Perhaps I couldn't have survived the kind of life we'll have with Jeremy before.

His mother hesitated and took his hand, squeezing it tightly. "And in spite of the frightening times you had to go through before Jeremy became saved, don't you believe that God provided him, as strong and clever as he is, knowing how to survive and teaching you all those things about protecting yourself and camping in the woods? You're such a different boy, stronger and wiser, and most especially, we have both learned to love and depend on the Lord more, and we know His Word better.

"So I am convinced that God gave our Jeremy to us, and I do not mean to let him go. I will marry him, and I will help him become a doctor and a preacher of the Word, and a pioneer, and whatever else God may want."

*****

Benny woke up early the next and looked out the loft window. He could see the small cabin across the field. Jeremy was already out chopping wood again. He hadn't come to the farmhouse for supper, though Benny had wanted to go get him. Uncle Tom had looked like a thunderstorm ready to burst out with lighting and an angry downpour, so he hadn't said anything. But he was done avoiding Jeremy just because it might make Uncle Tom drop something on somebody's fingers again.

Benny dressed quickly, climbed down the ladder, slipped out of the house, and was about to break into a run when his mother called to him from the kitchen door. She handed him a warm linen-wrapped bundle.

"Fresh biscuits and ham," she said. "Enough for both of you. Grab a bucket of milk from the dairy, and tell Jeremy I love him."

Jeremy was very happy to receive both the breakfast and the message. They sat down to pray and a heavy thumping on the door made them both jump.

"I've come to visit the free man!" thundered Doc Daniel. He almost filled the small room until he sat down and produced his own breakfast in a napkin.

"This place is much nicer than when Tom lived here," Doc Daniel said appreciatively. "That little woman back in the kitchen seems a bit fond of you, Jeremy. I thought you might not have noticed." Jeremy just grinned.

"I've had this thing knocking around my place a couple of years." Doc Daniel produced a flat leather bag attached to a belt. Benny realized that it was Jeremy's makeup and disguises kit.

"I won't have any use for this," Jeremy shrugged.

"Not so fast." Doc Daniel stopped him from tossing the bag under the small bed. "I also brought you a mirror. I see there's none here. That must've been Mrs. Laughlin's idea of kindness. But I have a thought to share with you."

Jeremy put his fingertips on the little metal mirror, the same one in which he had seen his scarred face for the first time in Doc Daniel's cabin. He did not pick it up, however.

"Ben has told me you're a wizard with your little bag of tricks there. What about trying to pretty up that face of yours?"

Jeremy turned away. "Now, stay with me," Doc Daniel urged. "Do you think you're the only one who's got something he'd rather not have people see? Look here."

He pulled off his black felt hat and lifted the hair on the left side of his head. Benny gasped. An ugly scar started at the top back part of his head and disappeared into his beard. The top half of his ear was completely missing.

There's more that the beard covers," Doc Daniel explained. He rearranged his hair and replaced his hat. "Let your beard grow, and the hair, just a bit, and see what you can do with some of your greasepaint. I think you'll find you can hide a lot of what's troubling you, just like I do."

"How did that happen?" Jeremy asked.

"A logger in Oregon who didn't like my style of preaching," Doc Daniel grinned. "Not many preachers have visitors to their services try to take an ax to them. It was lucky I had my needle and thread with me."

*****

Benny finished all his chores, but Doc Daniel and Jeremy still hadn't come out of the little cabin. Benny didn't say anything about the experiment to his mother or his aunt and uncle. He wasn't sure it was going to work. But when Doc Daniel and Jeremy finally entered the farmhouse at lunchtime, Benny whistled in appreciation.

"You look wonderful!"

"I never would have believed it," said Aunt Caroline. Jeremy had applied a false beard and combed his hair around his face. He had carefully applied makeup until his scars were almost invisible.

"Quite a difference," nodded Uncle Tom. "That stuff won't hold up under a day's haying, though, which is what I'm off to do."

"Jeremy isn't going to be a farmer, Tom," Doc Daniel said. "He's going to be a doctor and a preacher of the Word. I think it'll stop some of the distraction -- some of the prejudice."

"Mother, don't you like Jeremy's new face?" Benny demanded. "You haven't said anything."

Benny's mother blushed but still didn't speak.

"Mother, he looks almost as handsome as he used to," Benny persisted. "I know it's not real, but -- "

"Ben, let it rest," Jeremy interrupted. "I need to work on it some more -- it could be better. Let's go take care of Switch."

Benny started to follow Jeremy, then darted back to the kitchen for some sugar lumps.

"It was such a shock," he heard his mother say as he stopped outside the kitchen. "I didn't know what to say."

"He was looking for your approval more than anybody else's," Doc Daniel chided. "You must know how much his looks trouble him, especially when he loves a lady as lovely as you."

"I accepted his scars. I loved him for who he was. It wasn't necessary to hide behind that -- false face." Benny's mother shivered.

"Mrs. Richardson, Ben told me your Jeremy was once a very handsome man. It's no sin to paint a barn when it needs it."

"He should accept God's will. It is a testimony to the power of God. People could be convinced just by seeing what God has brought him through."

"Did you think this all through to convince yourself? Isn't it a kind of pride to wear medals of your old sins so people can compliment you on how forgiven you are? God doesn't remember our sins. He doesn't expect to see them lined up like trophies on a mantelpiece. I say let Jeremy bury that old face. Did you love those scars so much that you'd force him and yourself and everyone else to go on looking at them?"

Benny peeked around the corner and saw a tear trickle down his mother's cheek.

"No," she whispered. "I hated them as much as I loved him. I'm glad to even pretend they're gone. I'm glad to see him as handsome as I always imagined he must be."

"Then you'd better tell him so," Doc Daniel urged. "Mr. Jeremy's heart's very much of the tender sort, especially where the beautiful Mrs. Richardson's concerned."

Benny jumped into the kitchen at that moment and snatched some sugar out of the bowl on the table. He pushed it into his mother's hands and turned to run out.

"Jeremy needs that right away, mother!" Benny called over his shoulder. "I've got to help Uncle Tom."

*****

Dan Connors had bought Jeremy a fine new suit of clothes and a "proper doctor's hat" which covered his last few scars. Doc Daniel found an old used buggy and helped Jeremy train Black Switch to pull it.

The stallion did not care for the task at all. But with the buggy painted a jaunty green and yellow and the handsome black horse in the harness, Doc Daniel pronounced Jeremy ready to go and become a doctor after two weeks at Uncle Tom's. Doc Daniel took Jeremy over to give him a proper introduction to Dr. Shepherd. They returned and announced that Jeremy would be going to live with the doctor in his big old house.

"I think it's time Benny and I stopped imposing on you, too," Benny's mother insisted to Uncle Tom. "I've talked to Mrs. Anderson about working as a housekeeper and cook at her place. Benny and I can live there. They have two big rooms set aside. Mrs. Anderson wrote me a note and said to come by on the fourth. That's today."

"Abigail, if you leave this house, don't come back," Uncle Tom said angrily.

"Thomas!" Aunt Caroline exclaimed.

"We'll just see how long your dreams will last before they fetch up against reality," Uncle Tom said.

*****

"Abigail, I'm so sorry I caused this," Jeremy said to Benny's mother as they loaded their bags into the buggy behind Black Switch. "Why don't you just stay with Tom while I'm working for Dr. Shepherd?"

"The sooner we can earn the money we need, the sooner we'll go west," Benny's mother said firmly. "I can help if I'm working. Tom didn't pay me, you know." She smiled.

"I can get some work after school, too," Benny said eagerly. "If we live in town that'll work out great."

They were delayed by a stop to help some people whose wagon had broken a wheel. Jeremy stopped outside the Anderson's house in the late afternoon.

"There's no need to come in," Benny's mother said. "Doctor Shepherd will be anxious about you. You can bring our things by later."

"Say, Ben, isn't that your buddy Jason?" Jeremy asked as he helped his mother down.

"Hey, Ben!" Jason ran over from across the street and pounced on Benny. "Who's that man with your mother?"

"That's Jeremy."

Jason marched over and planted himself in front of Jeremy. Then he marched all around and stopped in front again.

"What happened to your face?" he demanded.

Benny's mother laughed. "Jeremy has been to a specialist," she explained. "He has a new face now."

"No kiddin'? Doctors can do that?"

"Remember how it says in the Bible, 'Behold, I make all things new'?" Jeremy grinned. He squatted down and looked Jason in the eye. "Touch it."

Jason hesitated, then reached out a hand. "It ain't real," he marveled. "But I like it."

"Thanks. This was one of my giants. He's not quite dead yet, but I think he's pretty well buried."

"My pa's not gonna believe it's you. He kept sayin', 'How's he gonna preach to folks lookin' like that? How's he gonna doctor folks lookin' like that?' Guess he don't know God can do anything, huh?"

"He can even make the dumb speak," Jeremy said slyly. Jason turned red. "I see you got your tongue back, Jason."

"I'm sorry – real sorry about how I acted."

Jeremy drove off in the green and yellow cart and Benny joined his mother again.

"Come on, darling. Mrs. Anderson will be wondering what happened to us." Benny's mother climbed the front steps of the Andersons' house and knocked on the door. No one answered. She knocked several more times.

"Hello, Abigail!" Mrs. Turner, the Andersons' next-door neighbor, appeared at her window. "My dear, the Andersons have been gone four days. They must be well on their way to New York by now."

"New York! I -- I don't understand. I had a letter from Mrs. Anderson..." Benny's mother dug in her purse while Mrs. Turner came out of her house and joined them. She took the letter from Benny's mother and glanced over it.

"Oh! That Lydia Anderson! Trust her to make such a muddle of a simple thing. They've shut up the house for the summer, Abigail. They've family in New York, and John is attending some sort of convention for his business. She wanted someone to come on August fourth, not June fourth."

"August!" Benny breathed. "Mother, what are we going to do?"

"Why, what's wrong?" Mrs. Turner asked. Haltingly Benny's mother explained that she could not go back to Uncle Tom's and why.

"Tom is the stubbornest man alive. Oh! Abigail! Oh, my dear! You've nowhere to go! That Lydia. Won't I give her a piece of my mind when I see her next? Come stay with us, Abigail. We'll make room."

Benny and his mother looked at the Turners' small house and Benny thought about their five children.

"Oh, thank you, but we should just ... Perhaps there are rooms to let in town somewhere?"

“Rooms? Humph! Not the Swenson’s Boardinghouse for certain. Nothing but bedbugs and whiskey bottles. Let me think ... The Godfreys have a room, but it’s much too small ... There’s Rosa Salter. You know her, don’t you? Plays the organ at the church. I think I just heard her say she wanted to take in boarders.

“Her place is run down -- It’s just her and that dog. Used to have a lovely dress shop, and made such beautiful things. Everything just went to pot somehow when her husband died five years ago. Maybe it would do till you found something better.”

“Mrs. Salter. Of course. Thank you, Mrs. Turner. Now if I can only find work...”

“That I’m afraid I can’t help you with. You poor thing. I’m so sorry. If Clyde or I can do anything to help ...”

## Chapter Four -- Mutter Salter

Benny and his mother found Mrs. Salter's house easily. It was large, very run-down, and built around a storefront shop. Benny thought about the woman that Jason Owens called "The Goosestepper." She marched around town with her large, cold-eyed dog, stiff and soldierly, and spoke to everybody in short, sharp sentences.

The dog began to bark, deep and warning, as they picked their way up the broken steps and knocked on the weathered front door. A thin, dark-haired older woman opened the door, her hand resting on the head of a big black and tan dog with pointed ears.

"Mrs. Salter, I'm Abigail Richardson, and this is my son Benjamin. I'm looking for rooms to rent."

"*Nein*. Children I do not vant. Noisy, destructive, especially boys." She started to slam the door.

"My son is not like that at all," Benny's mother exclaimed. "He is quiet and neat. He'll be no trouble to you, I promise."

"You promise much." Mrs. Salter opened the door again. "The name of Richardson I do not know."

"We've met at the church," Benny's mother said.

"Ah, *die Nachtigal* -- the lady who sings so sveetly. You are young. Vidow?"

"Yes. My husband died in Philadelphia about three years ago."

"You come here alone to raise your son? Vhy?"

"I have a brother who owns a farm near Osage. Thomas Laughlin. I was living with him."

"*Die* Laughlins *Ich kenne.*" She made the words sound so harsh, the way she emphasized the hard "ch" in the back of her throat. Later Benny learned that *Ich kenne* meant "I know" in German. "Vhy have you come here, then? Your brother, he has no more room for you?"

"I want to be near the man I love. I thought I had work with the Andersons, but I misunderstood. I need to find a place to stay, and employment."

"This man you love," snorted Mrs. Salter. "Vhy does he not marry you and make a home for you?"

"Mrs. Salter, I'm only asking to rent a room." Benny could see that his mother was growing angry at Mrs. Salter's blunt questioning, but he knew they had few choices about places to live. "If you're worried about payment, I have some money, and I'm sure I'll find work soon."

"Richardson. Now I remember. You do sewing. Fine sewing. Your vork I know."

Benny's mother had done some dressmaking work for the Andersons and a few other people in town.

*"Mein Mann* -my husband -- and I did fine sewing," Mrs. Salter murmured. "But he died ... Alone I could not do it. For help I did not ask. But perhaps you and your son -- who must be neat and quiet indeed, since no sound he has made all this long time -- perhaps you could help me. Together ve could vork to make the shop run again. For this I vill pay you, and for no rent you vill live in my house."

Benny and his mother looked at the broken display window, the peeling paint, and the faded sign dangling by half its chain.

"It would be a great deal of work, Mrs. Salter ..." faltered Benny's mother.

Jeremy and Black Switch spun around the corner just then. Jeremy leaped out of the buggy and ran up the walk. Benny and his mother came down to meet him.

"Abigail!" he exclaimed. "I got back to the Andersons' and you were gone. The house was empty and locked up tight. I couldn't imagine what had happened. Are you all right? Mrs. Turner told me you were here, but -- " He stopped and took a good look around. "There must be other places," he said in a low voice.

"So this is your young man?" Mrs. Salter marched down the steps with her dog close by. "He does not approve of *mein haus*?" She reached out a hand and touched Jeremy's suit. "A fine suit, a fine buggy, but Mrs. Richardson must vork for her own keep. Of course, he is *schöen* -- handsome, and that is vhy you love him. You can sneer at *mein haus, Herr* Fine Clothes, but I vonder if she makes a mistake to marry you."

"Don't talk about Jeremy like that!" Benny shouted. "He doesn't have any money, and he's got to learn to be a doctor. Mother, I don't want to live here. Let's go somewhere else."

"Thank you for your time, Mrs. Salter," Benny's mother said stiffly.

"Vait. *Bitte."* Mrs. Salter clutched at Benny's mother's arm. "I beg pardon. I am not used much to people. I speak too bluntly. Vhat I said before -- the vork -- the help -- I still need. Please ... "

Jeremy took a step forward and raised his hand to Mrs. Salter's face. The dog barked sharply, and she flinched.

*"Du bist blind, Mutter,"* Jeremy murmured. Mrs. Salter trembled.

"For ten years," she nodded. "It vent slowly. No vun knew but *mein Mann*. He helped, he vorked harder, finally he did everything. But he died so suddenly. I vas too proud -- to tell anyone. Fritz helped me." She buried her fingers in the dog's fur.

"But Fritz couldn't tell you your house and shop are falling apart, *Mutter Salter,"* Jeremy said. "Come. Look at this. Look with your hands."

He led her around and made her touch everything, even the broken window. At the end she sat on the porch steps and wept. Jeremy sat beside her and held her hand.

"Everything is gone. In my mind it vas beautiful, just as it vas ten years ago. I vas such a fool. Everyone has seen this, and if they did not guess the truth and pity me, they have sneered at my carelessness, to let everything go to ruin."

"One more thing to look at, *Mutter*." Jeremy took her hands and placed them on his face. Her fingers moved hesitantly at first, but then she found the false beard, the makeup, and the ragged scars beneath the surface and in his hairline.

"These scars -- how vas this done?"

"The Lord sent a representative to me. I call him a Cougar Evangelist. I robbed a bank and came west to build a gambling casino, but the Lord God of Heaven and Ben Richardson stopped me and I accepted Christ. You can see what almost no one else can -- the truth about what you called my handsome face. If God can make this new, He can do the same for your house and your business."

Jeremy helped her to her feet. "But it's too much work for two women and a boy. You've let your pride blind you a long time. Now that you can see again, I'll tell you what we'll do. Mrs. Richardson and Ben will live here with you, now that I've seen the place isn't really going to fall down tomorrow. I'm staying with Dr. Shepherd at his place, and he's teaching me medicine. When I'm not working with him or studying, I'll be here, helping you. Will that suit you?"

Mrs. Salter started to cry again. "Everything I thought about you was wrong." She patted Jeremy on the arm. "Mrs. Richardson has chosen well."

## Chapter Five – A Real Doctor

On Sunday Jeremy went with Benny and his mother to the little church in Osage. Mrs. Salter and Fritz came also, and Fritz settled down beside the organ. "Don't sit there, Jeremy, it'll tip over," Benny warned as Jeremy approached a pew. Jeremy looked around as they made their way to a pew that would hold their weight.

"Tell me, Ben, is there a place in this town that isn't falling apart?" Jeremy sighed. Mrs. Salter struck a few chords on the wheezy organ. The Owens family trooped in before Benny could answer. The younger children tumbled down the aisle and descended on Fritz, who thumped his tail in appreciation of all the attention. Jason dragged his father up to Jeremy.

"See, pa, I told ya. He got a new face!" Jason said excitedly.

Carl Owens shook his head in disbelief as he clasped Jeremy's hand. "You look fine. Real fine," he said with a huge smile. "Guess my faith ain't all it oughta be."

"Guess nobody's is," Jeremy grinned.

A few more people came in, mostly elderly. A new circuit-riding preacher had recently begun to fill the pulpit some Sundays, and was here today. After a moment Reverend Clark entered from behind the pulpit. He was a small, weary-looking young man. He led a few faltering songs, prayed earnestly, and launched into his message.

"My text is taken from I Corinthians 9:16. 'For though I preach the Gospel, I have nothing to glory of; for of necessity it is laid upon me; yea, woe is unto me, if I preach not the Gospel!'" Suddenly the platform flooring gave way under him. Jeremy and Carl Owens rushed to help him out of the hole.

"Thank you, Carl. Thank you -- I don't believe we've met," Reverend Clark said to Jeremy.

"This is Jeremy Carlisle. Friend of mine," Carl Owens said.

"That is a great recommendation, to have Carl Owens call you friend," the pastor smiled weakly. He tried to stand but his leg went out from under him. Jeremy helped him to a chair. "I fear my ankle is sprained."

Jeremy took a look. "I'm afraid it is too," he said.

"Well, the folks will miss their mid-morning nap. We'll just have to cancel the service. This message ... I was so compelled by the Lord to prepare it -- "

"Carlisle here's been studyin' preachin'," Carl Owens piped up. "Let him do the messagin'."

"Carl!" Jeremy exclaimed. "I'm not prepared to preach a sermon!"

"My friend, we must be 'ready always to give an answer to every man that asketh you a reason of the hope that is in you,'" the pastor said firmly. "If you mean to preach, you must not miss a single opportunity. Has not the Lord compelled you to preach His Word, as it says in the verse I just read?"

Jeremy looked around at the handful of people, then back at the pastor's face, a mixture of kindness, earnestness and a bad attempt to conceal his pain.

"We all come to hear a sermon," Carl Owens whispered. "There ain't nobody else."

"'With meekness and fear,'" the pastor said, and winked at him.

Carl returned to his seat after propping the pastor's leg up on another chair. Jeremy went to Benny and his mother's pew and picked up his Bible. "What am I going to say?" he hissed.

"Tell 'em about how God makes all things new, Jeremy," Benny prompted.

Jeremy walked toward the platform, then thought better of it. He turned to face the small group from beside the front pew. “I -- I’m going to read from Genesis Chapter 32, verses 24 through 32.”

Jeremy read the passage and looked up from the Bible at the faces in front of him. “I had a wrestling match that was a little like Jacob’s, only the Lord sent a representative. Some folks here don’t know what I’m talking about, but my point is this: God said Jacob had power with God and power with men. He said he prevailed.

“God blessed him there, at that place called Peniel. Jacob said he named it that because he’d seen God face to face. I’ve seen God face to face, too. Have you? I have this Book --” he held up his Bible “ -- that shows me His face.

“God fought with Jacob here. That’s the face that hates sin. He hurt Jacob -- pulled his hip right out of joint. Mrs. Richardson can tell you what it feels like to suffer a dislocation. That was the face of judgment on sin.

“God changed Jacob’s name. That was the face that took away the old sins and made a new man. He said Israel had power, and that he had won. That’s the happy face of God- honoring victorious Christian living. I love to look at God’s face. Don’t you?”

Jeremy bowed his head to pray. “Lord God of heaven, the people of this church need to see Your face a little better, I think. We all do. Help me and all these folks to see Your face, and look at Your house, and take the power You’ve given us with You and with men and make all things new. In the name of the Lord Jesus Christ, Amen.”

Jeremy and Carl Owens carried the pastor, chair and all, to the rear of the church so he could greet people as they went out.

“Reckon this place could use some fixin’ up,” Carl Owens mumbled. “Yer gonna get a reputation as the shortest preacher in the west, Carlisle. But you do pack a lot into a little space.”

“Reverend Carlisle, I thank you for what you said,” the pastor said. He gripped Jeremy’s hand and couldn’t seem to stop shaking it. “What school of theology did you study at?”

"Philadelphia Penal Seminary," Carl Owens laughed. The pastor stared at him in confusion. "Never mind, Reverend. We'll explain it to you another time. Reverend Carlisle, grab a side of the pastor's sedan chair and we'll convey him to my wagon and over to my place for dinner. You come along too. You can tell the Reverend all about your seminary experiences."

"I would be honored," the pastor said.

Jeremy glared at Carl. "Stop calling me Reverend," he gritted.

"Okay, Doctor," Carl smirked. "Let's go."

"You have a doctorate in theology?" the pastor said in awe. Benny clapped a hand over his mouth and spluttered.

"Well, not exactly," Carl told the pastor. "He's studyin' t' be a medical-type doctor an' a preacher both."

"*Ja, ist war,*" Mrs. Salter said firmly as she and Fritz joined the group. "*Der Herrn Doktor* Carlisle can preach the Vord, heal the sick, repair vhat is broken – he does all things vell. He does all things vell."

*****

Dr. Shepherd had been forced to take to his bed about a month after Jeremy had come to live with him. Jeremy had taken over his practice completely, though he consulted frequently with his teacher about patients. It was not a busy practice at first, because Dr. Shepherd's health had been failing so long many people had simply gotten used to doing without a doctor. Once the town learned that there was a new, strong and healthy doctor, though, Jeremy's calls began to increase.

He still made time to work on Mrs. Salter's house, and to fix up the church. Carl Owens discovered very quickly how much work he was trying to do.

"This is crazy. You can't fix Rosa's house and the church and doctor too."

"You volunteering to help?" Jeremy smiled.

So Carl Owens organized the men in the town to take over the repair work.

"We need you to be our doc," he explained. "And it's nice to have a fill-in preacher."

*****

The winter passed quickly. Everyone kept so busy. Benny's mother turned out dresses and shirts and suits on Mrs. Salter's treadle sewing machines. Benny kept them in running order and learned a lot about machine repair. Mrs. Salter knew every part by feel and taught him so much, blind as she was. She also felt Benny's mother's seams and made sure they weren't bunched or puckery. She was a hard mistress, but they had fun sometimes, too.

Every Saturday Mrs. Salter closed the shop at noon. She went to the cash drawer and counted out Benny's mother's salary as head seamstress and Benny's as machine repairman and delivery boy. Benny's box labeled "westward fund" grew a little fuller every week.

*****

One day in late spring Benny stopped in at the doctor's office. He was official errand boy of "Salter's Fine Tailoring and Dressmaking," and had been out delivering clothes his mother had made or repaired. Mr. Prentice, the schoolteacher, stood in the doctor's front room with Jeremy.

"Mr. Carlisle, I don't mean to sound ungrateful," he said. "You've done a good work in this town. But the fact is you are unlicensed. For a man to take the title of doctor, he ought to be licensed. Your training and study has been -- most irregular."

"I haven't taken the title of doctor," Jeremy said sharply. "I know I'm not one. I'm just filling a gap here; a gap you people helped to create by allowing Dr. Shepherd to go on for so many years, sick as he was, content that you had a 'real' doctor."

"People all over the area are talking about 'that young doc,'" Mr. Prentice said stiffly. "The town council feels a responsibility for the safety of its people. I was asked to bring this matter to your attention. As long as Dr. Shepherd is alive there isn't really much we can do, since he is responsible for you. But if you ignore our concerns, we may be forced to take action."

Mr. Prentice turned and left. Jeremy sank into a chair.

"What's he talking about, Jeremy? You're a good doctor. Everybody in town likes you."

"Mr. Prentice thinks that just because where he came from, the laws required all doctors to be licensed, he can come here to Missouri and bully me," Jeremy sighed. "Most states have overturned their licensing laws. But Daniel Connors says we need to go further than the law requires, to have a clean testimony for the Lord and to be above reproach even to people who have no cause to reproach us. He's right. Daniel said he could arrange for me to go to a medical school, Kemper College in St. Louis, take some tests and demonstrate my knowledge and skills. But most of all, I'd have to come up with several hundred dollars. I don't have it, and I don't know how to get it, unless I sell Switch."

"Sell Black Switch! Jeremy, you can't!" Benny heard a noise. Jeremy jumped out of his chair and ran upstairs with Benny following. They hurried into the room where Dr. Shepherd lay.

*****

He struggled for every breath. Jeremy mixed a powder in some water and helped him drink it. He knelt down beside the bed and took the old man's hand. Dr. Shepherd hadn't been able to talk for some time now.

"I sent for Doc Daniel, Dr. Shepherd. I don't know if he'll even get the letter. I can't do anything else for you. I'm scared."

Dr. Shepard patted Jeremy's hand as it held his own. He smiled and shook his head, then pointed up.

"Oh, no. Oh, no," Jeremy said. "You can't do that. Dr. Shepherd, I'm just not ready to have my first patient die on me yet. Wait for Daniel. Die when he's here."

Dr. Shepherd shook his head again. His hands went limp. His labored breathing stopped. Jeremy stayed on his knees, his eyes fixed on the old man's face.

"Jeremy, he's dead." Benny had seen his father's face as he lay on the sidewalk in Philadelphia. He knew the look of death. Someone banged on the door downstairs. Benny ran to answer it, but Jeremy didn't move.

*****

Doc Daniel stood outside. He took a look at Benny's face. "I'm too late," he said.

"Doc Daniel, Jeremy needs help. Mr. Prentice said the town won't let him practice medicine without a license. He's going to make trouble if he keeps doing it now that Dr. Shepherd is dead. But it costs a lot of money. Everybody says the town needs a doctor. Jeremy's been doing a real good --"

"Ben, Ben," Doc Daniels interrupted. "Let everything be done decently and in order. Where's Jeremy?"

"Upstairs with Dr. Shepherd."

"What -- you mean he just --" Benny nodded. Doc Daniel hurried upstairs with Benny following. Jeremy still knelt just as Benny had left him. He didn't even look up when they entered. Doc Daniel approached the bed and took Jeremy's hand out of Dr. Shepherd's. Jeremy jumped, then slowly got to his feet.

"I'm sorry," Doc Daniel said. "Jeremy, I'm truly sorry. I should have been here."

"I'm not even a doctor yet," Jeremy said in a weak voice. "I thought I'd at least be a doctor."

Doc Daniel took Benny and Jeremy each by an arm and pulled them out of the room.

"You having a piece of paper or not having one didn't make any difference to Jonas," Doc Daniel said. "You know that."

"It does to the town of Osage," Jeremy said wryly.

"Ben told me," Doc Daniel said. "As many times as we've talked about this licensing thing, I can't think why I didn't take care of this before. Here." He pulled a packet out of his shirt and handed it to Jeremy. "Open that."

Jeremy opened it and took out a handful of money. "What is this? Where did it come from?"

"Ben ran Black Switch in a horse race down in Farmington last summer," Doc Daniel shrugged. "Switch won. That's the prize. Five hundred dollars."

"But -- but --" Benny spluttered. "How'd you get the prize, Doc Daniel? We didn't have a bill of sale."

"Forgot to give you this, too," Doc Daniel said to Jeremy. He handed him a piece of paper.

"Let me see that!" Benny grabbed the paper and read it aloud.

"One horse, named Black Switch, sold to Mr. Jeremy Carlisle, on this tenth day of September, in the year of our Lord 18--, for the sum of two hundred dollars."

A description of Black Switch, a wax seal, and signatures followed.

"But -- but I didn't know you had a bill of sale! I thought you'd've lost it when the barge sank, anyway --"

"I bought Switch fair and square, with money I'd saved," Jeremy said. "I kept the bill of sale in my makeup bag, because anybody can accuse you of stealing a horse, especially a valuable-looking one, and the last thing I needed was to be accused of being a thief." He smiled wryly. "Sure, I played that trick on the trader to get him cheap -- he'd been a race horse, probably worth much more than two hundred dollars.

"But the bill of sale's legal and proper. The fine Italian gentleman stole poor Mr. Carlisle's horse after he whacked him on the head and disposed of his remains."

"Switch was a race horse?" Benny breathed. "That's why he knew how to run so well."

"I'm getting left out of all this," Jeremy complained. "You raced Switch? Why didn't you tell me? I'd've told you the whole story."

"There wasn't time before the race," Doc Daniel chuckled. "And I thought I'd have a little fun at poor Ben's expense and keep it as a surprise. I knew that money'd come in handy sometime."

"You had the bill of sale all along?" Benny asked.

"Jeremy gave it to me before he went to prison. He told me if anything happened to him, I was to sell Black Switch to get money to make sure you and your mother were taken care of. I couldn't keep the horse myself, because I travel so much, but Tom was agreeable to doing that. I told him the truth about the Bill of Sale later, after

I'd collected the prize. But I honestly forgot about the money."

*****

Doc Daniel preached Dr. Shepherd's funeral message.

"'I am the resurrection and the life,'" he read from his big Bible, standing in the remarkably full church. "'He that believeth in me, though he were dead, yet shall he live. And whosoever liveth and believeth in me shall never perish. Believest thou this?'"

Doc Daniel looked around at the crowd. "Well, do you?" he thundered suddenly. "Some of you darkened this church door for the first time today, maybe the second time, if you got married here. What are you doing here? Do the people of Osage understand what Jonas Shepherd knew with all his heart and soul?

"He lived the example of a godly, selfless servant in this town for fifty years. He buried his wife here. He saw his children grow up and move farther west, but he stayed and gave everything he had to this town. Now he's up in heaven hearing the Lord's 'Well done,' and peeking over the battlements, wondering if any more than half a dozen people from this town will join him there."

Benny looked around at the sound of all the uncomfortable murmurings and rustlings. Then he saw a group of men standing up in the back of the church. Mr. Prentice stood among them, and he realized it was the town council. Benny glanced over at Jeremy, who sat with Carl Owens and the other pall bearers and never lifted his head, much less noticed the delegation clearly just waiting for the service to be over. Doc Daniel did not miss them, however.

"There's more to life than just being prepared to meet the Lord, though, and Jonas knew that too," Doc Daniel continued. "There are people here who might have prayed a prayer and think themselves fine Christians, but they follow a bunch of man-made rules and despise the folks who think faithfully studying the Word of God and having an obedient heart are good enough.

“Sometimes we need man-made rules. But some man-made rules poison a person’s whole perspective on life. Matthew 23:4 says, ‘For they bind heavy burdens and grievous to be borne, and lay them on men’s shoulders; but they themselves will not move them with one of their fingers.’ These rules make man think he’s in charge of things. He becomes self-righteous. He forgets to be grateful. They make him attack people who might not think those rules are quite as important. He’ll spoil the good and pass over the bad and never understand why he can’t succeed at serving God.”

Benny thought a fight was going to break out in the back of the church. It started as a whispered undertone and continued after all the other people had gotten over being uncomfortable about Doc Daniel’s message. Quite a bit of foot-shuffling caught Benny’s ear and he peeked back just once more, seeing a flurry of hand-gestures and clenched fists as the town council propelled itself out of the church in a body and never came back. Doc Daniel closed in prayer, thanking the Lord for His ability to comfort and to soften hearts.

*****

After the graveside service and burial Jeremy and Doc Daniel were invited to Mrs. Salter’s for dinner. Just as they sat down at the table, a group of men, much smaller in number than the one that had been gathered at the back of the church, came to the door and asked to speak to Jeremy.

“Uh-oh! Looks like the town council to me,” Jeremy grunted.

“Mr. Carlisle,” Mr. Prentice said, “The matter about which I spoke to you has come to a head, now, as you know. I regret that we must force this upon you at this sad time, but the license --”

“Mr. Carlisle is leaving for St. Louis tomorrow,” Doc Daniel broke in. “I’m personally escorting him to see that he doesn’t experience any delays in the process. Odds are we’ll be back in two to three weeks at most with a shiny medical license for Mr. Carlisle to show off to you all. Will that satisfy the council, Mr. Prentice?”

"Why -- why of course, Dr. Connors," Mr. Prentice stammered. The wind was thoroughly taken out of his sails. The last of his supporters among the council glowered at him. Shame-faced, they herded Mr. Prentice out of the house.

Jeremy waited until the council had departed. Then he grabbed Doc Daniel by the arm and pulled him into the parlor, slamming the door behind them.

*****

*"Wass ist loss?"* Mrs. Salter demanded. "We have not had a bite to eat, only all these goings-on to upset *mein haus."* Benny's mother tried to reassure Mrs. Salter, but neither she nor Benny really had any idea what had happened now. What could Jeremy and Doc Daniel be talking about? Was Jeremy saying he wasn't ready to take the doctor's exam?

Benny couldn't help wondering how he could be ready. It must be a very hard test. And Jeremy had just found out yesterday that he had enough money to take it. He had been so busy, taking care of patients, repairing the church and Mrs. Salter's house, preaching at the church when Doc Daniel and Reverend Clark weren't there -- had he really had any time to study?

The day Jeremy showed up with Dan Connors in Jefferson City, Benny had scribbled down a list of things in the front of his father's Bible. He had done it that night before he went to sleep in the Connors' rented house. These were things that had to happen before they could all go west together. Almost a year had gone by since that day. But Benny's list remained completely unticked. He had looked at it every time he read his Bible and had it memorized by now.

He knew the first thing that had to happen was that Jeremy would have to marry his mother. He had been itching to tick that one off, sure that it was enough that Jeremy had asked, his mother had agreed. Uncle Tom believed it sure enough to remain angry about it. They hadn't even talked to Uncle Tom since they had moved into town. Aunt Caroline had sneaked peeks at them at church but even she hadn't dared to come and talk to them. They had gotten messages through some other ladies in town expressing Aunt Caroline's love but that was all. Still, Benny couldn't tick it off until it was a done deed. He knew too well how life could turn upside down and plans could change.

The second tick would be Jeremy becoming a doctor or perhaps an ordained minister. Benny hadn't been sure about how either of those were to be done, but he thought they ought to be on the list. He still didn't know about the ordination, but now the doctor path was pretty clear, at least what had to be done. There was money, money he could proudly say he had at least helped to secure, but was Jeremy ready?

Jeremy and Doc Daniel burst out of the other room before Benny could get any further down his mental list. Jeremy hesitated just a minute while Doc Daniel took his seat again. Then he scooted around the table and went down on one knee before Benny's mother. Mrs. Salter, who was seated next to Benny's mother, nearly jumped out of her chair, being unable to see what had happened. Jeremy laid a soothing hand on the older woman's arm.

"Dr. Shepherd left me his house, Abigail. I have a home for you now. I have the practice without any question as soon as the doctor's exam is passed. There still isn't much money, but I don't want to wait any longer. Daniel has flat-out promised to come straight back with me after this license thing is taken care of to perform the ceremony. Can we finally get married, Abigail?"

"Oh, yes," she answered, accepting his proffered hand. "Of course. I've been ready forever, I think."

"I think perhaps a month it will be," Mrs. Salter said. "The roses in *mein garten* vill be in bloom by then. These your flowers can be. Mrs. Jones at the hotel beautiful cakes bakes. I speak to her. *Und die Kleid vertig vollen."*

Benny and his mother had both been learning bits of German, because Mrs. Salter frequently became too impatient or excited to keep to English all the time. "The dress?" Benny's mother said faintly.

Mrs. Salter marched out and returned with a beautiful sky-blue satin dress, just cut out, still all pattern-markings and pins. Doc Daniel lifted it up so she could spread the skirt out.

"But -- that's to be -- Mathilde Hodgekiss's --" Benny's mother stared at the dress-to-be in disbelief.

"Mathilde never order a dress. I tell a little lie," Mrs. Salter said shamefacedly. "She is just your size, so from her ve take the measurements. I make you choose the fabric when she begs for help, because I know you get what pleases you, if you think it is not for you. Then I fuss and I pretend it must vait because, vell, because my daughters are coming, and they vill finish this for you. I could not have you make your own vedding dress."

"That silk was so expensive," Benny's mother whispered. "I can't -- "

"Cannot Mutter Salter give you a vedding present?" Mrs. Salter demanded. "And suits for your son and for Jeremy my daughters vill make also. As soon as they arrive, *zum arbeiten gehensie zeit*. To work they go. So, all vill be arranged, vhen Jeremy returns our doctor, ve vill be ready for the vedding."

## Chapter Six -- Plans and Trials

So many things had to be done before Jeremy got back from taking the doctor's test, Benny thought as he ran down the street from the doctor's house where Jeremy lived to Mrs. Salter's house where he lived with his mother and the seamstress. As he went by the little church he smiled to think how it had looked when they had come to Osage, and for a long time afterward. Only after Jeremy had preached his sermon on making all things new had people begun to fix and paint the run-down church. Now none of the pews tipped, none of the floorboards gave way, and a fresh coat of white paint really did make it look new. Once Jeremy had begun to work to fix it up people had gotten behind him. Now the church looked beautiful.

As he came around the corner Benny looked at Mrs. Salter's house and shop. It looked new, too. Jeremy had worked so hard on fixing the run-down place. At first Mrs. Salter, who was blind, had fussed at him for taking away all the creaks and cracks that helped her to find her way around the house. When people had seen how much Jeremy was doing, they helped with Mrs. Salter's house too. Bright yellow, it was one of the prettiest in town now, and her dress shop hummed with activity.

Benny grinned as he ran up the steps. It was as if God had planned the right time for his mother and Jeremy to get married. Mrs. Salter hadn't had any communication with her children back east since her husband had died. Since she became blind, she couldn't write to them or read their letters, but she was too proud to tell anyone. Her daughters thought she was angry with them and had stopped writing. After Benny and his mother had come to board with Mrs. Salter they had convinced her to let them write letters for her, and the misunderstanding and hurt had quickly been cleared up.

Mrs. Salter's two daughters were also dressmakers, and they and their husbands had arrived in Osage to help run the shop the day after Jeremy and Doc Daniel had left to travel to St. Louis for the doctor's exam. Benny's mother had worried about leaving Mrs. Salter ever since the day they had started working at the shop, knowing she couldn't run it alone. When the letter had arrived announcing that the daughters had set out for Missouri, they had all celebrated. And apparently, Mrs. Salter had begun her secret plans to get wedding clothes.

*"Hier bist Lotte, und hier bist Helga,"* Mrs. Salter had explained in her short, sharp way when her daughters had appeared at the shop. "They vill take good care of the shop. You can go and be our doctor's vife." Mrs. Salter had forgotten to introduce her daughters' husbands, Matthew Bolton and Peter Dreyfus, who planned to start a Mercantile in Osage and had brought two big wagonloads of supplies.

The two women had hugged Benny's mother and thanked her for reuniting them with their mother. Benny remembered the tears in his mother's eyes. He wondered if she was thinking of Uncle Tom and Aunt Caroline. Uncle Tom was still afraid of the hardships that they would suffer moving west. Jeremy filled in whenever Doc Daniel was away and no other traveling preacher was in the area so the church met more regularly than it ever had. Benny wondered why none of the town council objected to an unordained and unlicensed preacher, but since Mr. Prentice never came to church he supposed that was the real reason. Uncle Tom never said a word to them when he and Aunt Caroline were at services. He didn't want Aunt Caroline to speak either but sometimes she would sneak a quick hug and kiss when his back was turned.

*****

"There was a letter from Jeremy at the Post Office, Mother," Benny said rapidly as he came into Mrs. Salter's kitchen. He waved the short note, which he had already read as he ran around town on his errands. "He said thanks again for the lunch you packed for Doc Daniel and him for the trip. He admitted there was nothing but a piece of dry bread in his whole house."

"That man!" Benny's mother laughed. "He wouldn't eat if we didn't feed him, I don't think. What's this, darling?"

"A package addressed to you from Dan Connors," Benny replied as he handed his mother a small box. He would have thought she could have discovered that for herself by reading the outside of the box.

"But what's in it?" his mother persisted, shaking it.

"I don't know," Benny shrugged. "Oh, there's a letter from Mrs. Connors too." He fished it out of his pocket and grabbed a sandwich from the plate on the counter just as Mrs. Salter finished making it and set it there. His mother quickly opened the letter, though Benny would have preferred to know what was in the package.

> *My Dearest Abigail,* the letter said, *We were so thrilled to know Jeremy will finally get his doctor's license, and even more thrilled to hear of your wedding plans. We will surely do our best to be there, but in case circumstances prevent us, we have sent you a package of things that have very mysteriously come into our possession.*
>
> *We are given to understand that they belonged to Jeremy's mother, and were kept safe by a friend who sadly lost touch with Jeremy. Dan apparently failed to get the package in the mail before Jeremy and Father Daniel departed, so we have taken the liberty of addressing them to you, knowing that Jeremy would certainly want you to have them. With all our affection and good wishes, Elizabeth Connors."*

"Oh, if these things belonged to Jeremy's mother, I should hardly be the one to open the package," Benny's mother protested. "Imagine how he would feel, not having the opportunity to be the one to look at them first, his last mementos of his mother!"

"Come on, Mother, Jeremy wouldn't mind, I'm sure!" Benny exclaimed. "We ran Switch in the race without being able to ask Jeremy first, and look how well that turned out. Maybe there's money in there that we can use for our trip west! Maybe enough that we can go right away!"

"You are to be married," Mrs. Salter said gruffly. "Soon enough you vill open all Jeremy's mail, deal *mit* all his things, vash his undervear. Open the box, Abigail. Money I cannot think it contains, but surely if *Frau* Conners says it is for you, she does not say so lightly."

Reluctantly Benny's mother opened the plain little box. She pushed aside a lot of cotton wool and uncovered two boxes, a small blue velvet one and a long black velvet one. His mother cried out in astonishment. Lotte, who had gone out to have lunch with her husband, came through the door at that moment and heard Benny's mother cry out.

"What has happened?" Lotte demanded. "Have the doctors had an accident? Are they dead?"

"The doctors are dead?" Helga cried, coming in behind her.

*"Nein, meine zwei Gansen,"* snapped their mother. She often called her daughters silly geese, and Benny had to admit sometimes they were a bit silly. "Vhat is it, Abigail? Vhat contains the box?"

Benny watched his mother open the small blue box and take out a beautiful silvery ring with a swirling pattern of sparkling stones. "What – what--?" she gasped.

"Benjamin, *wass ist dass*?" Mrs. Salter demanded.

"Mother, is that what I think it is?" Benny demanded. They both stood there staring at the ring. Lotte and Helga finally got close enough to see why Benny and his mother didn't answer their mother. Lotte gaped. Helga sputtered. Benny's mother finally handed the ring to Mrs. Salter.

Mrs. Salter took the ring and felt it. *"Dass ist so schoen!"* she breathed. "How heavy it is!"

"This comes from Jeremy?" Helga gasped. "For you?"

"It was his mother's," Benny's mother whispered. "Some friends sent it to me from Virginia. Jeremy doesn't even know about it yet."

"What's in the other box, Mother?" Benny demanded.

"Put the ring on, Abigail," Lotte ordered. "It ought to be sized so you can wear it."

"I can't wear this. It's too much," Benny's mother said.

Helga snorted. "Of course you can wear it," she said firmly. "You are going to be the doctor's wife. Who better to wear beautiful things? Put it on."

Benny's mother slipped the ring on her finger. "It fits perfectly," Lotte exclaimed. "As if God made it for you."

"What's in the other box?" Benny asked again. With trembling hands his mother opened the black velvet case. In it lay a string of pearls and stud earrings, perfectly matched, glowing in the light of the table lamp.

"Mamma, pearls! Beautiful pearls!" Helga cried. "Perfect for the bride to wear on her wedding day!"

"We must put these away," Benny's mother exclaimed. She pulled the ring off and hastily shut up the cases in the box. "It will be up to Jeremy to decide what is to be done with them."

"Abigail, vhat are you saying?" Mrs. Salter asked. "He vill give these to you, of course, *Liebschen.*"

"They must be worth hundreds -- perhaps thousands of dollars," Benny's mother faltered. "He should sell them and use the money. Doctor Shepherd's house needs so many repairs, and we must get so many supplies to move west, a wagon, tools, household goods -- "

"He will be a rich doctor soon," Helga snapped. "Everyone in town says they miss him, need him, want him to hurry back and tend them."

"Doctor Connors is paying the expenses for their trip," Benny's mother said weakly. "Hotels and meals must be very expensive. And we must pay him back for all that. No, I'm sure Jeremy will want to sell the jewelry to pay for more important things."

"Nonsense!" Lotte sniffed. "You keep them, Abigail. You cannot always be practical. Sometimes you must let your heart have its way."

*"Nein,"* Mrs. Salter said. "It shall be as Abigail has said. She is a vise little woman. It is for Jeremy to decide vhat is done. Suppose you lock them here in *mein* safe, Abigail, *und* vhen Jeremy returns, he vill have his say."

Her daughters and Benny all started to protest. Mrs. Salter cut them off with a slice of her hand. "Silence," she ordered. "In the safe they go." Benny's mother left the room to go store the box in the safe in Mrs. Salter's bedroom.

"He would not be so heartless as to deny Abigail those jewels," Lotte said. "How her eyes danced to see them."

"Some men would be selfish and say the money mattered more," Helga frowned. "Perhaps he is like them."

"You don't know anything about Jeremy," Benny exclaimed. "He's never cared about money, except to use it to do what's right, to take care of us and everything he's responsible for."

"Most men are selfish," grunted Lotte.

"Jeremy never thinks about himself!" Benny shouted at her. "He's trying to fix up the doctor's house because he's said he's ashamed to bring us home to such a shabby, broken-down place," Benny said. "Jeremy's working so hard, and everybody just criticizes him. It's not fair!"

He ran downstairs to the dress shop, grabbed the pile of packages on the counter, and ran out.

*****

Benny hurried to get his deliveries done. He wanted to get back home and see if his mother was all right. He knew she wanted those pretty things, and he was afraid Lotte and Helga would pester her about them and make her cry. She had been so worried about the wedding, trying to get things together for the move to Jeremy's house, trying to finish up all the work at Mrs. Salter's. Lotte and Helga were not as good at sewing as his mother, and they were lazy sometimes, gossiping instead of working. As he left the last customer, Benny saw Uncle Tom's wagon parked in front of the dry goods store. Aunt Caroline came out the front door just as Benny raced by.

"Benny! Oh, stop a minute, dear," Aunt Caroline said. Benny stopped. Aunt Caroline hugged him. "How is your mother? Excited? Busy? Ready for the wedding?"

Right at that moment Benny didn't know how his mother might be. So many things had happened to upset her lately, besides both of them missing Jeremy. But he knew one thing that would surely help make her feel better.

"Are you coming to the wedding, Aunt Caroline?" Benny asked. "Mother really wants you and Uncle Tom to be there. Can't Uncle Tom just forgive her for wanting to marry Jeremy?"

"I'm going to come, dear," Aunt Carline said. "Thomas or no Thomas. I know he wants to come, too, but he won't give in. He's so stubborn."

"Do you think he'll change his mind?" Benny asked. "It would make mother so happy."

"Thomas has been trying harder than ever to convince everybody he's right," Aunt Caroline said. "He says, 'See what I told you? That fellow's runnin' all over the countryside already. He's preachin' at the church. He's drivin' clear to Farmington. He's neglectin' Abigail and they aren't even married. And now he's gone off to St. Louis to get a doctor's license so he can be busier and neglect her some more. And you want me to go to that wedding and give them my blessing? I guess I won't.'"

"I guess he's like I was when my father died and we had to move out here," Benny said. "I thought if I just dug in my heels and fought the whole way things would change to be the way I wanted them to be. They sure did change, but not the way I planned. Things were going to turn out wonderful when God was ready. I just made it a lot harder by being stubborn."

"So you think you're in a position to be givin' me advice, eh, Benjamin?" growled Uncle Tom as he appeared suddenly beside them.

"Now Thomas, don't you start on the boy. He spoke his heart, that's all," Aunt Caroline snapped. Benny had never seen her angry with Uncle Tom before. He looked at the two of them and saw worry lines and gray hairs that hadn't been there a few months ago. He wondered if this problem was making them as unhappy as it had made Benny and his mother.

"Uncle Tom, please, can't you like Jeremy just a little?" Benny begged. "He's got so much trouble right now. He ought to be happy that he and mother are finally getting married. But he can't be because people are trying to tell him what the Lord's will is and he knows what it is. He just hasn't got time to do it all by himself."

"Did I ever say I didn't like him?" Uncle Tom demanded. "That young fellow could make a dill pickle sweet. Why wouldn't I like him? I just don't want my sister to marry him."

"Did you want mother to marry father?"

"No. He was poor as a churchmouse 'cause he'd disowned that rich family of his. He was in Seminary, workin', teachin', preachin' --"

"But you liked him, too, didn't you?"

"There wasn't a better man on God's earth than Jon Richardson," Uncle Tom admitted.

"Then why can't you stop thinking about what you want and start thinking about what my mother wants?" Benny said. "She found two men who love God and want to serve Him with all their hearts. You didn't want her to marry either one of them. Now who's wrong about what they want, my mother or you? You'd better come to the wedding. Don't you stay away and break mother's heart. I'll -- I'll come get you, tie you up with that horsehair rope you gave me, and I'll drag you to it if I have to. But don't make me do that, because I'm the best man, and it might make me late."

Suddenly Benny heard a bunch of clapping. Half the people in town had come out to listen to his speech to Uncle Tom. Both of them turned very red.

"All right, Ben. All right. We'll be there," Uncle Tom promised. "Tell Abigail we love her. Tell her we love her very much."

*****

Benny hugged them both and sped off. He had almost reached Mrs. Salter's house when Matthew Bolton came by in his cart to pick up his wife from work.

"Can I give you a lift, Benjamin?" he asked. Benny smiled and climbed up in the cart.

"Thanks, Mr. Bolton. How are things going with your store?"

"Be ready to open next week, we hope," Mr. Bolton replied. "That is, if Lotte doesn't change her mind about the curtains and rugs again, and if Helga will let Peter have some peace about the yardgoods selection. I'll tell you, he and I were always good friends, but those wives of ours can be a trial. They are the most selfish women I ever laid eyes on sometimes. Everything has to be just as they want it, or we hear about it 'till our ears ring."

"Jeremy said Mrs. Salter was selfish and proud when we first went to live with her," Benny said.

"Selfish? Mother Salter?" Mr. Bolton raised his eyebrows. "We were so shocked to hear she'd gone blind. I was a little inclined to think she was kind of brave, fending for herself all these years, not wanting to be beholding to anybody."

"I thought that too," Benny replied. "We didn't even know she was blind, all the time we lived here, but Jeremy saw it right away. And he said she was foolish and proud, not brave. She made people stay away from her by being cross and short-tempered, when she and they both could have got a blessing if she had let people help her. She complained about what mother and I did all the time when we first came. Nothing we did was good enough for her. Or we did too much for her, when she wanted to be independent. Or Mother couldn't make her German bread just the way she wanted it. Or mother worked too fast, and we didn't always have enough work to keep us busy. "

"Guess I know where Lotte and Helga got it from," sighed Mr. Bolton. "But I haven't really seen their mother act like that since we've been there. Did your Jeremy find a way to cure her?"

"Um ... I'm not sure if I should say," Benny mumbled. "I don't want to seem disrespectful of Mrs. Salter, or make you think Jeremy is, either, because he loves her. It's just that -- well -- I told him she was making Mother cry almost every day, and Jeremy can't stand to have Mother cry."

"All right, now I have to know what he did, because I have seen nothing but love between Mother Salter and your mother, Ben Mr. Bolton said. "And frankly, I'd like to nurture a little more loving attitude in Lotte. I'm sure Peter would be happy to see the same in Helga."

"Well ... You see, Jeremy was doing all this work to fix up the house and the shop, and Mrs. Salter kept complaining because she actually used the creaky boards and peeling paint spots to find her way around. We wondered why she was so good at that, until those things started to disappear. She got more and more frustrated, but she hardly ever complained to Jeremy, or even to me. She took it out on Mother. And Mother would go to sleep crying.

"So Jeremy came over one day, all polite and chatting with Mrs. Salter in German, and told her he was taking her for a buggy ride. Mrs. Salter fussed at first, and said she was too busy, but Jeremy sweet-talked her into going. They were gone about two hours, and when they came back Mrs. Salter made a beeline to my Mother and hugged her and kept saying how sorry she was. She looked exhausted. We didn't know what had happened.

"Mr. Bolton, she had her hair full of twigs, her dress was ripped, and she even had cuts and bruises on her face and hands. Mother tried to stop all the sorrying, to find out what happened, but Mrs. Salter refused to tell her, or let her help her get cleaned up. She went off to her room alone. Mother turned to Jeremy and asked, 'What happened to her?'

"Jeremy didn't want to say at first. My mother figured out he'd done something she wouldn't like. Finally he admitted he'd taken Mrs. Salter out into the woods, slipped a muzzle on Fritz, led him away, and left her to try to find her own way out. He let her go like that for an hour. He said it was one of the hardest things he'd ever done, keeping close enough to help if he had to, but just standing by and listening to her storm and shout and finally break down and cry.

"At last he went back to her, took her by the arm, and said, 'The next time you make Abigail cry, *Mutter* Salter, back to the woods you go, till you learn to value the people who help you live your life. Understand?'

"It was a whole week before Mother would speak to him or let him come to the house to see her. She kept saying what a cruel thing it was, and how she couldn't believe he could be so heartless. I almost thought everything was over between her and Jeremy. But finally Mrs. Salter sat her down and said, '*Mein Liebe* Abigail, forgive your Jeremy for Mutter Salter's sake. We cannot do vithout that vise young man.'"

"Whew!" Mr. Bolton whistled. "Your Doctor Carlisle's a braver man than I am. And Lotte and Helga aren't blind so that idea wouldn't work with them if Peter and I dared to try it."

"Maybe you should talk to Mrs. Salter and ask her what she thinks you should do," Benny said, after thinking a little. "She is their mother."

Benny jumped out and ran into Mrs. Salter's house without stopping to see if Mr. Bolton took his advice. He did hope something would happen to make Lotte and Helga work a little harder and be a little less silly.

Benny found his mother with her eyes a little red, but when he told her Uncle Tom and Aunt Caroline were coming to the wedding, she grabbed him in a tight, tight hug and kissed him.

*****

Jeremy's second letter came from St. Louis about a week later.

"Even Daniel's considerable influence and his incessant quizzing and drilling the entire trip didn't quite prepare me for how hard the exams were. I've taken the written tests and I'm sure there's not a drop of medical knowledge left in me. It was squeezed out as if that hydraulic press I told you about came down on me head uppermost, and I'm limp as a rag.

“Unfortunately I’ve got only one day to recover and stuff my head full again because the second set of tests are still to come. I wonder if there’s any point in taking them. I’m sure I failed yesterday. There was so much I wasn’t expecting. Daniel tries to be encouraging. He says they ask so many questions that you can afford to get some of them wrong and still pass. I don’t know. I just don’t know. There are three sets of tests altogether. The first was written. Tomorrow’s is an oral examination by a roomful of doctors. Imagine twenty or thirty distinguished professors of medicine all looking inside my brain and finding it’s only an empty attic. I had a nightmare about that.

“The third test is practical knowledge. Oh how I dread that.

“I must demonstrate what I know -- measure and prepare dosages of medication, show how to set broken bones -- who knows what they will want to see? I cannot prepare for that, Daniel says. I just have to know it when the time comes, and I have to do it well enough to impress seasoned old men who’ve done it twenty or thirty years. My terror is inexpressible. Oh pray for me, my little family-to-be, or else find me another job before I come home in disgrace.”

Benny and his mother did pray every day for Jeremy. They prayed together and alone. Benny learned the real meaning of “pray without ceasing” during that time. He wanted to believe Jeremy was just nervous and unsure of himself and that he would pass. But Jeremy’s training and experience had been so short and so strange. Would it be enough?

“Some irregularity has occurred with my written exams,” Jeremy reported in his second letter, which they received a week later. “I do not understand it quite, and Daniel does not either. They have been invalidated by the panel and I must retake them. Thank the Lord they are not charging a second fee. Poor Black Switch did not look forward to a trip to the auction and I certainly had no heart to take him.

“I feel badly for Daniel because he has to stay for this delay. I cannot think what went wrong. There was talk of some candidates cheating, but I guess if they thought I had done that they wouldn't let me retake the exams. Nothing has been said about my orals or my practical. Perhaps they do not matter if the written tests are not acceptable. This added time of waiting is dreadful. We have been told new tests will not be ready for a week.

"Daniel has tried to "show me the town" but I have no heart for it. I miss my dear Abigail and my Ben so much and wish I could have brought you with me. It is fine if you have someone you love very much to share it with. I am also so anxious to be done with this testing. It is bad enough to go through it once. How can I endure it again?

"Of course I shall endure it, because I know you are praying for me and I cannot let that be all for naught. How I love you both. How glad I am that I am not like some of these hard, proud young chaps who swagger in to the tests and try to tell the great men a thing or two. I am just thankful that the Lord may be able to use my poor skills if I can get through this."

Benny and his mother waited a long, anxious week but they did not hear from Jeremy or Doc Daniel. Everyone in town asked every day if there was any news. Benny felt like hiding when he saw someone coming toward him on the street. He just didn't have any answers. He was so tired of waiting.

*****

Very late Thursday night three weeks after Jeremy and Doc Daniel had left Benny heard thumping and bumping at the front door. He dragged himself to the front room and squinted in a sudden bright light as his mother flew past him in her nightclothes with a lamp, then fetched up very suddenly just short of Jeremy's arms. Doc Daniel deflected .her into his own embrace and she blushed and smiled.

"Well? Are you a doctor?" Benny demanded.

Jeremy sighed and squeezed Benny's mother's hand very tightly when Doc Daniel let her go. Benny repeated his question, tired and cross. Jeremy and Doc Daniel looked over at Benny and burst out laughing. Benny caught a glimpse of his reflection in the long front window. He trailed a blanket behind him and his hair stood up on end. He scowled at them and tried to rub his hair flat.

“The reason Jeremy had to take his exams over was very simple,” Doc Daniel said. “They’d never had anyone get a perfect score on a written test before. They couldn’t believe he hadn’t cheated, so they made up a whole new, harder test just for him. But Jeremy got a perfect score on that one too. He did outstandingly well on his orals and practicals too. The board said they had no record of a better-prepared candidate. They almost pinched him to see if he was real before they gave him his sheepskin.”

Benny scratched his head, knowing it was making his hair stand up again and not caring. “Are you a doctor or not?” he asked Jeremy.

“Yes, Ben, I’m a doctor.”

“Good,” Benny said. “I’m going back to bed. G’night, Doctor Dad.”

## Chapter Seven -- Busy All the Time

It was lunchtime the next day before Jeremy made it back over to Mrs. Salter's. Fridays were half-days at the dress shop and Helga and Lotte had already left to go home to their husbands. Mrs. Salter had gone to practice the organ at church. Benny's mother brought out the box Dan Connors had sent and set it in front of him, along with Elizabeth's letter. Jeremy read the letter first. Benny wondered what it was about adults that made them read letters first when packages were so much more interesting.

"Look at what's in the box, Jeremy," Benny urged. "You won't believe it!"

"I shouldn't have opened it," Benny's mother said, keeping her eyes down. "I should have just kept it for you. I had no idea --"

"What in the world is in there?" Jeremy asked. "Abigail, what's wrong? You look as if you've done something terrible."

"Open it!" Benny cried. Finally Jeremy did. He held up the ring and stared at it for a long time.

"Jeremy, was it really your mother's?" Benny demanded. "I thought actors were always broke."

"We had good times and lean times," Jeremy said softly. "In one of the good times my father bought her this ring. Oh, how she loved it. In the lean times I remember she pawned it once or twice but she always redeemed it somehow. And when my dad really went to drink he tried to take it from her and sell it, but all of a sudden it wasn't there. We never knew what she did with it."

Jeremy stared at the ring a few more minutes, then seemed to wake up suddenly. He looked at Benny's mother, who was smoothing her skirt and looking at her hands while she did it, just like she had when they had first met up with Jeremy again in Jefferson City after he was freed from prison.

"It'll need to be sized, I guess," he said, and reached out for Benny's mother's hand across the table.

"No, it fits perfectly," Benny crowed. Benny's mother blushed so red and Jeremy looked startled.

"You already tried it on?" Jeremy asked. He finally managed to grab one of Benny's mother's nervously busy hands. The right one. "Well, good, then." He started to slide the ring onto her finger.

"No -- no -- don't!" Benny's mother cried, fighting to get her hand away. "Shouldn't you sell it, my dear? It's so fine, surely there are better uses for money than -- Oh, I can't -- I shouldn't -- " But her eyes were fixed on the beautiful ring.

"Abigail," Jeremy said softly, slipping the ring into place, "what would ever make you think I would sell the only thing that made my mother's sad life happy? How could I do anything else but make you happy with it?"

Benny's mother burst into tears. Jeremy brushed her cheeks and then kissed the wet off his fingers. Benny squirmed.

"Jeremy, there's something else in the box," he said. Jeremy dug inside and opened the pearl box.

"Whew!" he whistled. "Now I know my mother never owned anything like these. These are -- These came in the same box? Neither Dan nor Lizzie said a word about where they came from?" Both Benny and his mother shook their heads. "I wish I knew who sent these things and how they found me. I'd like to know a friend of my mother's who was good enough to keep a diamond ring for her and then find me and send it out here.

"But these pearls -- You're sure they weren't a wedding gift from Dan and Lizzie? I've never seen them before." Jeremy puzzled a moment longer, then held the box out to Benny's mother. "Still, Lizzie said they were for you, Abigail. You'll wear them, won't you? We surely can't raise money for the trip west off of them, since we don't even know where they came from. Let's see how they look on you."

It didn't take much persuading. Benny's mother slipped away to her bedroom.

"She doesn't look altogether happy, Ben," Jeremy fretted. "Did she really want me to sell those things?"

"Jeremy, she loves them," Benny assured him. "It's just that she always tries to be practical, and to figure out what God would want, not what she would want. But her face was so happy the first time she saw that ring."

"Well, practical is how I should be thinking," sighed Jeremy. "I had a trip out to Mort Sellwick's this afternoon that was going to shoot the rest of the day. But he just met me here in town and showed me that infected leg of his was so much better I have a free afternoon in front of me. I should work on the house, but right now --" He broke off as Benny's mother came in wearing the pearl necklace and studs and looking so pretty and happy Benny clapped his hands and shouted.

"Right now," Jeremy resumed, "I'm going to take the afternoon off to ask a beautiful lady on a buggy ride to the lake. What do you say, beautiful lady?" He held out his crooked arm to Benny's mother. She blushed, slipped her arm in his, and they left together.

*****

Benny sat at the kitchen table another full minute. Then he jumped up and ran all the way to the Mercantile Store, which still hadn't officially opened yet, since Lotte and Helga were still quarreling with their husbands about decorations and stock and everything under the sun. As a matter of fact, both couples were standing on the front porch of the building, practically shouting at each other. Benny didn't care what they were arguing about this time. He stepped into the middle of the four of them and shouted, "I need your help!"

They stopped talking and stared at him. "Benjamin?" Mr. Bolton spluttered. "What's wrong?"

"My mother, has she hurt herself?" Lotte demanded.

"Mrs. Salter's fine," Benny said impatiently. "I wanted to ask what you're all getting my mother and Jeremy for a wedding present."

They all looked at each other. Benny saw them screw up their faces in embarrassment. Benny grinned. "I thought you might need some ideas," he said briskly. "I've got a whole list. Come with me." He marched off, peeking over his shoulder just for an instant. The four adults stared at each other, stared at him, and then hurried to follow. Benny's grin got a lot bigger as he headed toward Dr. Shepherd's run-down old house.

## Chapter Eight – Tanta Troubluska

The day of the wedding, a week later, dawned perfect, clear and warm. The Osage church was full when Benny came out the side door of the sanctuary and took his place as best man with Jeremy beside him. Mrs. Salter played the little pump organ, which Benny had taken apart and repaired. He was finding that he was getting pretty good at cleaning and fixing mechanical things. The organ sounded so much better now. The rear door opened and Benny saw his mother in her beautiful blue satin gown and the pearl necklace and earrings. She came through the door on Uncle Tom's arm. Uncle Tom gave him a wink and Benny smiled even bigger.

Doc Daniel had kept his promise and was there to perform the ceremony. Benny was so glad. Dan Connors and Elizabeth sat down near the front. Benny's grandfather had met them in Philadelphia and come west with them, so he was there too. Beside Mrs. Connors sat a strange woman. She was very old, but her hair was dyed bright red and she wore a lot of jewelry and bright, flashy clothes. She wore a big, feathered hat and a thick veil that made it hard to see her face.

"I know that woman," Jeremy whispered. "But it can't be. It can't be."

Mrs. Salter stood up as Matron of Honor as soon as she finished playing. Her daughters had made her an elegant rose-colored dress and her gray hair was beautifully styled. Benny tried to listen to the service. He managed to hand over the ring at the right time. But he couldn't stop wondering who the mysterious old woman might be.

Jeremy sure took a long time kissing his mother, Benny thought. Doc Daniel had told Benny that the custom was for the first kiss to be in private and that the bride and groom shouldn't kiss at the wedding. Jeremy had laughed and said, "That's all right, Daniel. The first kiss was private, and we are going to kiss right in front of everybody."

Outside the church a big line of people came by to shake hands with everybody in the wedding party. Benny's hand got so tired and sore. Then someone with a very soft, very wrinkled hand took his.

"So you're my Cheremy's best man," the tiny, elderly, red-haired lady said in a very deep, strong voice with a funny accent. "Did he tell you who I am?"

"Uh ... no, ma'am," Benny said.

She laughed. What a funny, deep, nice laugh she had. "We will talk later." She kissed Benny on the cheek. When she lifted her veil Benny saw that her withered face was scarred by terrible pock-marks. Benny glanced sharply at Jeremy, who was craning his neck to get a look under the veil. The woman pressed Mrs. Salter's hand quickly, kissed Benny's mother with just the tiniest flip of her veil, and then stopped in front of Jeremy and gave a laugh like a big, fine old silver bell pealing.

My little Cheremy," she said, holding out her arms. She was no more than half Jeremy's size. "Come, come, no kiss for *Tanta Troublushka*?"

Jeremy blew out a breath and scooped the little woman into his arms. He whirled her around in the air. He laughed, louder and happier than Benny had ever heard him laugh before, and he had heard some fine laughs from Jeremy. Jeremy kept pushing her face tight against his. She kept trying to keep her hat in place. Finally they stopped spinning around and Jeremy set her down very gently and helped her rearrange the veil.

"Dan brought you here, didn't he?" Jeremy demanded. "Dan, how did you find her? I thought she was dead. Abigail, Ben, this is Alexandria Bogdonovitch. She was the greatest stage actress in Russia. She was my mother's best friend. You were the one who sent me my mother's ring, weren't you?"

"I didn't find her, she found me," Dan laughed. He took Miss Bogdonovitch's arm in his and she patted his cheek. "Do you know, she saw that Hollidaysburg newspaper about the bank robbery and she's been hunting you ever since to whip the living daylights out of you for stealing that gold? She said she knew your whole plot, because you'd joked about doing something like that since you were ten years old."

"'I work at a bank, I be nice to everybody, they give me the keys, I take all the money in a big black bag and run away!'" Miss Bogdonovitch said severely. "Your mother taught you better than that."

"I know she did," Jeremy said guiltily. "I gave it all back, though, *Tanta*. Ask anybody."

"I don't have to ask anybody. I look at your face, and I know that now all is well," Miss Bogdonovitch said kindly. "The pearls look well on your lady."

"Of course! They were your pearls!" Jeremy gasped. "*Tanta,* they were the pearls your husband gave you? We can't keep them!"

"Of course you can keep a gift freely given," snorted *Tanta*. "She is like your mother, you know. It made me happy to see those things make someone else happy. I kept them in a box for twenty-five years, my little Cheremy. The ring, the pearls. I could not give that ring to your father. Poor Ricky was long dead. And you -- I did not know what had really become of you, my Cheremy, until I met this sneaky underhanded lawyer who tried to keep you from God's just punishment." She hugged and kissed Jeremy again so everyone would know she was teasing. Her hand lingered on Jeremy's cheek.

"Yes, *Tanta*, God marked me like he marked you," Jeremy said softly. "But I didn't let it stop me, either."

"I am so happy for you, my Cheremy," she murmured. "I am so glad to see you again."

*****

Mrs. Salter and her daughters had made a feast of wonderful German dishes and Mrs. Salter's house was filled with people eating and talking and laughing. Benny was fascinated with Miss Bogdonovitch. She told story after story of her stage life and talked about Jeremy when he was a little boy.

"*Tanta* almost died of smallpox when she was only twenty-three, Ben," Jeremy whispered. "No one in those theatre audiences ever knew how terrible her scars were. They called her Helen of Troy, because everyone thought she was beautiful. I know she was before. There's a painting hanging in the Imperial Palace in Russia that she posed for when she was seventeen. They call it *Archangelina*, the Lady Archangel.

"She was a master with makeup. She taught me from the time I could open a jar. Oh, how I loved her. How my mother loved her. She nursed my mother when the cholera took her. She cried for two days, and then she disappeared. I was so afraid she'd gotten sick and died, too."

"I did get sick," Miss Bodgonovich said, sweeping up behind Jeremy. "Sick at heart. Sick of your wretched father. I went home to Russia. I went all over Europe. I tried to get away from my pain, and I left you in yours, stupid, selfish woman that I was."

"I'm just glad you're alive, *Tanta Troublushka,"* Jeremy said, pulling her down onto his lap. "Stay with us, won't you? I've got a great big house and Abigail would love to have you. Don't leave me again."

"Say, now!" Dan Connors exclaimed, "You can't take *Tanta* away from Elizabeth and me. She's promised to come to Virginia with us."

"Yes, Jeremy," Elizabeth said, taking Miss Bogdonovitch's tiny hands. "She can't go west with you, you know."

"Of course not. My traveling days are over," Miss Bogdonovitch said. "These sweet young people are going to fuss over me and give me Russian chocolates every day. I am no pioneer. It will take me a year to recover from this trip." She comically aped a bent and crippled invalid and hobbled away from Jeremy.

"You see where I get it from?" Jeremy laughed. All that evening he and *Tanta Troublushka* sang silly operatic songs in strange languages, banging on Mrs. Salter's old piano. They recited lines from plays they'd done or seen. *Tanta* disappeared into a bedroom while Jeremy entertained the crowd with a hilarious dumb show about a drunken peddler. He reduced everyone to tears of laughter.

Suddenly Miss Bogdonovitch came out of the bedroom. Benny stared in disbelief. She wore a silver ball gown and a white powdered wig. Her face was perfectly smooth and so beautiful Benny couldn't believe it was she until she began to sing in her strong, low, magnificent voice. She told them afterwards that it was an old Russian love song especially for Jeremy and Benny's mother.

"Now go! Go! Take your lady and get out of here," Miss Bogdonovitch said to Jeremy. "It's time for the honeymoon. You have a new life, and you can't stay reminiscing with an old relic." Benny saw as she came close that her makeup was so heavy it made her look as if she were a china doll. "Go at once. *Tanta Troublushka* dismisses you from her presence. *Do svydanya*, my Cheremy. Go with God."

*****

Benny could hear Jeremy and his mother stumble up the porch steps. Someone giggled and someone else hurriedly shushed him. Jeremy and Benny's mother had returned from their wedding trip in Jefferson City after dark, just as they had written that they would. Benny knew they had first gone to Mrs. Salter's, expecting to collect Benny. But Mrs. Salter's house was locked up and completely dark, just like every other place in town. Benny knew there was a note pinned to Mrs. Salter's front door, telling them to come here, but everyone had whispered that they had come into town so long ago. Benny imagined Jeremy and his mother going to other houses, Lotte's and Helga's, looking for him, and he was worried that they might really be getting upset.

"Do you know that this whole town is dark, Abigail?" Jeremy's voice said, fumbling to unlock the front door. "There's no one here. The door's locked." He stopped and someone shuffled and stepped on Benny's foot. "Ouch!" He hissed. "Shhh!" someone hissed back.

"What in the world is going on?" Benny's mother's voice asked. "Should we go out to Tom and Caroline's, do you think?"

"Maybe the fair was early this year," Jeremy's voice speculated. "Ouch," someone behind Benny muttered. More shushing and shuffling. Benny couldn't believe Jeremy hadn't opened the door yet. "I'm sure everything's all right. We'd've heard if they evacuated Osage."

"Enough is enough!" Uncle Tom exclaimed at last. "Light 'em up, everyone, before we all suffocate in here!"

Suddenly every window of the house lit up with three or four candles or lamps. People poured out all the doors. Some even jumped out the ground-floor windows. Everyone carried candles or lamps. Everyone in Osage, the Owens, Uncle Tom and Aunt Caroline, every soul had crowded into the Carlisle's "new" home, Doctor Shepherd's old place.

Welcome home! Welcome home, Mother and Jeremy!" Benny shouted. "Do you like it? Do you like it?"

"Why -- Does the house look like it's been painted, my dear?" Benny's mother asked, blinking in all the lights.

"It does at that, my love," Jeremy replied.

"Mrs. Salter's daughters and sons-in-law got everybody in town over here and we spent all week fixing and painting and cleaning!" Benny pulled them into the house as people shook hands or patted their shoulders. Benny, along with Mrs. Salter and her family, stayed to give them the "grand tour."

"There are new braided rugs in every room," Benny exclaimed, dragging them from room to room. "The woodwork's so shiny I can see my face in it. That banister thing doesn't fall off when you grab it anymore -- It's like a new house."

"This is -- this is wonderful!" Jeremy said. "How can we thank everyone?"

"And where did they all go?" Benny's mother realized suddenly that the rest of the townsfolk had vanished.

"Doc, ever since you came here, we heard you been makin' things new," said Peter Dreyfus. "And, well, this young fellah," he mussed Benny's hair, "has been doin' some talkin' about all you and your Missus done, especially for Mother Salter, and we figgered everybody in the town owed you, and owed you a lot, us especially, so we all pitched in to fix the place up for you while you were gone. We wanted t' make all things new for our new doc."

"And by the way," Matthew Bolton added, "If we forgot anything you need for your house or your new life, come on over to the Grand Opening of the Bolton & Dreyfus Mercantile tomorrow and pick out whatever you want. Your money's no good there. Never will be, for the first month we're open. It's only thanks to Ben we're opening the store at all. You folks have a good evening."

The Boltons and the Dreyfuses hurried away with Mrs. Salter in tow. Jeremy and Benny's mother watched them go, too astonished to speak.

"I have a feeling we missed something," Jeremy ventured, looking sideways at Benny.

"Lotte and Helga helped fix up our house?" Benny's mother asked. "All they've done since they arrived was quarrel and gossip and put everything off. I don't know how Mrs. Salter got them to finish the wedding clothes she promised us."

"I ... um ... I gave Mr. Bolton and Mr. Dreyfus some ideas about how to get them to stop being selfish," Benny said reluctantly. "See, the day you gave mother the ring and the pearls and went on that ride, I heard what you said about needing to get the house fixed up. I knew you'd been so busy, you needed some time off, and time with Mother, and that you'd never really get the house done without help. So I was trying to think of who could help get the work done while you were on your trip. Everyone here in town is as poor as we are, but the Boltons and the Dreyfuses at least had lots of things for stocking their store that they could use.

"But when I went to ask them for help, they were arguing about the store again. I got them to come here to look over the house, but Mrs. Dreyfus and Mrs. Bolton started right in arguing again, about drapes, about rugs, about what kind of paint, and their husbands just stormed away. I ran after them and told them I really needed their help. And I -- well -- I made a suggestion. I had told Mr. Bolton about -- um -- about how you got Mrs. Salter to stop yelling at Mother all the time, Jeremy --"

"You didn't!" Benny's mother gasped. "But what could they -- How could they --"

"Mrs. Bolton and Mrs. Dreyfus left here, realizing their husbands had gone, and when they got to the store the doors were all locked. They went to their houses and those were locked too. They couldn't get their husbands to answer their calling or knocks. Finally they went to their mother's house and found it locked up too. Their mother let them bang on the door awhile. Then she called out from the window.

"'*Wass ist loss, meine zwei Ganzen?'* she asked them. They started to complain about how their husbands had gone off somewhere and locked them out of the houses and the store.

"'They have not gone off. They are *herein* visiting *mit* me,' Mrs. Salter told them.

"'Well, let us in!' Mrs. Dreyfus said to her. *'Nein,'* Mrs. Salter said. 'Ve have no room for selfish, quacking geese here. Go live in the pond *mit* the rest of the gaggle. Or learn to live at peace and appreciate vhat you have, your homes and your husbands and your jobs vith me and your new store. You shall have none of them until you stop this bickering and complaining. No vork you do, no peace you allow, so no homes you shall have. Go be *Ganzen* if you vill.'"

"Surely that didn't work!" Benny's mother exclaimed.

"Well, it took the whole four hours you and Jeremy were gone, almost," Benny grinned. "They banged on the door, they stormed, they threatened to call the sheriff, and they cried. I was listening the whole time, hiding out in my room, but you couldn't help hearing it all. Nobody in town could help. Mr. Dreyfus and Mr. Bolton wanted to give in a half a dozen times. A crowd gathered outside to watch them. Nobody said a word when they tried to get someone on their side. Not even the Sheriff.

“Mrs. Salter wouldn’t give up her keys. She wouldn’t budge. She admitted that she’d spoiled her daughters, that she was to blame for them being so selfish and stubborn, and that she finally knew how to fix them. She told those men that it was her house, and if they wouldn’t stand by her and let her have this out with her daughters, none of them would ever be welcome back. So they waited it out. Finally Mrs. Dreyfus and Mrs. Bolton said they understood, that they’d been wrong for years, and they cried, really cried, and asked their mother and their husbands to forgive them,

“Mrs. Salter let them in, and they all sat down at the kitchen table. She made them tea and got out some of her best cookies, and she apologized to her daughters, said she was just like them, and had raised them just like herself, but that God had made her change, and she prayed they would really change as well. They all prayed together, and cried some more. Then Mr. Bolton came and got me, and said, ‘Now, let’s get to work planning what we’ll do with the Doc’s house while they’re gone.’“

“I -- I did notice Lotte and Helga seemed much quieter that last week in the shop,” Benny’s mother said uncertainly.

“The wedding clothes did get finished,” Jeremy added. “Nicely done, too. And the house is beautiful, and the store is opening.”

“God can make things new, even when you’re not around, Jeremy,” Benny smiled.

## Chapter Nine – Ben of All Trades

"Two bad cuts, a case of croup, a broken finger, and a baby who swallowed a button," Jeremy sighed as he sat down in the kitchen. "And it's only eleven-thirty. I guess we can stop praying in the patients now, my love."

Jeremy took his wife's hand and squeezed it. Then he grasped Benny's hand and led them in prayer for their lunch. When he finished he looked around.

"I'm sorry Dr. Shepherd turned the dining room into a consulting room," he said with a grin. "I'm sure it used to be a lovely dining room."

"I don't mind eating in the kitchen," Benny's mother smiled.

"Me, neither," Benny said. "Doctors usually get rich, don't they? With all these patients you should have enough money for us to go west in no time."

"Umm ... Mrs. Carlisle, would you tally up the morning's earnings for our junior partner, please?"

"Why, yes, Doctor," Benny's mother said, taking a pad out of her apron pocket and reading. "Let's see ... One promise to shoe our partly barefoot horse, three bales of hay to feed him, two dozen eggs to feed us, one new buggy wheel, and ... ummm ... two dollars and ten cents and an IOU for ninety cents." She had to dig in her pocket for the money and the crumpled slip of paper. "But Mrs. Olsen said she may pay the ninety cents in yard goods if we don't mind."

"Oh, no," Benny groaned. "It's going to take forever!"

"God will send us west when He's ready, Ben," Jeremy laughed. "We won't starve while we're waiting, anyway, and neither will Black Switch."

Black Switch had caused a lot of talk around town. No one else had such a fine horse. But Mrs. Salter had come to Jeremy's defense, snapping out that Osage wanted to be proud of its doctor, and that a fine horse helped him make a good appearance as he went around town. Black Switch saved Jeremy a good deal of time on his house-call rounds. Sometimes Jeremy used the green and yellow buggy, such as when Benny or his mother went along with him.

Jeremy had paid dearly at first for his efforts to make Black Switch appear high-strung and for all the tricks he had taught him. It took a long time for Black Switch to accept the fact that the buggy was there to stay. Jeremy always had to be prepared for sudden stops or to fix a harness strap cunningly chewed through when he came back to the buggy after a call.

Benny ran to the front door as someone knocked sharply. Benny opened the door and found Jason Owens on the front porch. "Hi, Jason, what's up?"

"Pa sent me for the Doc," Jason answered. "Ma's havin' some kinda trouble. Can he come right now?"

"I think so. Come on. Let me check." Benny brought Jason back to the kitchen and told Jeremy what Jason had said.

"Mrs. Owens?" he said, getting up. "Sure, I can go on over there. What could be the matter with her? After nine children she works harder than her husband. She's the one who always snuffs and sticks her nose in the air -- " He imitated her perfectly and Benny and Jason both laughed, "-- whenever somebody talks about bringing their children to see me. 'Doctors!' she says. 'We get along all right taking care of ourselves!' Well, I'd better get going." He kissed Benny's mother and followed Benny and Jason out into the yard.

"Can we take the buggy, Dad?" Benny asked.

"I don't see why not," Jeremy shrugged. "But let's be quick about it. Mrs. Owens won't think the better of me for taking too long to get over there." Switch was quickly hitched up with all three of them working together.

*****

Carl Owens waited out in front of the farmhouse when they arrived. He took Black Switch's headstall as the boys and Jeremy jumped down.

"I'll care for your outfit, Doc," Carl said. "Go on inside. Martha's -- she's not doin' good."

Jeremy stared at the man. Jason's father looked drained and very worried. "Carl, what's wrong? Is it something serious?"

Carl snorted and led Black Switch away. Jeremy hurried into the house with Benny and they found Suzie Grimsby pacing in the front hall. The teenage girl went to school with Benny. She, too, looked strained and nervous. "Ma's upstairs with her, but somethin' ain't right," Suzie reported. "Ma didn't wanna call fer y', but she can't do nothin'. Mr. Owens he said he was gonna call you anyhow. Don't reckon she'll make ten."

Jeremy had started up the stairs when what Suzie had said finally hit home to him. Suzie Grimsby's mother Sally was the town midwife. And Martha Owens was carrying her tenth child just now, due to deliver most any time.

"But I --" Jeremy broke off. "Uh -- Suzie, would you like to take a ride in my buggy?"

"I'd like it fine!" Suzie beamed.

"Good. You go as quick as you can to my house and just ask my wife to come over. I may need her assistance."

"Sure thing!" Sally flew out of the house. Jeremy grabbed Benny by the arm and pulled him close.

"Ben, pray hard. I've never delivered a baby. I've never seen it done. Doc Daniel truly believes in the skills of a midwife, so didn't tell me how to do it. Dr. Shepherd felt the same as Daniel. The Medical Boards talk about hospitals and forceps and never say another word on the subject. It's something midwives always do in a home birth. And this one's a bad one-- even the midwife can't handle it. The only thing I was ever taught about childbirth was how to -- to cut a baby out of a dead woman. Oh, Ben. Pray, pray, pray."

*****

Benny followed him up the stairs. Jeremy had no trouble locating Mrs. Owens' room. Never in all his life had Benny expected to hear that strong, self-possessed woman weep and cry out so. Jason's older sister crowded three of the younger children down the stairs past him. Jeremy paused with his hand on the doorknob.

"Lord, help me," he whispered as another scream came from inside. "Help Martha Owens. And bring my Abigail here quick."

Quickly he slipped inside. Benny came close to the door. He heard Mrs. Grimsby say in an angry voice, "This ain't no place for men!" Apparently Jeremy decided to ignore Mrs. Grimsby for now. "Mrs. Owens, I'm here to help," Jeremy's voice said. Benny had seen Jeremy with many sick or scared people. He knew the first thing Jeremy always did was try to calm them down. He could picture Jeremy kneeling beside Mrs. Owens' bed and taking her hand in his firm, strong grip.

"She don't hear you!" Sally Grimsby's voice shrilled. "Can't nobody help her. Baby's turned bad, probably dead, an' it won't come out."

Mrs. Owens gave another terrible cry, and the room became very still. Benny's heart sank. But a moment later he heard Mrs. Owen's voice, weak but still with some of her old spirit.

"Well, well, if it ain't the doc. Sally, don't tell me you gave up. Mustn't mind her, doc. It ain't easy to admit you're licked. It ain't easy for me, either. This one just ain't goin' right. Sally says the baby's dead. You think so too?"

"Martha, I can't feel anything moving," Jeremy's voice said uneasily. Benny wondered what Jeremy was thinking. How did you get the baby out, even if it was dead? It couldn't stay in there. Mrs. Owens wasn't dead. But Benny had to admit that might still happen, as terrible as her condition seemed to be. Then Benny heard Jeremy and Mrs. Owens both gasp.

"It's alive!" Jeremy crowed. Then Mrs. Owens began a kind of sobbing, gasping, wailing sound. Benny wished he could help instead of just standing outside the door. He wished he could go outside where he didn't have to hear the awful sounds of Mrs. Owens' pain. But Jeremy had asked him to pray, and he wanted to be close and not distracted.

"Martha, God knows I want to help you. He loves you, and he loves this child. The Bible says a lot about women having children. It's something that's real important to God. Let's ask him to help us. I'm going to pray, and you pray with me, and while we do that, I'm just going to be turning you and pushing a bit here and there, all right?"

"All right, Doc," Mrs. Owens said. Jeremy began to pray, and Benny whispered his prayer right along with him. Several minutes passed. Jeremy kept on praying, though his voice seemed to get a bit hoarse and he breathed heavily as if he were working hard.

"Oh! Oh! Oh!" cried Mrs. Owens. Sally Grimsby gave a startled grunt, and then Benny heard a baby cry. Mrs. Owens laughed out loud.

"Ben!" Jeremy shouted a few minutes later. He flung the door open. Benny peeked in and saw Sally laying a swaddled-up bundle in Mrs. Owens' arms. "Go tell Carl and the kids to come see this little pip. I mean this big, fine, healthy boy!"

"Oh, why not?" snapped Sally. "Just fill the whole room up with men!"

When Benny and Jeremy came downstairs, Suzie was just arriving with Benny's mother in the buggy. Jeremy scooped her off the seat and hugged her very tightly.

"Oh, my Abigail," he sighed. "I guess I really didn't need you, but I sure wanted you."

"We're still beatin' 'em, Ben," Jason confided to Benny. "Now it's six boys to four girls. Pa says thanks a lot, Doc. We're gonna call 'im Peter, an' it'll be Pip for short, 'cause pa says you're right, he is a pip."

"Jason, why didn't you tell me what was wrong?" Jeremy asked. "Your mother and Pip could both have died if we'd kept lollygagging around."

"No foolin'?" Jason's eyes went wide. "But it's just another baby. An' all ya did was pray an' it popped right out. That's what Miz Grimsby is sayin'."

Jeremy glanced up at Mrs. Owens' bedroom window. Sally Grimsby's scowling face looked down at them. Then her expression softened, almost into a smile but not quite, and she waved at Jeremy.

"Well, Jason, I guess you're right," Jeremy grinned. "All Pip and your mama really needed was God. He's delivered a lot more babies than I have. Come on, you Carlisles. I have afternoon rounds to do."

*****

"Hi, Mr. Carter. Do you have any chores or errands I could do for you today?"

"Well, hello, Benny," said the owner of the dry goods store. "Need to earn some spending money?"

"Not exactly," Benny replied. "I'm trying to help earn the money we need to move out west."

"I should've thought Doc Carlisle was earnin' money hand over fist," Mr. Carter said, surprised. "Never saw a doc so busy as he is."

"Oh, Jeremy's working as hard as he can," Benny said quickly. "But people pay us in eggs and yard goods and hay bales. We'll never get to move west if we don't get some money."

"Hmmm. I can see where that might be a problem. But say, you've already got your school, and you're still doing a bit of work for the Widow Salter, aren't you? Sure you're not going to be too busy to help me? I need somebody reliable."

"Mr. Carter, if I say I'll be here to help you, I'll be here. I won't let you down," Benny promised.

"All right, then. Stop by tomorrow after school, and I'll have some work for you. I'm sure I can count on you, Benny. You and your mama and the doc, you're good folks."

"Thanks, Mr. Carter. Thanks a lot!" Benny hurried out. Next he went to the livery stable. The boss there, Mr. Ludlow, agreed to Let Benny help clean the stalls and take care of the tack before school. He agreed that Benny had probably had a lot of experience taking care of farm chores and Black Switch. After that Benny went over to the Andersons' big house and Mrs. Anderson told him he could sweep the walks and porches and mow the grass.

Benny's mother wondered at first why Benny was suddenly getting up so early. He began fixing his own breakfast and disappearing before she saw him in the morning. Jeremy told her not to worry. Benny was getting his chores at home done just as he always had, and they knew he had occasional odd jobs. Benny began coming home late, too, sometimes barely making it to the supper table. He was short with his mother when she asked him why.

"You don't complain when Dad misses dinner," Benny grumbled.

"When your dad is late, at least I know why, darling," his mother replied. "You're not being kept after school, are you? Are you having trouble with your classwork? Can we help?"

"School is fine. Mother, I'm tired. Can I go upstairs and do my homework?"

Benny's mother went up to check on him and found him asleep at his desk with his head on top of his geography book. She woke him and chided him for not finishing his studies. Later, when Jeremy came home, she mentioned how tired and cross Benny seemed.

"Well, at least you've seen some of him lately," Jeremy commented. "He never seems to be around anymore. What's he so busy doing? I'd think he was a little old for secret clubs."

"He's not doing anything with Jason Owens," Benny's mother frowned. "I just heard them arguing outside the other day. Jason was saying that Benny never wanted to do anything with him anymore. Benny said he was too busy. Very short and sharp, he spoke to poor Jason. I made him apologize, but he said it was only the truth."

"Well, Mr. Carter said he's doing a fine job at the dry goods store," Jeremy smiled.

"Benny's working for Mr. Carter?" Benny's mother stared at Jeremy. "I didn't know that. Perhaps Mrs. Salter didn't need him anymore. Poor thing. He worries so about us getting enough money to move west."

"Ben's still working for Mrs. Salter, too," Jeremy said. "I saw him running across town with a package from the sewing shop yesterday."

"Oh, my! Two after school jobs seems like a lot."

Jeremy got up to answer a knock at the door. It was Mr. Ludlow from the livery stable. "Evenin', Doc. Sorry to bother you at home, but Ben left this on the hay bales this morning. Figured he'd need it before too long." Mr. Ludlow handed Jeremy Benny's jacket.

"What was Ben doing at the stables?" Jeremy asked. Benny's mother came up behind him.

"Didn't you know he was workin' for me?" Mr. Ludlow asked. "Doin' a bang-up job, too. He's mighty handy with the horses. Customers like him 'cause he's so polite and all. You oughta be might proud of 'im, Doc. Evenin', Mrs. Carlisle. Tell Ben I said I'll see him in the mornin'. Fine boy. Hard worker. G'night, now."

Jeremy stood looking at Abigail, Benny's jacket still in his hands. Abigail finally took it from him, brushed it off and hung it on a hook in the hall.

"Maybe I'd better go talk to Ben," Jeremy said finally. Abigail nodded. Jeremy climbed the stairs and knocked softly on the door of Benny's room. There was no answer. He opened the door quietly and found Benny huddled over his desk, feverishly writing. His hair was mussed and his face looked heavy and flushed in the lamplight.

"Ben, you ought to be in bed by now," Jeremy said softly.

"I didn't quite finish my homework," Benny muttered without looking up. "Just a few more minutes."

"Just how many jobs are you working now?"

Benny started and looked around at Jeremy. "Six," he said in a low voice.

"Six!"

"Not all of them every day," Benny said defensively. "I still get all my chores done, and Mr. Prentice says my school work is better than anybody's."

"Are you sure you're all right?" Jeremy asked. He sat down on the edge of the bed.

"I'm doing fine. Everything's fine. Can I finish my homework now?"

"I think maybe you ought to slow down a little bit, Ben. You're not going to be able to keep up with all this."

"You're keeping up with everything you do," Benny said. "You get up in the middle of the night, you go out early in the morning, you drive twenty miles to one patient. Nobody's asking if you're doing too much. Mother gets up early and works hard all day, scrubbing floors and baking bread and tending her chickens and helping you. How come you and mother think I'm doing too much? Why do grownups work and work and work and nobody ever tells them to slow down, but kids can't do everything they can to help without somebody telling them to take it easy? I don't understand!"

Jeremy reached over and pulled Benny across to sit by him on the bed. Benny burst into tears and sobbed against Jeremy's shoulder.

"We've got to have the money or we'll never get to go west, Dad. Don't you understand? I just want to help."

"All right, Ben. Easy now. I think you're absolutely right. You work as much as you can and earn as much as you can. You keep up with your schoolwork and everything will be fine. But hear me on this. There's a line you've crossed and it's an important one. You think your work is so important that you can fight with Jason and be short with your mother and fall asleep over your studies. All of that is okay, says you, because you're getting everything done. Not so. The Lord Jesus would stay up all night in prayer and then spend the day teaching, healing and loving men. He didn't spend the day growling at them because he was short of sleep and too busy. Don't you do it either. Understood?"

"Understood, Dad." Benny smiled and wiped his eyes. "Thanks. I'm sorry I've been a bear."

"You'll tell your mother that, and Jason, too, eh?"

"I sure will. Goodnight, Dad. I love you."

"Goodnight, laddie. I love you too."

## Chapter Ten – A Disappearance

Benny trudged home from school through the deep snow. He was gladder than he could say that school was out for Christmas holidays. Jason Owens walked beside him in rare silence. Benny considered Jason by far his best friend, but he was glad for the occasional break from Jason's almost non-stop talking.

"Didja hear Caleb Sutter -- I mean Caleb Prentice -- Is comin' home tomorra?" Jason said abruptly. So much for silence, and so much for Benny's light mood. Benny had always feared Caleb. Even though the older boy had been away at boarding school, Benny still had nightmares of the time when Caleb had caught him after school and beaten him so badly he hadn't been able to straighten up for three days.

"I thought he was staying in Ohio for Christmas, and the Prentices were going to see him there," Benny said, trying not to let his dread show in his voice.

"Change of plans, I guess," Jason shrugged. "When I was takin' my turn haulin' the firewood Mr. Prentice told me he'd got a letter sayin' Caleb was comin' home. He seemed surprised about it, too, but I guess he's comin', all right."

Surely Caleb would have got over hating him after all this time away, Benny told himself. He'd been studying cartography, meeting new people. Maybe he'd found someone in Ohio who was more fun to terrorize than Benny. After all, it had been almost a year. He might have forgotten Benny existed. Benny wished he could forget Caleb. He could scarcely even be thankful that Caleb had rescued his mother from drowning when she had fallen into the cataract in the woods and dislocated her shoulder. Caleb had made his venomous hatred of Benny so clear even after he had left Benny's mother safe at the doctor's. That was another nightmare. He could see Caleb, naked from the waist up, muscles bulging, long blond hair like a lion's mane around his harsh, angry features and blazing pale blue eyes.

"If it had been you in that river, Richardson," said the nightmare Caleb, "I'd've let you drown." Benny knew that Jason was jabbering on, talking about his family's plans for Christmas. Benny couldn't make himself pay attention. He left Jason still talking and ran up the steps and into the house.

*****

Throwing off his heavy clothes, Benny ran upstairs to his room. He ignored his mother's greeting and shut the door of his room. Quickly he plunged his hands into the big chest at the foot of his bed. He dug under the things inside, becoming more frantic. At last he pulled out the handsome black dragon-ornamented case he had been searching for. Pressing the hidden clasp, he popped it open.

Benny gazed at the beautifully polished throwing knife inside the case. He set the case down on his bed and picked up the knife. First he tested the balance in his palm. It was perfect. Then he flipped the knife around into throwing position and drew back. All of this took only a second. The knife streaked across the room and lodged in the eye of the cougar drawing hanging by the window. Benny grimly crossed the room and pulled the knife out of the wall. He turned to walk back to the bed and saw his mother standing in the open doorway. Her eyes were wide with shock.

"I -- I knocked, but you didn't answer," she said faintly. "Benny -- what -- what are you doing with that knife?"

"Just making sure I haven't gotten rusty," Benny said. He put it back in the case and slipped the case under his pillow. "I wonder if Dad will let me have the sheath now?" He mused.

“I thought you’d just packed that knife away,” his mother said.

“No, mother. I practice with it every day. Every single day. Now I’m almost as good as Dad was.”

“Does Jeremy -- does your dad know you’ve been doing this?”

“Well, he helped me a lot at first. I don’t know if he knows I’ve kept practicing. Mother, it’s kind of a sport, like fishing.”

“I’ve never heard of anyone being killed with a fishhook.”

“Don’t worry. I’m certainly not planning to kill anybody. Who would I want to kill?”

Benny’s mother had never found out about the beating Caleb had given Benny, or the constant threats and taunts Caleb had made. She knew that Caleb had been a bully, but he had made such an outward show of reforming when the Prentices had adopted him that no one knew he had never changed, just gotten smarter and craftier. No one, not Benny’s mother, not Jeremy, not even Jason, who knew Caleb disliked Benny more than anyone, knew how much Benny feared Caleb’s Christmas homecoming.

*****

It quickly became apparent after Caleb arrived home that something was wrong. The Prentices stopped their proud bragging about how well he was doing in school. The big welcome home party they had planned was cancelled. Benny saw Caleb lounging around town with several bad characters. Thankfully, Caleb seemed no longer to know that Benny existed. Benny did ask for, and received as a Christmas present, the ankle sheath Jeremy had used to carry the throwing knife in his wilder days before he became a Christian. Benny got a lecture on never wearing it to school.

*****

In the middle of the night after Christmas day, someone knocked loudly on the Carlisle’s front door.

Benny got there first, and found Mr. Prentice on the porch.

"The -- the doctor -- is he in?" Mr. Prentice stammered. Benny knew that Mr. Prentice had never seemed to like or trust Jeremy. He couldn't forget that Jeremy had robbed a bank before he was saved. He couldn't forget he had spent two years in prison in Philadelphia. Jeremy had won friends all over town with his fine doctoring, friendly ways and Christian love, but the Prentices had never been friendly with them, and had never sought his medical services before.

"What's wrong, Mr. Prentice?" Jeremy came up behind Benny. Benny felt him staying back in the shadows and realized Jeremy still felt very self-conscious about being seen without the makeup that hid his terrible scars. He didn't wear any to bed, of course.

"It's Caleb," Mr. Prentice said. "He's had some kind of accident. Some of his friends just brought him home. We can't wake him up -- please, can you come quickly?"

"I'll be there in five minutes," Jeremy said, disappearing from the doorway. Mr. Prentice hurried off.

"Get my bag, Ben," Jeremy ordered as he vaulted up the stairs. Benny ran into the surgery and fumbled around for things Jeremy might need. Maybe Caleb had fallen and hit his head. Maybe he had a bad fever -- Benny wasn't sure what to pack.

"Want to get dressed and come along?" Jeremy asked. Benny was surprised. Usually Jeremy took Benny's mother along if he thought he would need help. Benny left Jeremy finishing the bag and ran upstairs to throw on his clothes. He was down again in a moment. "It takes your mother much longer to get dressed," Jeremy said with a grin. "Come on."

*****

They decided to walk, since the Prentices' house was not that far and it would take time to hitch up the buggy. Very soon they were let in to the Prentices' house. Mr. Prentice reached out to take Jeremy's coat as he finished stomping the snow off his boots and turned around into the full light of the hallway.

Mr. Prentice gasped and pulled his hand back. “Your -- your face!” he croaked. “What -- what --?”

Benny quickly took Jeremy’s coat and found a hook for it himself. Jeremy went red, then white, but he said nothing in reply. Benny knew that most people in town knew about Jeremy’s scars, and many had even seen them. Obviously Mr. Prentice had not known about them. Jeremy grabbed his bag from Benny.

“Where is the patient, Mr. Prentice?” Jeremy demanded. Still Mr. Prentice just stared. Finally Jeremy pushed past him, pulling Ben along, and went into the front room. Mr. Prentice seemed to wake up at last and hurried after them.

Caleb lay sprawled on the settee in the front room. His long legs dangled onto the floor and one arm hung over the back. His face was buried under a pillow and his breathing was ragged and loud. Mrs. Prentice jumped up from a stool beside Caleb’s head, took one look at Jeremy, and gave a little shriek of fright. Again Jeremy’s color changed, but he moved by her and knelt beside Caleb. With Benny’s help he rolled the young man onto his back, lifting one of his heavy eyelids. Jeremy moved Caleb’s head from side to side and felt it all over. He felt his pulse, listened to his chest, and finally opened his mouth and smelled his breath. Jeremy reeled back and stood up. He turned to look at Mr. and Mrs. Prentice and saw them close together, shrinking away from him and looking anywhere but at his face.

“Um ...” Jeremy stopped. Benny could see how hard it was for him to be professional while the Prentices were behaving like that. “I ... I examined Caleb for any head injuries, any bumps or bruises. I checked for fever or any symptoms of illness of any kind. Caleb isn’t hurt and he isn’t sick, Mr. and Mrs. Prentice. He’s drunk.”

“Drunk!” Mr. Prentice exploded. “Drunk! That’s impossible!”

“Ridiculous!” Mrs. Prentice agreed. “Caleb does not drink. He just went to a little Christmas party with some of his friends.”

"Caleb is drunk," Jeremy repeated. "Judging by his general appearance and condition, I'd say he's been drinking a great deal, and doing it for some time."

"He's been at school, Mr. -- er -- Doctor Carlisle--" Mr. Prentice insisted. "They would never allow the boys to drink."

"Well, he has been drinking," snapped Jeremy. "And if he doesn't stop, he'll die. I had a brother who died of drinking. He was nineteen, Mr. Prentice. How old is Caleb?"

"Nine -- nine--" Mr. Prentice couldn't finish.

"He's got to stop now," Jeremy said. "And you've got to stop pretending it isn't happening."

"How dare you?" shrieked Mrs. Prentice. "John, make him go away! If he can't help Caleb, why is he here?" She fell down beside the settee.

Jeremy brushed past Mr. Prentice and he and Benny went out to the hall to get their coats. Mr. Prentice followed them.

"Doctor Carlisle, I'm sorry," he said, touching Jeremy on the arm. "I'm sorry about the way we behaved. Caleb -- Caleb has been drinking. He's been dismissed from school because of it. My wife -- she doesn't know. I didn't know how to tell her. Caleb -- he laughed -- he bragged about it. I beat him, I threatened him, but he won't stop. I don't know what else to do. We can't control him. He -- he frightens my wife, yet she still wants him to be -- to be the boy we could never have ourselves. What can we do?"

"You've had a good look at my face, now, haven't you, Mr. Prentice?" Jeremy took both Mr. Prentice's shoulders in his strong hands and made him face him. "I can keep it hidden most of the time, but it's never really gone. It's like our sin. We can cover it up for a while, but it keeps peeking out. For some people, like Caleb, it comes raging out. You've got to get rid of that sin, Mr. Prentice. Caleb's sin, your sin, your wife's sin. The drink is just Caleb's way of filling that empty place where God should be.

"I don't know what you put in your empty space -- pride, maybe, thinking you're better than a poor ex-convict doctor with an ugly face -- whatever it is, I'll bet it doesn't work. Only Christ can take away the sin and fill the emptiness. As Caleb's father, you might be the only one who can help him come to Christ. You dare not neglect that any longer. Won't you submit to Christ yourself, and be the father to that boy that he desperately needs?"

"We've done the best we can to provide a home for Caleb," Mr. Prentice said coldly, pulling out of Jeremy's grasp. "He's been difficult -- always -- difficult. I can't do any more -- my wife can't do any more -- than we already have."

"Good night, Mr. Prentice," Jeremy said sadly. "Come on, Ben."

*****

They walked in silence back home. Just before they reached the house, Benny put his arms up and hugged Jeremy as tightly as he could.

"I love you, Dad," he said.

"Do you ever wonder what would have happened if your mother really had adopted Caleb back when his family died? Would he have turned out differently, do you think?" Jeremy sighed.

Benny's stomach lurched. How long ago he had run to his mother and begged her to take Caleb in. How long ago had he felt that much compassion for Caleb? Lately he had not felt sorry for him at all. But Caleb was in deep trouble. Benny had never tried to see things Caleb's way before. He had lived with a father who was always drunk and never worked. He had found his mother and sister frozen to death in their shack one winter morning, and his father had died in jail the same day. Caleb had gone to live with the Prentices, but Benny knew they had not loved him. His schemes to escape Osage hadn't worked. His life was a ruin, and at nineteen he was hardly a grown man.

"Isn't there something we can do to help him Dad?" Benny asked

"Maybe we can try," Jeremy said. "Come on. You must be frozen, Ben, know I am. We've got to get some sleep. We'll talk about it in the morning."

Jeremy and Benny's mother went to see the Prentices about Caleb the next day. They were cold and unwilling to discuss anything that might help Caleb. Mr. Prentice had told his wife the truth after Jeremy's visit, but she was still denying it. Mr. Prentice informed them that Caleb would be working for Mr. Black the wheelwright, that he would be kept very busy, and that there would be no further opportunity for him to be around his "unsuitable companions."

Benny had to pass by the wheelwright's shop every day on his way to and from school. He would see Caleb there, shirtless sometimes, even in the coldest weather, sweat covering his broad back, shaping wood, pounding metal, working as if he could sweat the trouble out of his body.

Benny was shocked to see scars crisscrossing Caleb's back. Mr. Prentice used a thin stick sometimes to discipline children at the school, but only a few switches through their clothing. He had admitted he beat Caleb, but Benny had never seen anyone scarred like that. Caleb never even seemed to notice Benny. Benny was glad for that.

*****

One day Benny got sick at school. Jeremy had caught a fever with cramps and vomiting from one of his patients and had been in bed two days with it. Benny had gone to school feeling light-headed and queasy, and by lunchtime had felt bad enough to beg Mr. Prentice to let him go home. Benny stumbled toward home and stopped outside Mr. Black's shop when a wave of nausea washed over him.

"Well, if it isn't sweet little perfect Benny," growled a voice. Benny had been so dizzy and sick he hadn't noticed where he was. He looked up and saw Caleb and two other young men. They passed a bottle around among them and guzzled the liquor with noisy slurping sounds.

"Skippin' school today, Little Benny?" sneered Caleb. He swaggered over, bottle in hand.

"I -- I'm sick," Benny said faintly.

"Aw! Ain't that too bad. Well, look here, I got some medicine. Just the thing. Here, drink some!" He grabbed Benny by the hair and forced his head back. The bottle came up close to Benny's face and liquor began to pour out, filling his nose with the smell. Benny vomited suddenly, right on Caleb's leg.

"Hey!" snarled Caleb, cursing as he kicked Benny hard. Benny fell to the sidewalk. Caleb kicked him again.

"You've always been such a good boy, haven't you, Benny? You've always made your mama proud, and everybody loves you. Precious Benny! You even came out on top when I beat the livin' daylights out of you. And you wanted your ma to adopt me. Didja think I'd forget that? You even made me save her -- Can't you just leave me alone? You're always in fronta my face, showin' me how I oughta be, and I don't wanna be like you!"

Kick after kick slammed into Benny. He rolled this way and that but he couldn't escape. The pain was terrible. He threw up again and cried out in pain and hopelessness. He could dimly tell that some people had gathered and somebody was yelling at Caleb to stop, but he was so strong no one could drag him away.

All at once there was silence and the blows stopped. Benny opened his eyes and looked up. Jeremy, only partly dressed, his shirt hanging open in the freezing air, his hair wild, his scars standing out in the terrible paleness of his angry face, had grabbed Caleb by the collars and slammed him back against the wall of the building. Benny knew Jeremy was still sick himself. Where he had gotten the strength to do what he had done to Caleb Benny did not know. How he had even known to come, Benny could not imagine.

"Don't move," Jeremy ordered Caleb. "You stir and I'll make you wish you hadn't."

Caleb hung frozen against the building as Jeremy knelt beside Benny. "Ben, are you all right?" he said fiercely. He probed Benny quickly here and there. Benny started to get up. "No. Stay put. Ralph, Marshall!" he shouted at two men who stood by. “Get Ben over to my house. I’ll be right behind you.” The two men quickly hitched up Mr. Black’s delivery wagon and put Benny on a horse blanket to lift him up into it. Jeremy went back to Caleb. Benny had never seen such terror in anyone’s face as he saw in Caleb’s.

“We’ve tried kindness and patience, Caleb,” Jeremy said. “Now we’ll try this. I can see you’re afraid of this face of mine. Good. You be afraid of it. You remember it every day and every night. And you remember that if you ever attack my son again, I will kill you. Never doubt that I can. Never, ever doubt that I will.”

Caleb bolted and ran, slipping, falling flat in the snow, tripping in the drifts, getting up, running again. He was not headed for the Prentice house. Jeremy jumped up into the wagon and steadied Benny on the short trip to the house. Benny’s mother waited on the porch, crying and trying to throw a blanket over Jeremy.

“What happened? What happened?” she kept asking. “I was in the kitchen. All of a sudden I heard you come flying down the stairs. I didn’t even see where you’d gone.”

Jeremy shrugged her off. “Bring him into the surgery,” Jeremy ordered the men. “Abigail, never mind me. It’s Ben who’s hurt. Thank you, fellows.” They left hurriedly. Jeremy took Benny’s mother’s face in his hands. “My love, be calm. I need you to help me with Ben.” Suddenly Jeremy sagged. “I’m still so confoundedly weak,” he said. “Caleb Prentice attacked Ben. When I got there he was kicking him -- he might be bleeding inside -- help me get him undressed. Ben, tell me where it hurts. No, I know, it feels like it hurts everywhere, but stay with me and think. Where’s the worst of it?”

Benny responded feebly to Jeremy’s gentle examination. His mother helped turn him and clean his bruises. Benny felt so dizzy and sick and hot.

“He’s got my fever,” Jeremy grunted. “Is that why you were coming home?”

Benny nodded. Even that hurt. Jeremy dragged up a stool and sat down heavily.

"Dad, you're still sick," Benny whispered. Jeremy looked so white, and his hands hardly seemed to be able to move. "How could you come? How did you know? How did you stop Caleb when nobody else could?"

"Maybe nobody else loves you like I do, Ben," Jeremy said with a tired smile. "I was lying there in bed, too pooped to even lean over the basin, and all of a sudden I knew I had to get up and go after you. I knew something was wrong. And when I got there, God just gave me back my strength for that minute or two it took. God told me you needed me, Ben. That's all. And He helped me."

*****

By nightfall it became clear that Caleb was gone. No trace of him could be found anywhere around town. He hadn't gone home for any of his things. He had vanished. The next day some men searched the area. But more snow fell and a bitter, freezing wind howled until it drove them home. Benny, miserably trying to throw up with bruised ribs, could hardly understand the news that Mr. Prentice had told them not to continue searching.

"But, mother, what if Caleb should be lost out there in this weather?" Benny whispered as she put a cold cloth on his forehead. "Why doesn't Mr. Prentice want to find him?"

"He's so ashamed of what Caleb has done, darling," his mother said. "He told us that he wanted no more to do with Caleb. He feels Caleb is a man now, and I suppose he's right. I wonder what will happen to him?"

"I wonder that you can have so much compassion on that fellow, Ben," Jeremy said, coming into the room and sitting on the bed beside Benny. "He was trying to kill you. You do understand that, don't you? Everyone who saw it was sure he was going to succeed."

"Don't you remember what I used to tell you when you first said you'd kill me, after I found out you were a bank robber, Dad? I said if you killed me, I'd go to heaven. But if you died, you'd go to Hell. And it's the same with Caleb. Don't you see how much he's like you? God made him see Christ in me, and he hated it and wanted to stop seeing it. That means he could get saved. You did."

"You shame me, Ben. I really wanted to kill Caleb. I still do."

"Dad, if someone's trying to kill someone you love, then you have to do whatever it takes to stop him. There's nothing wrong with that. That's not the same thing as wanting someone who needs Christ to find Him instead of wanting him to die without finding Him. I never loved you so much as when I saw you saving me from Caleb. You did something no one else could, Dad. I've been so afraid of Caleb for so long. But now I know that if Caleb ever does come back, I don't need to be afraid."

"Whoa, Ben. I took Caleb by surprise and scared him a little bit. I'm not really so sure I could fight him off again."

"You don't understand. All I mean is that now I can trust God to protect me from Caleb. This time He chose to use you. Another time He'll do it some other way. But however God chooses to do it, I can stop fretting about it. You showed me that God is able to protect me. That's why I don't have to be afraid of him anymore."

## Chapter Eleven – Neglected Business

By the time school ended for the winter session everyone knew that the Prentices were leaving. Caleb had never returned. Some people wondered what would happen if he did come back. Mr. Prentice only said they were going to move back to Boston.

"If Caleb did come back, would the Prentices take him to Boston with them?" Benny asked Jeremy one day.

"I don't know," Jeremy shrugged. "I wonder if he'd want to go with them. But I don't expect him to come back, so it doesn't really matter."

*****

Slowly but surely the Carlisles were collecting the things they would need to travel west. Benny couldn't understand how it was happening, since hardly anyone paid them in money. One day his mother took him out to the storage shed where they were filling up crates and barrels of things to take west.

"Look here, darling," she said, leading him to a crate. "Here are nails and woodworking tools. Look over here now. Seeds to grow our own garden. Over there are some beautiful quilts and braided rugs. And we have flour, dried beans, sugar, and a barrel of salt pork. Don't you see that God can give us what we need without giving us money?"

"We still need a wagon and oxen," Benny said.

"We need quite a few things, darling," his mother said, hugging him. "And God knows about every one of them. What's bothering me is what Osage's going to do for a doctor when we leave. Your father's been so busy we've hardly had time to pack and prepare the things we've got."

*****

Later, Benny met Jason in town where several boys were eyeing the new wood models in the window of the mercantile. Benny listed all the things they had accumulated for the trip west. "I didn't really see anything happening," he admitted. "But God is getting us ready, little by little."

"Someday I'm gonna go west, too," Jason said. "I'm gonna build roads and bridges so the towns can grow."

"You're not," sneered Joe Walker, the wheelwright's son. "And I don't guess Benny will, either. Doc Carlisle's got a chance to get rich if he just plays it smart. He'd be stupid to go out west. If I was a doctor I'd go back east where they get rich."

"My dad's not interested in getting rich," Benny snorted. "He wants to serve the Lord."

"How come you call him that?" Joe asked.

"What?" Benny had started to walk away to Mrs. Salter's shop to see if she had any deliveries or sewing machine repairs for him to do.

"The doc," Joe answered. "How come you call him your dad?"

"Why -- why shouldn't I?"

"He's not your dad just 'cause he married your ma. He'd have to adopt you. But I guess he doesn't want to or he'd have done it by now."

"You're crazy," Jason scowled. "Doc Carlisle is as good a dad as mine or yours. Maybe better."

Joe ignored Jason, looking straight at Benny. "How come he hasn't adopted you? The Prentices adopted Caleb right away, the same day his folks died."

Benny was silent a minute. "I guess it's just something he never thought about," he answered finally. "He's been really busy."

"If it was important to him, he'd've done something about it!" Joe challenged.

"What's it to you, Joe?" Jason demanded. "You oughta mind your own business, maybe."

"What if your ma was to die?" Joe persisted. "The doc could just -- well -- he could just leave you, or get rid of you -- give you to the orphanage --"

"As if he would," Jason snorted. Benny didn't say anything. He listened in silence to the flood of words still coming out of Joe's mouth.

"Even if he kept you, he could be a rich doctor if he went someplace else, like I said, and he'd get so busy he wouldn't have time for you. Maybe he would go back east and set up a fancy city practice, and put you in a school far away so you wouldn't bother him, and --"

"Are you done?" Benny asked finally. "Anything else you want to say?"

"You think it ain't true," Joe said, "but it could happen. I just read it in a book, something just like that."

"You read it in a book," Benny repeated. "You mean this book?"

He grabbed the dog-eared illustrated serial out of Joe's back pocket and opened it. Joe tried to grab it away but Benny started to read out loud.

"'What happens when the light first pierces the dark dampness in which we have waited? We are slapped and cut loose. If we are lucky, someone is there to catch us and persuade us that we are safe. But are we safe? What happens if, too early, we lose a parent? That party on whom we rely for only everything? Why, we are cut loose again and we wonder, even dread whose hands will catch us now?"

"Give that back!" Joe cried. Benny was taller than he was and he held the book up in the air. Joe danced around him.

"You want it back?" Benny asked. "Then try really reading this. It's a story by Charles Dickens, called *Nicholas Nickleby*. It's about a man who was selfish and mean almost his whole life, who never tried to do what was right. It has nothing to do with my dad. Take back what you said about him. It's not true, any of it. He's always wanted to go west. And he's never going to get rich being a doctor. And as far as adopting goes, the Prentices never loved Caleb. They had a fancy legal piece of paper but they were selfish and proud, and when they couldn't be proud of Caleb, they gave up on him."

"Ask him how come he's never adopted you," Joe challenged, still trying to get his serial back.

"I couldn't do that." Benny brought the book down suddenly and Joe grabbed it away.

"Why not?" demanded Joe. "You oughta go and find the doc right now and ask him."

"But I --"

"Go on. I dare you! Go ask him!"

Benny spun on his heel. He saw Black Switch and the buggy parked out in front of the Millers' storefront. But when Benny started up the stairs to the Miller's house, which was above their millinery shop, Benny saw Jeremy on his way down the steps and backed up to wait for him. Some of the boys, Joe included, followed at a little distance.

"Jeremy, I need to talk to you about something," Benny said quickly. Jeremy looked up, startled, as he came off the bottom step.

"Ben! I didn't see you," he said. He glanced behind him, and Benny saw that Sheriff Tanner had followed Jeremy down the steps. "What is it? Is your mother all right?"

"Jeremy, how come you never adopted me?" Benny blurted out.

The sheriff came up close behind Jeremy. Jeremy glanced at him again. Then he looked back at Benny.

"How come I never adopted you?" Jeremy had a very odd expression on his face. He held on to the stair rail as if he were dizzy. The sheriff put out a hand. At first Benny thought it was to steady Jeremy, because he really seemed to be having some kind of trouble keeping his balance. He put a hand on his forehead.

"We've got to have that talk, Doc," Sheriff Tanner said. He took Jeremy firmly by the arm. "I got to have it for the official report."

"Now -- now wait just a minute," Jeremy waved his free hand. "Wait, Abe. This is important, what Ben has just asked me. I've been so busy I -- This is so important I've got to take care of it right now."

“Doc!” The sheriff looked angry and impatient. Jeremy shook off his hand. He grabbed Benny by the arm. “Come on, Ben. You and I are going to get your mother and go over to the magistrate and get this taken care of right now.”

“You can’t just walk off, Doc!” the sheriff spluttered.

“Watch me. Come on, Ben.”

*****

An hour later Benny and his mother and Jeremy came out of the magistrate’s office, really just a room in Osage’s little *Traveler’s Rest Hotel.* Benny studied the sheepskin parchment in his hands. He saw Joe Walker across the street but Joe Walker didn’t seem all that important at the moment.

“They’ll have to send for the final paperwork from Philadelphia,” Jeremy explained, “And they’ll make copies of the rest of the documents here and deliver them to the house. Is that good enough for now?”

Benny smiled sheepishly. Jeremy had pestered the clerk and finally got the magistrate to see them. Everything was signed and sealed. What a lot of paperwork they’d had to do! Some of the things didn’t seem to have much to do with just adopting Benny. Jeremy had gone over all kinds of legal papers relating to the house, the medical practice, and things Benny hadn’t even known about before. His mother had seemed a little puzzled by all the things Jeremy had her study and sign. Jeremy actually became sharp with Benny when his attention wandered.

“Pay attention to this, Ben. Your mother can’t go through this alone again. You have to help her if the time comes.” Benny had tried hard to understand it all, but the one thing he didn’t understand was why Jeremy was so serious and so concerned. Benny thought that maybe Jeremy just felt bad about putting the adoption off.

In Benny’s hands was a legal certificate stating that Jeremy Gladstone Carlisle had completed all the procedures for the adoption of Benjamin Jonathan Richardson Carlisle.

"It's great," Benny said, finally waking up and realizing what Jeremy had just said to him. "What did the sheriff want to talk to you about, Jeremy? I mean -- Dad?"

"The sheriff?" Benny's mother echoed.

"The same thing he still wants to talk to you about," Sheriff Tanner said, coming quickly up behind them as Jeremy helped Benny's mother up into the buggy. He looked very angry. "I don't want to make a scene, Doc. You can save us both a lot of trouble if you come along with me now."

"All right," Jeremy nodded. Benny saw that he didn't seem as troubled as he had been when Benny had first seen him outside the Miller's store. "Abigail, you and Ben go on home. I think -- I guess I'll be along later."

"What is it?" Benny's mother asked, frightened. "My dear, what's wrong? Mr. Tanner, what is it?"

"I'm investigating the disappearance of Caleb Sutter -- Caleb Prentice," the sheriff said. "The doc here was one of the last people to see him before he took off. And I guess they had words."

"What are you saying?" Benny's mother demanded. "Caleb attacked Benny. He would have killed him. My husband stopped him. He --"

"Mrs. Carlisle, I have a job to do," the sheriff said. "Your husband threatened to kill Caleb. And now Caleb's missing. I have to get a statement from him and ask him some questions. That's what I'm going to do."

"Are you going to arrest my dad?" Benny asked, horrified.

"Ben, Abigail, please go home," Jeremy urged. "Please. The sheriff does have to do this. You're just making it harder. Ben, you hang on to that paper, and make sure you get the rest of the documents as soon as they're ready. Abigail, everything's in order at the house. If something happens, you won't have any trouble selling the practice and Switch, too, if you need to. Go to Ben's grandfather or Tom if I'm -- If I can't come back. Promise me you won't just try to get by on your own again. Promise me."

"Oh --" Benny's mother leaned down and seized Jeremy and held onto him, burying her fingers in his hair. "I love you so much."

"I love you, Abigail," Jeremy whispered. "Ben--" he reached out a hand and Benny grabbed on to it. "Ben, I love you too, son. I love you, too. Take your mother and go home."

Benny grabbed the leads and Jeremy untangled himself from his wife's grasp. Benny snapped the reigns and Switch took off for home. Benny had to help his mother into the house. He made her lie down on the couch in the sitting room. She was crying so hard Benny couldn't stay in the room and listen to her. First Benny unhitched Black Switch and put him up in the stable. Next he went out to the storage shed and looked around at all the things that represented their hopes and dreams of going west. He felt like picking up an ax and smashing the barrels and crates into a thousand pieces.

"The sheriff was there to arrest him at the Millers' place," Benny said out loud, pacing wildly around the little shed. "I came there with some stupid, selfish idea that Jeremy didn't care about me, because Joe Walker read about it in a serial, and I came right out and asked him about that stupid adoption, when the sheriff was taking him to jail. And he cared so much about us he had to go and get everything legally written up and ready because he doesn't think he's ever going to come back home."

Benny wondered how anybody could be so stupid as to think Jeremy would really kill Caleb. Then he remembered the fury on Jeremy's face. He remembered the amazing strength with which Jeremy had pulled Caleb off Benny and slammed him into the harness shop wall. Jeremy was still sick with a fever then, but he had stopped Caleb when no one else could. Benny remembered what Jeremy had said to Caleb. He knew Jeremy never said anything he didn't mean. And Caleb had never been seen again since that snowstorm.

"Jeremy didn't do anything to Caleb," Benny told himself. "He wouldn't once he knew I was safe. That was all he cared about. He just wanted to take care of me. He only cared about me. He wants to stay with us and take care of us forever. God wouldn't take him away from us, not after he took my father. We can't lose Jeremy too."

Benny fell down on his knees. "Lord God, please protect my dad and bring him back home. Oh, please, don't let anything happen to him. We love him, and we need him so much. Please let my dad come home."

Benny pulled out one of the quilts his mother had been showing him and wrapped himself up in it, lying down on the shed's dirt floor. He continued to pray until he fell asleep.

Benny woke with a start. It was pitch dark in the shed. He scrambled out of the quilt, but he was so stiff from lying on the cold dirt floor that he could hardly get the door open to go out of the shed. In the twilight he hobbled out and came around the front of the house just as Jeremy came up the walk.

"Dad!" He cried. He flew to Jeremy and hugged him as hard as he could. Then, finally, he began to cry.

"Oh, now, don't son, please," Jeremy begged. "Everything's all right. The sheriff did his duty. He asked his questions, and then he said I'd only acted like and done what any father would have. He has no evidence that I had anything to do with Caleb's disappearance, except that I might have scared him into running away. And he admitted that if he was in my place, and it was his son likely to be killed, he'd have made sure himself that Caleb wouldn't want to come back and try again. He said that's what fathers are supposed to do for their sons.

"All his talk about my being a father, and me taking care of my son really warmed me up inside. I used to think I'd never want children, Ben. I was such a fool. I'm so glad I have a son. I'm so glad we got that taken care of. Ben, I might have brushed you off if it hadn't been for the sheriff. If I hadn't been just a little bit afraid of not coming home, I might have left you and your mother in a bigger mess than you had when your father died. Now, if anything does happen to me ..."

"Don't say that, Dad," Benny pleaded. "You can't ever leave us. When my father died, the world just sort of crumbled out from under us. It was so awful. I don't think mother would make it if it happened again."

"Ben, I can't promise nothing's ever going to take me away from you and your mother. You have to remember that it's God you have to rely on, not me. Surely you learned that during our trek here before I was saved."

"God gave you to us," Benny said stubbornly. "Nobody else could have gotten me to Uncle Tom's. And He saved you, and he led you to marry mother. He wouldn't take you away."

"So if I were taken away, that would mean you'd stop trusting God again?" Jeremy scowled. "Do you have any idea what it was like for me those two years in prison? When I got saved I thought everything was going to be wonderful. I thought I'd get a little slap on the wrist prison sentence and be right out again. I thought I'd be headed west in no time at all. And then I was inside those stone walls, looking at ten years stretching ahead of me like eternity, more than a thousand miles away from you. I thought I'd never see you again. I thought I might not survive ten years in that place. Getting your letters just made it worse. I knew I'd never be a doctor, or a preacher. I thought God had just dropped me -- or worse, that none of what you and Doc Daniel had told me about was real or true. I thought I was alone."

Jeremy shook Benny by the shoulders. "But I wasn't alone. Back in Jeff City, before you even came that first time, I realized that God was there with me. I had His Word and I could talk to Him even when I was exhausted and hurting and had nothing but more exhaustion and hurt to look forward to. I submitted to His will and I thanked Him for His love, which I could believe in by faith through His Word, even in prison. And the next day you and your mother showed up to visit."

"So what you're saying is that I have to trust God even when there's no good and sensible reason to do it?" Benny asked.

"Here's the good and sensible reason, Ben," Jeremy chuckled. He opened his doctor bag and pulled out his Bible. "We always have this reason to trust God. Because He says in His Word, 'I will never leave thee, nor forsake thee.' Somebody used to quote that verse to me all the time."

Benny's mother came out onto the porch then, saw Jeremy, and flew into his arms.

"I prayed and prayed and prayed, and then I just fell asleep," she said guiltily.

"I did the same thing," Benny admitted.

"It's all right," Jeremy said. "'It is vain for you to rise up early, to stay up late, to eat the bread of sorrows. For so He giveth His beloved sleep.' Maybe that was God's way of keeping you both from worrying too much."

"But I haven't fixed dinner," Benny's mother said.

"Let's go down to the hotel and have dinner there tonight," Jeremy suggested. "We've got cause to celebrate. Les Miller paid me for tending all five of his kids when they had the measles. He paid in cash, Ben. We're rich!"

*****

Laughing, they went into the house to get ready. On the way into the hotel, Benny saw Joe Walker. "I'll be right in, Mother, Dad," he said, and turned over to where Joe stood.

"Wasn't the sheriff gonna arrest the doc?" Joe said, wide-eyed. "How'd he get rid of Caleb? Was it self-defense?"

"Thanks, Joe," Benny said.

"Thanks for what?"

"For giving me a chance to prove that my dad doesn't do anything for himself, unlike Ralph Nickleby. He does everything for the Lord, and my mother, and for me, because I'm his son. For real."

## Chapter Twelve – The Doctor's Assistant and the Schoolteacher

"Now, dear, it's only temporary. The board is desperate," Benny's mother reasoned. She had just come back from a school board meeting with an announcement that had sent Jeremy leaping off his chair. Jeremy paced around the kitchen.

"Temporary?"

"Four weeks, they think," Benny's mother said timidly.

"Four weeks? Abigail, school begins in two days. This new teacher goes and breaks her legs. Not one leg. Two legs. Temporary? Four weeks? She'll be lucky if she can do it in four months! This won't be temporary. You'll be there the whole winter term. I don't want you to teach school, Abigail. I need you here, helping me with the practice. I can't do without you."

"There's no one else, my dear," Benny's mother set her bonnet on the table. "Really, you know there's no one else. We already had to lose the summer session because the Prentices were gone and no one answered the advertisement. These children need schooling. Do you want Benny to lose another whole year of school? I have to do this. We'll manage somehow."

"The board will manage by getting someone else. Abigail, I had to do my evening surgery without you. I couldn't find anything. I couldn't see the women patients. It's impossible. You can't do it!"

"I'm going to ... um ... see if Switch is all right," Benny said. He sidled out onto the kitchen porch, but he knew Switch was fine and he was too cold to leave the porch as the argument continued.

A light coat of new snow had fallen that day and a hard frost had set in on top of it. Everything sparkled in the moonlight like it was diamond-coated. Benny shivered but he didn't think he should go back in.

Why was Jeremy so opposed to his mother helping out at the school, he wondered? His mother was right. Osage was practically a one-horse town. It was certainly a one-doctor town. And there had never been a school before Mr. Prentice had come. Benny hadn't thought he would miss the summer school session but he had. The news that the new teacher couldn't come had even made Jason Owens complain about growing up in ignorance. If Benny's mother didn't become the schoolteacher there just wouldn't be one.

Jeremy did seem helpless when it came to organizing things, though. Benny had found everything he needed for the evening surgery pretty quickly when Jeremy had howled for help. Jeremy was so smart but he didn't really know how to plan for ordinary, everyday things and he was hopelessly absent-minded. Benny or his mother always checked the black doctor bag in the morning to make sure Jeremy hadn't put in a wrench instead of a stethoscope. Jeremy did need a wrench sometimes but it was supposed to be in the tool chest under the buggy seat. Benny had found the stethoscope in there more than once.

Benny had an idea suddenly. He threw open the kitchen door and burst in as Jeremy was just opening his mouth to say no in some other way.

"I've got it," Benny exclaimed. "I know how Mother can teach and you can still get your work done, Dad," Benny said to Jeremy. "I've been an idiot. I should be helping you too, not just Mother. Mother and I will get everything arranged just like you want it before we leave for school in the morning. We'll go over your appointments the night before and make sure you can just take off in the morning without worrying about anything.

"Now there's one thing you'll have to do for this to work," Benny continued. "I'll bring some extras of the stuff you always run out of to school. Dad, you'll swing by the schoolhouse during recess or lunch -- whenever you can -- and I'll set your bag up again. Mother will be here in the evenings so you can have your surgeries. I'll help with the grading, Mother, so you won't get behind. Most of the kids here are in lower forms than me. It'll be easy for me to grade their work. I'll do whatever else I can to help mother and you, and it'll all get done, Dad. How about it?"

"But --" Jeremy began. He looked from Benny to his mother. "You really want to have school, don't you?" he laughed. "All right, all right. Maybe the two of you can prop up my inadequacies. I was afraid you were just doing this because you think I'm not earning enough, Abigail. I know it's slow going to get us on our way west, but I'm trying."

"Oh, my dear, that wasn't it at all," Benny's mother said, kissing Jeremy. "The town needs a teacher. That's all I thought about. Thank you, darling, for wanting to help." She kissed Benny too. "I was worried about your dad's poor old medical bag and how it would get filled up."

*****

By the next day everyone in town knew the school was going to open on time. Benny and his mother had a practice drill with Jeremy to make sure their system for taking care of Jeremy's bag was going to work. Jason saw them that afternoon as Jeremy stopped to get his bag refilled. Benny had been helping his mother put up dried flowers and other decorations in the schoolroom. He hurried out with supplies for Jeremy and the good doctor was quickly on his way again for afternoon visits.

"Hey, Ben!" Jason shouted from across the street. "Guess I don't need to tell you school's startin' tomorrow!"

"Guess you don't," Benny grinned.

*****

"This is something we didn't consider when we agreed that you could teach the school, though," Jeremy was saying soberly to Benny's mother as he came home from his livery stable job. Benny stopped in the middle of heading to the sink to wash for dinner. "Are you sure you'll be well enough, considering your condition, Abigail?"

"I'll be fine," Benny's mother scoffed. School had been in session for weeks, and everything had been going fine.

"Mother? Are you sick?" Benny asked. He looked from Jeremy to his mother.

"No, darling, I'm fine!" Benny's mother kissed him. "Don't worry. Really, I'm just -- well -- "

"Is it that -- that thing you had to have surgery for after the barge sank?" Benny struggled to figure out what was going wrong now.

"No, darling, darling -- I'm going to have a baby," his mother finally admitted.

"A baby!" Benny cried. "Dad, maybe she shouldn't be a teacher. What if she has trouble -- what if it's like Mrs. Owens?"

"Oh, darling, no, there's nothing to be afraid of!" his mother exclaimed. "Mrs. Owens had nine children without any trouble. I had you without any trouble. You mustn't think it's dangerous to have babies. It's a wonderful, precious gift from God."

"Ben, I'm sure your mother's right," Jeremy said, but he seemed uneasy.

"Mother, Dad's a doctor," Benny said sharply. "If he isn't sure this would be safe, why don't you listen to him?"

Jeremy and his mother both tried to reassure him but Benny continued to worry. He had never forgotten his experience going with Jeremy to the birth of Peter Owens, who was now old enough to toddle around, but whose coming into the world had almost ended his mother's life. The next day after school Benny ran into Mrs. Grimsby, the midwife.

"Could I talk to you for a minute, please, Mrs. Grimsby?" Benny asked.

"You want to talk to me?" Mrs. Grimsby looked around to see if anyone else was there. "What about?"

"My mother's going to have a baby," Benny said uneasily.

Well, that's fine," Mrs. Grimsby smiled. "Unless you're worried about competition, of course."

"Competition?"

"You've been your mama's one and only a lot of years. A baby's bound to take away some of that attention."

Benny flushed. "I'm scared," he said in a low voice. "I was there when Mrs. Owens had Pip. What if my mother--?"

"Oh!" Mrs. Grimsby looked embarrassed. "I should have known better, a fine boy like you. Listen here, Benny. I ain't a educated lady like your ma, nor a doctor like your pa neither, but I delivered a heap of babies. Sometimes things go good, sometimes things go bad. You can't change that by frettin'."

Benny was not at all reassured. Mrs. Grimsby usually didn't bother with sparing people's feelings, but she studied Benny closely, then spoke again.

"Usta be, when I started midwifein', we didn't care much about all this cleanin' and such like the doctors preach on," she confided. "Dirt's a natural thing, we thought, but educated people and doctors taught us that was wrong. More mothers are livin' through babies' births, more babies are livin', too, now than have in a hundred years, so I hear. It's still up to God, I reckon, to make wrong things come right, like when little Pip was comin' wrong.

"But as for your mama bein' in danger, if ever there was somebody the Lord was lookin' out for, it's you and your mama. One of the ways He's lookin' out for you that I think is a fine, big way, is givin' you that dad of yours. And for your mama's particular situation right now, between your Doctor Dad, and me, because there ain't no better midwife in three states, and God, and you and your fine, serious, prayin' ways, your mama's pretty well as safe as any soul on Earth can be. Don't you quit bein' concerned, don't you quit praying, but remember what I said."

Benny hugged Mrs. Grimsby. She blushed and kissed him on the cheek.

*****

Benny bounded down the stairs early one morning during the summer session of school and swung around the banister post as he always did. He stopped dead in shock, however, when he saw his mother lying in a heap on the little cushioned hall bench where patients sometimes waited to see Jeremy.

"Mother! Are you all right?" Benny cried, alarmed. He knelt beside her and patted her shoulder. She muttered and stirred a little but did not wake up. Benny had not seen her look so completely exhausted since they had traveled on the barges through Pennsylvania. There didn't seem to be anything wrong with her. Benny knew that she had been working very hard lately, teaching school, keeping house, and helping Jeremy with his patients.

"Little Mother doesn't know how to slow down, Ben," Jeremy had sighed a few days ago when they were putting up Black Switch for the night. "The only thing we can do is try to spare her work if we can. Now that she's expecting a baby, that will make her extra tired too."

Benny pulled an afghan over his mother and helped her into a more comfortable position on the narrow bench. Then he went into the kitchen. Someone had to make breakfast. Benny knew that Jeremy had come in very late from an emergency. His mother needed all the rest she could get.

"Well, I guess it's campfire breakfast today," Benny said to himself. He remembered the first time he had tried to make breakfast when he was traveling west with Jeremy. Jeremy had taught him how to cook over a campfire. He got out the fat, salt, milk, flour, and leavening and started a batch of biscuits. He made coffee and fried bacon.

While things were cooking, he looked at the stack of books his mother used to prepare for her lessons at school. He had helped his mother a good deal in the classroom lately. He was close to fifteen now. Caleb Sutter had taught classes before he left for boarding school. Benny stole another look at the books as he turned the bacon.

Jeremy stumbled sleepily into the kitchen a few minutes later. He looked around at the neatly set table, hot biscuits steaming on a tray, and coffee and bacon warming on the stove. Benny sat in the middle of a sea of books laid open around him.

"Where's your mother? Big test today?"

"You might say that," Benny said.

"Where is your mother?" Jeremy repeated.

"Didn't you see her asleep on the hall bench?" Benny went back to his books. Jeremy poked his head around the corner into the hall.

"Is she all right?"

"I think so. She just seemed really tired, so I made breakfast."

"Well, that was thoughtful of you, Ben." Jeremy patted him on the shoulder. "We'd better get her up, though, so she can get over to the school."

"I was thinking, Dad ..." Benny hesitated. "What if we gave mother a day off and I taught school today?"

"You?" Jeremy exclaimed. "Why, Ben, do you really think you could?"

"Yes," Benny replied. "It's only a half-day today, because it's Saturday. I'm sure I can do it."

"I'm afraid the students might give you a hard time," Jeremy warned. "And what will the parents say if they find out your mother wasn't there?"

"I know how to handle that," Benny said mysteriously. "I mean, both of those things. Is it all right if I take some things to school with me?"

"What things?"

"Jason calls them my 'Wonder Stuff.'"

"Hmmm ... Going to resort to bribery? You're right about your mother needing the rest. And it is only a half day. All right, Ben, if you really think you can handle it."

Jeremy carried his wife gently up the stairs and put her back into bed. She hardly even made a sound. He took Ben and his books and his box of 'wonder stuff' over to the school with Black Switch and the buggy after they ate breakfast together.

"Please pray for me, Dad," Benny said as they parted. "I hope I'm not just doing this to show off. I really do want to help."

"I will pray for you, Ben. Have a successful day. Remember how many times God told Joshua to have courage and not be afraid."

"Right," Benny nodded. Before he left Jeremy prayed with Benny.

Benny stacked the books neatly on the teacher's desk in the order he would need them, then walked around the classroom to see that everything was ready. His stomach would not be easy.

"Oh, Lord," Benny whispered. I want to do this for mother, and for You. Help me to do it well."

*****

"Where's the teacher?" Benny turned at the snapping, girlish voice. Two girls, alike as he and his mirror-face, stood before him. Rose and Violet Mitchell had started school the day before. Both had straight black braids and blue eyes. Both wore pink muslin sack dresses. Benny knew their names, but he had no idea which was which.

"Aren't you too old to be in school?" one girl snapped. "Boys as big as you should be earning a living, my pa says. I wish I was big enough to quit school. Ma says maybe when I'm thirteen. That's six whole months. I could help her a lot at home. Don't care much about school anyhow. Where's the teacher, I said? Don't you talk? Benny, that's your name, ain't it?" How come you don't talk, hey?"

"Because you don't give him a chance, Rose," her sister said in a soft but firm voice. "His mother is the teacher, you know, so he's much too smart to talk to ignorant girls like us. Come and sit down and stop being pesty."

"Actually, I'm your teacher for today," Benny blurted out. His voice squeaked just a little, but he managed not to sound too childish. "So you can call me Mr. Carlisle. It's a very good idea to take your seats. The other pupils have come, and we should begin."

Both girls looked at him in astonishment. "Where's your ma?" Rose demanded. "Who said you could be the teacher? I don't --"

"Rose, for goodness' sake, come and sit down!" Violet grabbed Rose's hand. "Everyone is staring at you."

She pulled Rose away. Benny walked up to the front of the schoolroom. The other children looked around for Benny's mother.

"Let's open in prayer," Benny said firmly. "Please rise and do honor to the Lord God of Heaven."

"We don't pray first. We pledge first," Rose argued.

"Today we pray first," Benny said. "Unless you wish to stand until recess, Rose, you had better not interrupt again."

Rose opened her mouth. Violet poked her hard in the ribs. Benny knew that he would never confuse the two girls again. Rose glared at Violet but her mouth shut tight.

"Lord God," Benny prayed, "Help us this day to draw closer to You through what we learn. Amen."

He led them in the pledge and told them to be seated. "I am your teacher today," Benny said. "Please call me Mr. Carlisle. We will carry on lessons as usual."

"I still want to know who said he could be the teacher," Rose said in a harsh whisper.

"I want a roomful of people who can behave well all morning, and who can keep a secret forever," Benny went on. "In this box I have surprises for everyone who can do those two things."

"What kind of surprises?" demanded Rose.

"Who can recite the Scripture we learned yesterday?" Benny asked. Several children put up their hands. Benny called on Violet.

"'All we like sheep have gone astray. We have turned every one to his own way. And the Lord hath laid on Him the iniquity of us all.'"

"Very good, Violet," Benny smiled. "Here. This is for you." He took a small object out of his box and carried it to Violet's desk. Violet took the flat rock, puzzled. Suddenly she gasped.

"Look, Rose, it has a fern in it!" Violet traced the faint grooves that formed the fern fossil's leaves and stem. "It's a fern carved in stone!"

"It was carved by God," Benny said. "During the great flood plants and animals were crushed by the water and mud and their impressions became frozen in stone forever."

"It's so beautiful," Violet whispered. She gazed at it a few moments, then handed it back to Benny.

"Oh, no, Violet. That's yours to keep. Remember to keep the secret."

"What secret?" Rose muttered, so quietly Benny could hardly hear.

"You will not learn the secret until the morning is over," Benny said.

He was amazed by how quickly the children fell into line. Even the boys who were older than Benny were eager to earn something from the Wonder Stuff. Benny had hardly believed Jason's admiration for these things he had collected over the years, in Philadelphia, on his journey west, and as gifts at one time or another. Each thing had a story and a memory behind it. Some his grandfather had given him and had belonged to his father when he was a child. Benny hated to part with his seashells, his whole snakeskin, other fossils, and the rest of the Wonder Stuff.

But Benny knew he was rich in "things." They were not truly valuable, but they were in most cases more than these frontier children could hope to possess. Even Rose was cowed and awestruck by the prism that made rainbows. Benny knew it was only a crystal from Grandmother Richardson's chandelier back in New York.

"The Lord doesn't want us to love things," Benny told himself as he sadly watched his wonder stuff dwindle away. "That's as good a reason as any for getting rid of some of this stuff."

The morning ended quickly. As they stood for closing prayer, Benny saw Rose fingering her crystal and stealing glances at him. He knew she and others were dying to ask about the secret, but she had been quiet and well-behaved the whole time.

"Before we pray and are dismissed I am going to tell you the secret you must keep for me. I've rewarded your good efforts today with these little objects from my box. I've also tried to secure your good will, because I want all of you to promise that you won't say anything about who your teacher was today. That is the secret you must keep forever."

"But what if --" Rose started to pipe up. Before Violet could even poke her she raised her hand. "Yes, Mr. Carlisle," she said meekly. "I think you're a swell teacher." All the children agreed to keep the secret. Benny prayed and dismissed them.

*****

He started off toward home, intending to come back with Jeremy later to pick up the books in the cart. Then he realized Violet and Rose were following close behind him.

"Mr. Carlisle," Violet began. She stopped and looked at Rose.

"Humph!" said Rose. "I don't know why I can't hear what you're going to say."

"Because you can't, that's all," Violet said sharply, her cheeks bright red. "I'll see you at home, Rose."

Rose flounced off and broke into a run. Benny did not know whether to continue walking or wait for Violet to have her say. He believed Violet and Rose lived on a farm in the opposite direction from his house. It would take Violet a long way out of her way to follow him home.

"Shall I ... shall I walk you home?" Benny asked.

"Please, Mr. Carlisle, if it wouldn't be too much trouble," Violet said softly. Benny turned down the lightly wooded path where Rose had disappeared. He was glad he had refused Jeremy's offer to pick him up right after school with the buggy.

"Did you want something, Violet?" Benny asked after a few moments. "It's not school, and I'm not the teacher anymore, so you don't have to call me Mr. Carlisle."

"All right, Benjamin. You -- you won't be coming back to school anymore, will you?"

Benny was startled. Until this moment he hadn't thought about it. But the answer came easily to him.

"No, I don't suppose I will."

"Your mother knows such a lot," Violet murmured. "But I can tell you know a lot too. She's probably taught you all she can."

"I want more schooling," Benny said uneasily. "I mean, I don't want to apprentice -- not yet. I like helping my dad on his rounds -- "

"I don't see you as a doctor," Violet chuckled. "Certainly not as a tradesman. I don't think you really want to be a teacher, do you?"

"I thought I might, until I actually did it. It's hard."

"I want to be a teacher, though. I'd like to go as far west as I can and start a brand new school for the first people in a brand new town."

"I want to go west too. I guess it doesn't matter what I do once I get there. They'll need people to do everything."

"What do you really like to do best?"

"What does that matter? My mother had to sew and cook and clean house to earn a living after my father died until she married my dad. She didn't just do what she wanted. My dad hated sick people and preachers before he became a Christian. He wanted to run a gambling casino in Kansas City. People don't usually end up doing something they like when it comes to earning a living."

"You're so realistic about everything," Violet sighed. "I guess it's because you've had so many troubles in your life. Are you bitter toward God about the things you've suffered, Benjamin?"

"What makes you think you know so much about me?" Benny snapped. "You saw me for the first time yesterday. How do you know what I've been through, or if I've suffered anything, or what I think about God?"

"The Owens's have the farm right next to us," Violet answered. "I asked Jason Owens's sister Faith about you."

"So now you think you know everything about me, do you?"

"I know that you try to do what's right, and you love the Lord, but I think you serve Him without joy, because maybe you're afraid He'll turn your life upside down again if you make any plans for the future. That's bitterness, Benjamin."

"So I'm bitter?" Benny stopped and stared at her. Then he looked up. He saw that they stood at the edge of the trees near the path that ran between the Owens farm and the next one. "That must be your farm, right? So you're home now. Good-bye, Violet."

*****

Benny turned and ran, knowing with his long legs that Violet could never catch up with him. He ran back to the school, snatched up the heavy stack of books, and ran all the way home, panting and staggering. He didn't stop until he dropped the books on the kitchen table with a crash.

His mother and Jeremy looked up in surprise from their lunch. Benny saw a place was set for him and food was ready, but he didn't sit down.

"I'm not going back to school anymore," Benny said as he tried to control the heaving in his chest. Benny's mother opened her mouth to speak.

"You know, I was just talking to Daniel about that very subject the last time he was here," Jeremy said before Benny's mother could say anything. "Daniel thought you might be getting a little beyond our school here. He recommended a boys' academy in Detroit where they help a fellow to prepare for a career or college. I guess you're ready to talk about it now."

"Detroit?" Benny's mother broke in. "That's so far away. When would we see him?"

"He'd come home at holidays, perhaps in the summer if he isn't working in town. Many of the boys find jobs that help them train while they're there."

"How soon can I go?" Benny asked.

"Is it very expensive?" Benny's mother asked. "How will this affect our plans to go west? You do still want to go with us, don't you, darling?"

"Ah, now, Abigail, there's plenty of time to talk all this out. Eat your food, Ben, and get to your chores. We'll discuss it more at dinner."

Benny went through his chores in a daze. The day had begun like any other day, but suddenly nothing was the same. Then he realized that his mother and Jeremy were standing on the back porch, talking in raised voices. Benny pitched the last fork of hay into Black Switch's manger and walked to the door of the stable.

"You should have spoken to me about this first," Benny's mother said angrily to Jeremy. "How could you just tell Benny so casually, as if it were a certain thing?" Jeremy said something Benny couldn't hear, and he moved closer.

"Abigail, Ben's fifteen now," Jeremy said. "I've seen him going through those books Mr. Prentice left at the school -- Geometry, Philosophy, Latin -- he's ready for more than you can teach him. But I think he was afraid to suggest going away, because of how you'd take it. You see he was right to be."

"We haven't money for boarding school. How can we still save for the trip west?"

"And what will you do if Ben decides he doesn't want to go when we go?" Jeremy held Benny's mother gently by the shoulders. "You can't keep him forever, Abigail. It's not the money or the plans that bother you. It's letting Ben go. Well, you'll have to do it. Daniel's already arranged for Ben and Jason Owens to go to the school in Detroit. As far as money is concerned, your father-in-law has offered to pay both Ben and Jason's costs," Jeremy said. "He didn't want you to know, because he was sure you'd object to it as charity. But it's foolish to look at it that way. The man had no other children. Ben's the only heritage he has, and he wants to do this for him. So I don't want to hear you say you're not going to accept it."

Benny's mother looked up suddenly and saw Benny listening. She straightened her shoulders. "I suppose it's all settled then," she said. "Of course Father Horace can pay for Benny's schooling. Why would I object? It's a wonderful gift, Benny, and I hope you're properly appreciative."

She picked up a flowerpot and started to walk away with it. Then she began to tremble. The crockery fell to the floor and smashed. Jeremy leaped forward and hugged his wife tightly.

"Now, little mother, he'll be all right without you," Jeremy soothed. "Grandfather Richardson and Trevor and the whole household are moving to Detroit. They will spoil Ben rotten every chance they get. And think of the fun we'll have -- You and me alone for the very first time."

"Until our daughter arrives," smiled Benny's mother. Jeremy wouldn't let her bend down to clean up the broken pot. He held her upright while Benny took his cue and quickly dove down and swept everything up.

"How can you be so sure it will be a girl, Mother?" Benny asked. He was glad the subject of boarding school was over for the moment. Even though he was thrilled by the possibility, he hoped it wouldn't come up again right away. Otherwise he might be the one breaking things and crying.

"I know, that's all," his mother smiled. "Goodness, Benny, how did you make out with the class today? Did you like it? Did they learn anything? What about those twin girls? Could you tell them apart? Did that one who talks all the time give you trouble?"

Benny opened his mouth. Monday his mother would go back to that little one-room school. She would get to know Violet and Rose. But she might never know what had passed between Benny and Violet today. Benny would certainly never tell her. Would Violet? Benny doubted she would say anything about it to his mother. That was not Violet's way. She apparently delivered her messages sparingly, to the ones who needed to hear them. But Benny was not quite ready to admit that he needed such a message.

"Everyone did exactly what I wanted all day," Benny grinned. "I bribed them with my wonder stuff. They know you don't have to do that. And no, I didn't like it. I don't ever want to be a teacher again."

Benny's mother looked at him closely. "When you teach," she said, "you open your self to your students. If you can't bear it, then you should be something else."

Benny nodded. He threw the crockery pieces in the trash and kissed his mother. "You are the most amazing person in the whole world," he said. "Isn't she, Dad?"

"That she is, my boy," Jeremy said. "That she is."

## Chapter Thirteen – Off to Brigham

"So this is Brigham School for Boys," Jason said. He looked around at the handsome grounds and tall brick buildings. "Ben, there's still time to lite out for the woods. I don't know why your grandpa thought I wanted ta go ta some prissy boarding school. I mean, it was nice of him ta wanna pay my way, but I ain't sure there's much difference between this place and the Prison in Jeff City."

"Don't be an idiot." Benny laughed. "You said you wanted to be an engineer -- build bridges and all that. How are you going to do that if you don't get some more schooling? They're going to need bridges and roads and all kinds of things out west."

"But what if I turn out like that guy Trevor? My dad won't let me back in the house!" Jason complained.

"If 'that guy Trevor' may offer an opinion," said the British man who served as Benny's grandfather's valet, Trevor Channing, coming up behind them, "even pig iron looks better with a little polish, Master Jason."

"Aw, sorry, Trevor," Jason said with a blush. "I only meant I don't wanna be so stiff an' proper that I ain't fit fer my own folks anymore."

"Master Benjamin has a good deal of polish," smiled Trevor, "and he fits in well with any company. One of the things an education should do is teach you how to act properly with all kinds of people. You'll have a hard row to hoe here if you don't take some of the polishing to heart. And I don't think Mr. Richardson would appreciate the money and the trust he's invested in you wasted."

“Yeah, sure. I’ll do the best I can,” sighed Jason. He fingered the stiff material of his school uniform. “But do I gotta wear this hat?”

“Yes, we both do. Everybody will be wearing one, Jason, so it won’t be that bad,” Benny said. “Stop complaining. I can’t wait to start classes.”

“Welcome, fellows!” A tall, handsome, blond young man with a cheerful smile and a slight limp hurried up to them. “I’m Jack Williams. You’re the new lads, Owens and Carlisle, right? I’m to be your orientator. Glad to have you.”

“What’s an orientator?” Jason demanded. Benny could tell Jason had immediately decided he didn’t like Jack Williams. Jason had a natural dislike of tall people. Benny felt very thankful that Jason had made an exception for him as his growth spurts had begun to hit. Jason had grown a lot, too, but he was still so short no one realized he was actually a year older than Benny.

“Sorry,” Jack grinned. “I’m the fellow who shows you where things are and how things are done here. Every senior gets a new student to break in. But we’re short a bit on seniors this year, so you’ll have to share me. Any gear I can help you cart?”

Jason and Benny looked around at the bags Trevor had taken out of Grandfather’s carriage. Benny glanced, without trying to show it, at Jack’s dragging leg. The boy caught him at it and slapped his thigh good-naturedly.

“Don’t worry about my gimp,” he said. “I can pull my weight and yours too, I’ll wager. Is this your man?” Jack looked up at Trevor. “He’s not allowed to assist you with your things, you know. We have to work together and do things ourselves here.”

“Right you are, Master Williams,” Trevor said with a smart salute. “I’ll be off then, gentlemen. I think you’re in good hands. Farewell, Master Benjamin, Master Jason. Do let your grandfather hear how you’re doing, young sir.”

“Good-bye, Trevor. Thanks for everything. Thanks, Jack,” Benny said as Jack tossed a bundle up onto his shoulder. They gathered up the rest of the things and set off across the campus. Jack gave a running lecture as they walked about each building they passed and talked about how the classes would be conducted.

"Here's Manchester Hall," he said at last. "This is our dorm. I'll introduce you to the headman first, and then we'll get you to your room so you can settle in. It's good you arrived early. We can take a better tour after lunch if you like so you won't be so overwhelmed when class time comes. Ah, Mr. Stanford. Mr. Stanford is our Science Instructor. These are Carlisle and Owens, Two-oh-four."

"Carlisle and Owens, eh?" The portly gentleman had been standing with his back to the door, shifting papers at the front desk of the dormitory. "How do you do, Gentlemen? Owens, I'm afraid we don't wear our caps at quite such a rakish angle." He adjusted Jason's uniform cap. "And do watch those collars, Carlisle," he said as he fussed with Benny's shirt. "You'll brief them on inspections, of course, Williams."

"Absolutely, sir," Jack nodded. "Follow me, gents. Up these center stairs and to the right. The end stairwells get locked promptly at seven each night, so you won't be able to enter that way evenings. There's always a monitor on duty at the desk nights and you must sign in and out after supper. Heaven help you if you haven't got a good reason for being out of the dorm at night. Here's your room."

Jack led them into a small room with two bunks and a single bed, two desks, footlockers and two small closets. Jack tossed the bundle he carried up onto the top bunk.

"You two fight over the bunks," Jack explained. "The other bed's for your mummy."

"Our mummy?" Benny echoed.

"That's the pet name. You room with an upperclassman who's responsible to make sure you keep the rules, written and unwritten. He's got a technical title, but he's really your mummy, long and short. I don't expect he'll tuck you in, and if he sings lullabies you'd better plug your ears. In all other respects besides feeding you he'll do what your mum and dad can't."

"So who is our mummy?" Jason grumbled.

"You know, I should know that, but I don't." Jack scratched his head. "Someone late coming back, anyhow.

Remind me to ask old Stanford if he's about when we go down. Look, I'm in Two-oh-seven. Stow your gear and come by for me when you're ready. Lunch is in --" he glanced at a fine old gold pocket watch with obvious pride " -- forty-seven minutes. We must be on time for all events. You have read your handbooks, right?"

Benny and Jason nodded. "And try to get the wrinkles out. Stanford's not the only one who picks at every little rumple. All the faculty and staff are supposed to keep after us to look sharp. And we do, so don't disgrace us. See you in a bit."

"'Don't disgrace us'!" Jason mocked in a prissy voice when they were alone. "It's gonna be a long year." Quickly they began to unpack. Linens and blankets were provided but they had to make their own beds. Benny, more used to bed making than Jason, had his things arranged in very short order. He helped Jason hang his uniform jackets.

"I think Jack's a really nice guy," Benny commented. "You're going to have to get used to this, Jason, because it's not going to go away."

"I know. And I have to speak using proper grammar and avoid slang at all times," Jason sighed, tossing his handbook in a desk drawer. "This is gonna be tough. But I guess you're right about Jack. We could have somebody who's a real stuck-up snot for a -- a -- what's that word again?"

"Orientator. You know, if our roommate's already late, maybe it would help if we made his bed for him. There's supposed to be an inspection first thing in the morning. He might be in a rush when he gets in, and it could help him out."

"I'm gonna have enough trouble with my own bed," grunted Jason as he went back to struggling with his sheets. "How did my ma ever make beds for thirteen people every day?"

"I told you that you should've practiced. Nope. Do the corners like this." Benny showed him. "Come on, we've got to meet Jack. What room did he say?"

“Uhh ... I think it was two-oh-seven. Yeah. That’s it.” They knocked on the door and a skinny boy with messy red curls and freckles poked his head out.

“Hey, men, right on time,” Jack called from behind the stranger. “This is Lee Granger, a second-year man and the proud recipient of a record forty-five demerits in a single day -- today -- since he arrived two hours ago, all of them for appearance infractions. Hair not cut, shoes not polished, shirttail out, stockings sagged ... and the list goes on.”

“Forty-five!” Jason crowed. “Let me shake your hand, Brother. I can see we’re going to get along swell.” Lee accepted the handshake with an unrepentant grin.

“Lee, you don’t want to be late for lunch on top of it all,” Jack sighed. “No sense waiting for him.” Benny and Jason stared as Lee began wildly throwing on clothes. He had been clad only in pants and one drooping sock when they arrived.

“Dining Hall’s this way,” Jack directed. “Mason-Talbert Hall’s the name. Oh, we forgot to inquire about your mummy, didn’t we? Well, I’m sure he’ll turn up.”

“Say, how’d you get that bum leg, Jack?” Jason demanded.

“Yessir, that’s my shy violet pal,” Benny groaned.

“Not a problem,” Jack replied. “I like the open, honest type. I got this leg when I was five and visiting my dad at his sawmill in upstate Vermont. Fell through a railing into the flume. Nearly died. I was mighty lucky to be left with nothing worse than this to show for it. Dad and Mum never believed in coddling. I had to keep up with the rest or be left behind. Nothing much I can’t do except long-distance running.” His voice fell to a whisper. “Enter the Dining Hall in silence, remember. You know your table assignments, right?”

*****

The boy separated and Benny and Jason checked the numbered cards on each table and found their places. Benny had not realized how large Brigham really was. He found himself at a table with seven other boys and a man who introduced himself as Mr. Talbot, the English

Master. They all stood behind their chairs until the headmaster, Mr. Greyson, offered prayer. Then they sat down and the boys who had kitchen duty for this meal hurried out of the kitchen with steaming bowls and platters. Watchful kitchen staff made sure the boys worked neatly and quickly but did none of the serving themselves.

Mr. Talbot had each boy at the table introduce himself and tell where he was from and what he intended to study. Benny, as a first year student, didn't have much choice in his course assignments, so he hadn't made a decision on his area of special study yet. One or two of the other boys had not decided either, so he didn't feel so odd. None of the boys at the table seemed to know each other before, and the conversations Mr. Talbot tried to start usually died out with shy, one-syllable responses. Mr. Talbot seemed a kind, good-hearted man to Benny. He was young, thin, and small, with an odd accent. Benny remembered that he had said he was from Scotland.

*****

After lunch Jack collected them and gave them a tour of the classroom building. Benny hoped he could remember where to find his classes in the morning. More boys kept arriving all afternoon. Everyone was supposed to be present at supper, and a general meeting was to be held after the meal in the Peal Auditorium. Still the third bed in Benny and Jason's room remained empty.

"Most odd," Jack remarked. "Perhaps your mummy's been scared off at the thought of having to nurse a hopeless case like Owens." Jason socked Jack in the arm. Jack got him in a headlock that made Jason squeal like a piglet. His leg did not hamper him at all as he held rock-steady against Jason's struggles.

"Now, Owens, do straighten your cap," Jack said wickedly as Jason wheezed and twisted. "We don't wear them at quite such a rakish angle, you know." He let Jason go so suddenly that he fell flat on the grass. "You can get ten demerits for striking an upperclassman, my lad. Not that I'd turn you in, but some chuckle-heads would if they saw it."

"What do upperclassmen get for beating up new guys?" demanded Jason.

"Commendations usually," Jack said coolly. He helped Jason up and brushed him off. "Seriously, it's nearly dinner time. I can't think why your man isn't arrived yet. Let's see Mr. Stanford."

They found Mr. Stanford out front talking to Drake, the groundskeeper. "Ah, roight, two-oh-four," The man said quickly as Mr. Stanford looked absent-mindedly at his lists. "Sorry. sair. I meant t' inform y'. Them sent me o'er wi' th' messig but you was out an' it slipped me moind til jus' now. You'll 'a'fter move summun, Mr. Stanford, sair. That feller ain't comin' back. 'E's missin' -- dead, they thinks."

"Dead?" Jack exclaimed. "Who was it?"

"Are you sure, Drake? How awful. Murray Jacobs." Mr. Stanford finally found the spot on his list. He leafed through some other pages. "We are short of seniors after that unpleasantness last year. Perhaps a Junior ... hmm ... Joseph Banks! He might do. Yes. He'll have to move his things directly. Terrible thing about young Jacobs. Drake, how could you forget to tell me?"

"Murray Jacobs dead?" Jack breathed. "How did it happen?"

"Them said 'e were a-boatin' yestidy -- sturrum -- washed overboard," Drake spoke in grunts. "Got t' finish they leaves 'fore dinner." He hurried away.

Jack turned away and Benny saw that he was struggling not to cry. "Was he a really good friend of yours, Jack?"

"He was the best fellow I ever knew," Jack said softly. "Murray ... I can't believe he's dead. He wrote me just last week. We were going to hike up to the lake over the weekend. I can't believe he's dead."

"I'm really sorry," Benny said. Jack squared his shoulders.

"I must write his family. They were so close. I'm sure they're taking it very hard." Jack seemed to forget Benny and Jason were there. Jason grabbed Benny's arm.

"C'mon, Ben. We can find the dining hall ourselves. Let Jack alone for awhile."

*****

Benny nodded and they went off to dinner. The evening meal was more formal than lunch. Dining Hall staff did the serving this time, since the boys were expected to take time to get to know everyone at their tables and all the faculty and principal staff would be introduced. Benny saw that Jack was in his place on time, but he was pale and red-eyed.

Conversation came a little more easily at the table this time. Benny met two boys his own age and told everyone the story of his dramatic turn as a hunchback with the added realism of having to cover up a beating by Caleb Sutter which left him unable to straighten up for three days. Mr. Talbot laughed heartily and said he'd like to meet such a fine acting coach as Jeremy.

*****

After dinner the boys filed into the auditorium for the opening night meeting. Jack met them outside the dining hall and managed a smile but did not speak. The three of them sat together for the meeting.

"Let me say how saddened we all are by the shocking news that just reached us a few minutes before this meeting," Mr. Greyson said soberly after they had opened in prayer and had a Scripture reading. "Senior English Major Murray Jacobs was lost overboard in a boating accident yesterday." Benny heard many gasps and knew that Jack wasn't the only one who had considered Murray a friend. "This young man was a credit to the school, a fine Christian boy. We grieve for his family and for our own loss, for he was one of us. Please send a card or letter to the Jacobs family if you can. Memorial services will be held on Saturday, and those of you upperclassmen who were close to Murray may request a pass to go and attend. Unfortunately we cannot bend the rules for our younger students. They must remain on campus as is customary the first weekend school is in session."

The rest of the meeting proceeded as Benny expected. New students were welcomed. Older students were told to be a help and encouragement to them. Mr. Greyson emphasized that this was a school where Christ was honored and the young and inexperienced were to be led in the right path with kindness and firmness. He summarized some of the most important rules. He read the handbook statement on hazing and secret societies and repeated strongly that they were absolutely forbidden. Other school administrators announced a few schedule and class location changes for classes the next day. Soon the meeting was over.

*****

"Well, chaps, lights out is at ten," Jack said as they arrived back at the dorm. "If you need anything I'm just down the hall. But don't, positively don't, think of getting out of your room after lights out. That's something they do frown on here. Mr. Stanford and his monitors patrol the halls and security checks the grounds throughout the night."

Benny marveled at Jack's self-control. How would he feel if he had heard so unexpectedly that Jason was dead? The two boys looked at each other and Benny saw that Jason was thinking the same thing. Jack smiled as if he had read their minds.

"Murray was to be your mummy, fellows," he said. "He'd have done for you proper. Since he can't be here, he wouldn't want me to go all to mush and neglect the job. This fellow Banks, I don't know him really, but I think he's all right. There will be a dorm inspection tomorrow morning at six-thirty. Everyone tidies their rooms and then we line up in the hall for Mr. Stanford to pass judgment on our collars and cuffs and so on. It's a first day best foot forward kind of thing. Breakfast's at seven, so it'll be quick. Then class at eight, and you're off and running. Come and see me whenever you need anything. Really. Goodnight, then."

*****

Benny and Jason went into their room. They stopped short in the doorway. Large trunks filled almost all the floor space. Boots, cases, and various kinds of sports equipment lay everywhere. A young man straightened up from digging in a trunk and turned to survey Benny and Jason with cold gray eyes. He brushed back his straight dark hair.

"Look here, I'm going to need more space for my stuff," he complained. "First years don't get so much space. What's this?" He raked across the top shelf of the closet with a fencing foil and a bundle flew out and burst open. Benny and Jason both cried out in dismay as Benny's cougar skin and the black dragon-decorated case that held his throwing knife spilled onto the floor.

"Say, let Ben's stuff alone!" snapped Jason.

"What the blazes is that?" exclaimed Joseph Banks, poking at the cougar skin with the sword. "Why did you bring that mangy animal skin? I don't think that's allowed. And what's in the fancy box? Perfume?" He snatched up the box before Benny could get to it over the sea of trunks. Joseph fiddled with the box, but he couldn't find the hidden clasp. Benny rolled up his cougar skin and put it on his bed.

"It's a gift from my dad," Benny said. "May I please have it back?"

"I want to see what's in it. How do you open this -- thing?" he swore.

"Now I know that's not allowed," Jason said sharply.

"Go and tattle on me then, Priss," Joseph sneered. "It's only twenty demerits. But it'll hurt you a lot more than it will me. See if it doesn't." He threw the box in a corner, knowing Benny wouldn't be able to catch it. "Who cares about your stupid perfume? Don't bother to introduce yourselves. It's Carlisle and Owens and I really don't care which is which. But I do need more space. So hurry up and get your stuff moved."

Benny and Jason compacted their things as much as they could while Joseph shoved things around and made little headway unpacking. They had to hurry to get ready for bed as the warning bell sounded. Benny put out the lamp and dived under the covers of the bottom bunk just as a monitor poked his head in the door. “Good night!” He sang out and shut the door quickly.

“Weren’t we supposed to have devotions together before lights out?” Jason whispered.

“Not enough time tonight,” Joseph hissed. “Look, I’m sorry I was short with you fellows. Rough getting moved in and then having to change like that. I shouldn’t have taken it out on you. We’ll get everything straightened out tomorrow. Welcome to Brigham, lads. Sweet dreams.”

## Chapter Fourteen—Puzzle in a Box

"This is amazing. Just fantastic!" Jack Williams sat on Benny's bunk and stroked the cougar skin after classes the next day. "Carlisle, I can't even imagine owning such a treasure. No, I'm sure there's no rule against it. We're allowed mementos from home, as long as they don't take up too much space. Too bad you can't roll it out as a rug. You say Banks ragged you about it? Maybe he was jealous. I know I am."

Jack lay down full length on the skin. "You don't mind, do you?" he asked, starting to get up. Benny assured him it was all right. Jason had gone to an informal ball game with Lee. Benny had gone to Jack's room to ask if it was really against the rules to have the cougar skin and Jack had demanded to see it.

"As I said, I really don't know Banks well," Jack shrugged. "I guess I'd be short-tempered, too, if I got all moved in, then had to shift. And he does have a lot of stuff, doesn't he?" Jack gazed at Joseph's trunks. Mr. Stanford had been understanding of the disarray of their room for morning inspection, but had emphasized that Joseph must get his things arranged quickly. Joseph had worked hard at being pleasant to Benny and Jason before they parted for breakfast and classes. Benny wondered if his first impression of Joseph might have been unfair.

Benny brought out the black case and showed his knife to Jack. "Whoa, now, that's another matter, my lad!" Jack held up the handsome knife. "I'd give that to Mr. Stanford to hold onto for you. In the first place, it looks valuable. In the second place, we're only supposed to keep pocket knives. No lethal weapons. But my, oh my, is this a beauty."

"I didn't even think," Benny said. "Will I get in trouble for having it here?"

"Hard to say," Jack mused. "As long as you give it up straight off there shouldn't be a problem. I'll go along with you, if you like." He snapped the box shut.

"There's that jewel box again! What's in it?" Joseph Banks walked into the room "Let me see it."

He snatched the box from Jack's hand and tried to open it. Benny couldn't help laughing as he fought with the catch.

"See what I mean?" Jack said ruefully. He grabbed the box away from Joseph and quickly returned it to Benny. "No good having a thing like that around. Somebody's going to think it's a toy and want to play with it."

"I just want to know what's in it that's so special," Joseph sulked. He glared at Jack. Jack ignored him.

"We'll go straight down to Stanford. By the way, hello, Banks. We met at last year's Christmas party. Your little misunderstanding with my lads from last night is all ironed out, right?"

"Oh, absolutely," Banks said, quickly shedding his dark scowl and putting on a big smile. "I can make do very well with the space I have. Taking that -- er -- whatever it is -- to the dorm daddy, eh? That's much the best idea."

"I'm glad to hear you're a sensible fellow," Jack said, rising to his full height and towering over Joseph. "So you'll be a good mummy to my boys, eh? Just like Murray would have done if he were here."

"Nobody could be as good a chap as Murray Jacobs, Williams," Joseph said. Benny believed he meant it. "He'll be setting the angels straight."

Jack stared at Joseph for a moment. "Come on, Carlisle. Bring your box."

Benny rolled up the cougar skin and stowed it in the footlocker he shared with Jason. He picked up the case and followed Jack out.

*****

Mr. Stanford was horrified when Benny snapped open his case and he saw the knife. He dragged Benny off to Mr. Greyson's office immediately. He refused to allow Jack to come along. They had to wait some time before Mr. Greyson was free to see them. Drake, the groundskeeper came out of a door marked "Records" and shuffled through the lobby as they sat waiting.

"What were you doing in there, Drake?" Mr. Stanford demanded. "I thought you were out of records."

"Yessair, yessair," nodded Drake. "Jist returned m' key t' Mr. 'Opper, sair. On'y returned m'key, sair." He nodded to Benny.

"Pardon my speakin' young sair," he said politely, "but it's Master Carlisle, isn't it?"

"Yes, sir," Benny answered.

"I were just noticin' that fine case, sir. Japanner, ain't it?"

"I was told it was Chinese, Mr. Drake," Benny replied.

"I were fairst mate on t' Brig *Omega* out a' Bristol, England afore me lungs went bad," Drake explained. "Some calls 'em Chinee, they does, but Japanners makes 'em. Sometimes they be all differn't, natur'l colored woods, in the design, not lacquered black and set wi' stones like yourn. Be they some kinda puzzle, then, Maister -- ta open it, I means?"

Benny glanced at Mr. Stanford, who blew out an impatient breath.

"Go about your business, Drake," he ordered. "This is a disciplinary matter."

"Sorry, sair," Drake said, backing away and bowing as he went. "No 'arm meant, sair. No 'arm."

*****

When they entered the office Mr. Stanford clapped the case on the desk. "Just look at what this boy has brought onto the campus, Mr. Greyson," he exclaimed. "Just look at it." He had thought the case would just pop open, dramatically making his point. But it didn't.

"Well, it looks like a very nice... er ... box, Mr. Stanford."

Mr. Stanford grappled with the case, red-faced, trying to force it open. Benny reached out. "Let me help you, sir," he said. The case opened. Mr. Greyson looked at the knife, then at Benny.

"What a magnificent knife," he said. "May I?" Mr. Greyson lifted the knife and looked it over carefully. "Splendid. I assume you know how to use it properly?"

"I've never used it on anything but mice and lizards, sir," Benny replied.

"Mice and lizards beware," Mr. Greyson chuckled.

"Sir, the rule concerning weapons is very explicit," Mr. Stanford said sharply.

"Of course. No student may have in his possession any dangerous weapon," Mr. Greyson said. "Mr. Stanford, I believe I can deal with this. Thank you very much for calling it to my attention. We won't keep you any longer." Mr. Stanford bustled away.

"Suppose I keep the knife here in my safe, Mr. Carlisle. Any time you see a rising epidemic of mice or lizards -- or if you just want to keep your aim true, come and ask me for it. Did I hear Drake out in the lobby speaking to you just now?"

"Yes, sir. He was interested in the case. I guess he's seen something like it before."

"Mr. Drake has a colorful history, apparently, that we were not fully aware of when he came here," Mr. Greyson explained. "Did he seem very interested? Does he know what was in the case?"

"He wanted to see how the catch worked. Mr. Stanford wouldn't let me open it, though."

"Let us just take a little precaution, Benjamin. I shall keep the knife, as I said, but I shall return the case to you. You take it to Mr. Stanford and tell him I said he should keep it for you, safely locked up. We shall not mention that the knife is no longer in it. And I would not inform anyone else that you have such a knife."

"Jack Williams already saw it, sir. Jason Owens knows about it, of course. Joseph Banks saw the case, but he doesn't know what's in it."

"Well, we may safely trust Williams and Owens, I think. I confess I do not know Banks too well. Of course that may mean he simply isn't a discipline problem, which is a good thing. All the same, let us hope he remains ignorant. A knife like that could be a temptation."

"I'm sorry, sir. I shouldn't have brought it."

"Well, to you it is a memento more than a weapon, I am sure."

The headmaster made Benny show him the secret of the case's clasp before he put it in his pocket. Benny stroked the knife fondly and handed it to Mr. Greyson.

"Missing your Doctor Dad, are you, Carlisle?"

Benny crushed a powerful urge to cry. "Yes, sir. Very much."

"May we hope he will visit you here sometime?"

"His practice keeps him very busy, sir." Benny also knew that Jeremy dreaded meeting new people because of his scars from the cougar attack. He was never sure that the makeup he applied so skillfully covered enough.

"He is a towering testimony to God's grace if half of what Daniel Connors has told me is true. Tell him he would honor me if I could make his acquaintance."

"I'll tell him, sir. He likes to let me show him off, though he won't admit it."

"The place is still standing, so your comrade Owens must be adjusting."

"He's only been here two days, sir. Give him time."

Mr. Greyson burst out laughing. "Now, just a word about John Williams. He'll treat you and Owens like princes, but make him take some time to grieve. Murray Jacobs was very, very dear to him."

*****

Jack was trying not to look as if he were hanging around the administration building when Benny came out.

"What happened? You're not to be sent home, are you? I thought Stanford was going to burst!"

"Everything's fine." They returned to the dorm and Benny handed the case to Mr. Stanford with Mr.

Greyson's explanation. Mr. Stanford took the case reluctantly, muttered something that sounded like, "Most irregular," and shut the door in Benny's face. Benny decided not to mention the truth about the case to Jack. He felt as if Mr. Greyson had trusted him with an important secret, and he wasn't sure if even Jack should be in on it.

"Say, Jack, I'm sorry I dragged you into this. If you have some studying or -- or something else you need to do, you don't have to baby-sit me."

"No," said Jack, giving Benny an odd look. "But if you want me to shove off --"

"I didn't mean that."

"All right, then. Greyson told you to give me some space, right? Well, I've got too much space by half, Ben. There's this huge, huge--" he stretched out his arms and made a wobbly circle "-- really huge hole where Murray used to be. I was sitting there alone in my room after class, afraid I was going to get sucked down into that hole and never get out. Then you walked in with that little pinched, worried look that Murray always used to get when he was afraid he'd done something bad. Banks wasn't kidding about how good Murray was. But he always came to me if he thought he'd strayed. And he was always so broken if I stepped out of line. Anyway, I thought, maybe God's given me somebody new who's worth being good for. Do you -- do you play chess, Ben?"

"I'd love to play chess with you, Jack," Benny smiled.

*****

"Say, Carlisle, Owens, I'd like to introduce you to some fellows I know," Joseph said to Benny the following Saturday. Normally there would have been morning classes, but they were cancelled to allow attendance at Murray Jacobs' memorial service. Jack had gone and Benny and Jason had finished their chores and schoolwork and were sitting in their dorm room writing letters home because there was nothing else to do.

Jason looked at Joseph with undisguised suspicion. "What kind of fellows?" he asked. Joseph had been fidgeting on the edge of his bed for the last half hour, watching them while Benny and Jason had finished their writing. As soon as the envelopes were sealed up, Joseph had blurted out his proposal.

"Fellows. Friends of mine. Chaps who can keep things from getting too dull around here. Look, you don't have any plans for the afternoon, do you? Daddy Jack's away, and Lee's pulled kitchen duty. You'll find Saturdays a trifle long if you don't get out and meet a few more people. I'm just offering to help you along, like a good mummy. D'you want to come or not?"

"Sure," Benny said abruptly. He jumped up from the desk. "C'mon, Jason. Joseph's right. We should meet some of the other students. It might be fun. We'll just put our letters in the mailbox," Benny said to Joseph.

"Meet you over by the post office, all right?" Joseph said.

*****

"What's his game, d'y' think?" Jason asked after they left the dorm.

"Maybe he doesn't have a game. Maybe he's just being nice," Benny shrugged.

"Jack doesn't trust him and neither do I," Jason grumbled. "Anybody who's got that many clothes in a place where ya wear uniforms five and a half days a week has something loose somewhere. Didja see all his fancy duds? Snakeskin boots and silver belt buckles and silk ties. Who's he tryin' ta impress? Where'd he get the money for that stuff?"

"Stop being so suspicious, Jason. We don't know anything bad about Joseph. He's trying to be nice to us. Just relax."

*****

Neither of them felt very relaxed, though, when they walked with Joseph to the small lake at the back of the campus. They came into a clearing in a grove of trees where six other boys waited for them. Benny and Jason looked uneasily at the rich-looking clothing of Joseph and four of the other boys. Two others seemed to be new to the group like Benny and Jason.

"Welcome to the Omega Society, gentlemen," said a slim, slick-haired boy who waved a diamond ring under their noses. Follow me." He led them into a shed that housed gardening tools. The boy went to the back wall and shoved a block of wood, then moved aside a hidden doorway. "Enter our secret chamber," he said mysteriously.

The small back room of the shed was close and dusty. Three tables were folded up against the walls. Folding chairs leaned against the wall beside them. A dartboard hung on one wall, and the boy walked over and leaned against a large cabinet. He dangled a brass key from his fingers. "Let's have introductions first. I am Dereck Sheraton, president."

"President pro-tem, you mean," another boy growled. "We haven't had elections yet."

Dereck laughed breezily. "As you say, Scott. This rude fellow is Scotty Sullivan, vice-president and the man who would be king." Scotty had straw-colored hair and a sour expression. "Next is Raymond Greene, secretary." Dereck indicated a heavy boy with dark hair. He did not look happy to be there either. Benny glanced at Jason. Both of them were wondering how these grumpy fellows could possibly provide any good fellowship like Joseph had implied. "Joe Banks is our treasurer, and this last is Bob Lawrence. He's our Sergeant at Arms. Introduce the new recruits, those of you who brought them."

Joseph gave Benny and Jason's names. The other two new boys were Teddy Baxter and Gus Downing. The old members directed them to set up a table and some chairs. Then Joseph grinned. "Have a seat, gentlemen," he said, producing a deck of cards.

"Is that what this is all about?" Teddy demanded. "Gosh, I thought it was some kinda hoity-toity secret society. If we're just gonna play cards, that's all right!"

"I thought we were gonna have elections," Gus said uncertainly.

"Lads, lads," Dereck sighed. "The Omega Society is one of the oldest and most influential clubs on campus. We are brothers united to make a difference in the world. We seek out new, lost fellows like yourselves and give them purpose and a sense of belonging. We perform all kinds of worthy deeds. But we can't just broadcast ourselves openly.

"What would be the meaning of our charitable acts if we sounded a trumpet before us? We must meet in secret, and plan our work in secret. And we do not open our ranks to just anyone. We tap those who have special gifts, something to offer the society. Later we shall conduct our business and have our elections. But first there is time for a little recreation.

"The fact that we occasionally indulge in these harmless games should not trouble you. Remember that the rules clearly state that no card-playing is permitted in the dormitory. This obviously is not the dormitory. If you do not wish to join, you may go. But you may be sorry to have missed this opportunity. It will never be offered again."

Benny looked at Jason. Jeremy had been a master card player before he had become a Christian. He had earned their way for most of the trip from Pennsylvania to Missouri by gambling. Benny had watched him play a thousand times or more. Jeremy had shown him trick after trick. Benny had tried not to pay attention because he knew gambling was wrong. Yet Benny wondered if there would be any harm in showing these older boys that he could teach them a thing or two. Jason seemed to read his thoughts. He grinned but quickly covered his mouth.

"Let's play a little while, Ben," Jason suggested. "Just for fun, right, Joe?"

"Oh, absolutely, if you wish," Joseph said hastily. The other Omega society members scowled at him. "A game or two for fun, until you fellows get the hang of it, right? We usually do play with a bit of a pot."

"Here, Carlisle, how about you dealing?" Dereck invited, taking the cards from Joseph and thrusting them at Benny. Dereck, Joseph, Benny and Jason sat down. Bob, Teddy, Gus and Ray set up a second table. Scotty stood between the two tables and looked on.

Benny tried a fast shuffle as he had seen Jeremy do. The cards slipped and shot out of his hands all over the table, the floor, and into the laps of the four boys at the table. Everyone burst out laughing. Benny reddened. It wasn't as easy as it looked. He'd never even actually held a deck of cards in his hands before. Quickly they gathered up the cards. Clumsily Benny shuffled them and dealt out a hand of Faro.

"I say, Carlisle, you were funning us with that rotten shuffle, weren't you?" Scotty said after Benny won the first hand.

"I've never played cards before," Benny said truthfully.

"Rot," said Joseph. "You played straight through, named the wild cards, never asked one question, won hands down, and you want us to believe you've never played before?"

"You don't have to believe me," Benny shrugged. "Are we playing another hand?"

"Swap," Scotty demanded. "I want a crack at him."

The new foursome was Benny, Jason, Teddy and Scotty. No one else played -- they all stared at Benny. Benny fixed the game so Jason would win this time. He was getting better at shuffling. There was a trick to that, too.

"He's a -- professional!" snarled Scotty, cursing and jumping up from the table and throwing his cards aside in disgust. "I watched every move he made, and I still don't know how he did it. Banks, did you know about this?"

"No, I didn't," Joseph insisted. "But look, there's no harm done. We weren't playing for money. Don't you see how perfect he'd be? Nobody can beat him unless he lets him. We have got to have you, Carlisle."

Benny gathered all the cards into a neat stack. He stood up and pushed the deck toward Joseph, glancing at Jason.

"No thank you," they said at the same time. "'Bye, Joseph," Benny added, and they left the shed. As they emerged from the woods and started across the ball field, Joseph ran up to them.

"What's the matter with you fellows?" he demanded. "You're fantastic, Carlisle. We need you badly. Owens can come along. Look how the two of you flummoxed us. We really thought you were greenies. Think of the money we'll rake in."

"Joseph, we're not joining," Benny said sharply.

"Well, at least you've got to promise not to say anything about the society," Joseph urged. "Really. You've got to promise."

"We don't know anything," Jason reminded him. "Except that you all look like sourpusses and you want to sit around and waste time playing cards. So what could we tell anybody?"

"Right," Joseph grinned. "Still friends, though, aren't we?" He shook hands with them. "Good. Sorry it didn't work out."

*****

Benny and Jason spent the rest of the day exploring the wooded area at the opposite end of the campus from the Omega Society meeting place. They were startled to come upon Drake wheeling a barrow of leaves and clippings to the edge of the woods when they emerged near dinnertime.

"Young maisters could get lost out 'ere in this part o' th' groun's," he cautioned. "They be bogs an' thick briars. Best 'andle yersel's careful. Plays a bit o' cards, does thee, Maister Carlisle? Is that what thee keeps in thy puzzle box?"

"Uh, no, Mr. Drake. I don't own any cards. I just played the one time for fun," Benny said. "But it wasn't really much fun, so I doubt I'll do it again."

"That be a shame, maister," Drake said. "I mark thee as a man o' talent, an' talent shouldn't be wasted."

"How did he know about that already?" Jason asked after they had left.

"We were in a tool shed," Benny reminded him. "Drake probably came to get some tools and overheard us."

"Do you think he'll tell Mr. Greyson?" Jason fretted. "I wish we hadn't done that, Ben. It was funny to see their eyes pop out, but it made me feel kinda dirty."

"Me, too," Benny grunted. "I don't think Mr. Drake will tell on us, but God saw us all the same. And I'm sure He wasn't happy."

*****

"Ah, Mr. Carlisle and Mr. Owens!" Mr. Stratford, the language master, called out as they passed by the library on the way back to the dorm to change for supper.

"Hello, Mr. Stratford," Benny said. Jason mumbled a quick greeting and took off. He wasn't faring very well in Latin class. Mr. Stratford fell in beside Benny.

"You're a natural student of language," Mr. Stratford complimented him. "You were too modest when you told me of your previous studies. Have you actually been to Japan?"

"Japan, sir? No, I've never been there."

"Oh, my mistake. I understood you had some sort of curio -- a Japanese puzzle box."

"That was a gift from a friend. He got it in New York. Excuse my asking, sir, but how did you know about that box?"

"Understood you had to give it up to Stanford for safe-keeping," Mr. Stratford said. "How did I know? Why, I don't really recall. Perhaps Stanford showed it to me. I'm interested in foreign things, you know. Those boxes are fascinating. One might keep a treasure in such a box, something quite valuable, and no one could get at it without smashing the box."

"It'd be hard to do, sir," Benny said. "That box is at least fifty years old, I was told. It's been banged around a lot and hasn't broken yet."

"I wonder what a boy like you would keep in such a box, hmmm?" Mr. Stratford asked.

"Another gift -- something my stepfather wanted me to have," Benny replied. He felt funny calling Jeremy his stepfather, but Brigham seemed like such a formal place he didn't want to call Jeremy "dad" as he usually did.

"You are blessed with people who think a great deal of you," Mr. Stratford said. "I myself find you a fascinating young man. I hope we can get to know each other better. And I should welcome a chance to examine your box."

Benny left Mr. Stratford very puzzled. Why was the teacher so interested in his box? And Drake had asked about it again too. Mr. Greyson had been right. He had brought a big temptation with him.

*****

Shortly after dinnertime Jack returned from the memorial service. That evening Jason took on Lee in a no-holds-barred wrestling match in the gym and Jack and Benny played chess in the recreation hall. Just before it was time to go to the dorm for the night, one of the staff brought a crinkled, dirty envelope to Jack.

"Been searching for you to deliver this, Master Williams," the man said. "It was brought to the school earlier, but it only had the name Jack on it and we couldn't tell who it was for. We've made the rounds of all the Johns and Jacks here, but no one could make sense of the hen scratches. Might it be for you, sir?"

"Ah! A mystery, eh?" Jack pulled the much-handled letter out of the envelope. He opened it and looked at the crude message, which seemed to have been scratched with a charred stick. Many hands had smudged what little message there was. Jack held it close to the lamp on the chess table. His face went white and he stared at the man who had brought the message.

"Where did this come from?" He demanded. "Who brought it?"

"I believe it was a fisherman, sir," the man said. "He just left it without an explanation. What is it? Is something wrong?"

"Where can I find this fisherman?" Jack persisted.

"No one seemed to know him. They said he hardly spoke any English, and wouldn't stay for a reply."

"That can't be! Someone must know where to find him. I must speak to him."

"I'm sorry, sir. You might question the kitchen staff. But I don't believe they will be able to help you. I think the man is a foreigner who lives on a houseboat on the river. He could be a hundred miles away by now."

"Jack, what's the matter?" Benny asked, putting a hand on Jack's arm. The older boy looked so startled Benny thought he must have forgotten his presence.

"Carlisle, come along." Jack leaped up, clutching the note, and tore out of the recreation hall. Jack ran all the way back to his dorm room with Benny on his heels. By the time they arrived Jack was limping badly and threw himself down on his bed. "You see?" he chuckled dryly. "No marathons for me." He turned up the lamp on his desk and spread the note out again.

"Look at this," Jack said hoarsely. "Look at it."

Benny looked at the crude note. He could not recognize any of the scratched marks at first. "Wait. This is Hebrew. That's 'Rabbi' -- but I can't make out -- the next word is -- 'Lives'?"

Jack read in a low voice. "Rabbi lives," he said. "Float and hide. Help me."

"What does it mean, Jack?" Benny asked. It made no sense to him, but somehow it frightened him anyway.

"I know it means this, Ben. It means Murray Jacobs is alive."

"What?" Benny gasped. "Jack, how can that be?"

"Murray was a converted Jew," Jack explained. "No one here knew it except Greyson and me. Lots of fellows and maybe even parents would have given him a hard time. So we kept it a secret. But I used to call him Rabbi *BenJacob* as a joke. This note is from Murray. But I can't understand what he's trying to tell me. How can I help him if I don't know where he is? Should I contact his parents? What will they think? How can I raise their hopes when this doesn't tell us anything? I don't know what to do."

"Jack, it looks like there's blood on this note," Benny said. "Murray could be badly hurt. Maybe that's why he needs your help. He could have survived falling overboard in the storm, but now he can't walk or he's trapped somewhere. I think you should go see Mr. Greyson."

The hall monitor on duty did not want to let Jack out of the dorm. Jack wouldn't tell him why he wanted to see Mr. Greyson. He had asked Benny to come down with him, but Benny feared he wasn't very convincing either, since Jack had made him promise not to reveal that the note was from Murray. Jack became loud and angry when the monitor told him he should wait until Monday to see Mr. Greyson. The monitor ran to fetch Mr. Stanford.

"Williams, I'm astonished at your behavior," Mr. Stanford said. "We've never had cause to reprimand you before. What is the meaning of this outburst?" He stared suspiciously at Benny, as if he were responsible somehow.

"I've received a very important message," Jack said. "I've got to talk to Mr. Greyson about it right away."

"What can Mr. Greyson help you with that I cannot?" Mr. Stanford demanded.

"It's a private matter, sir. It concerns the safety -- maybe the life -- of another student. I have to see Mr. Greyson."

"Out of the question. You can't just come to me with cryptic riddles and expect to have your way. Lights out in one half hour. Good night, gentlemen."

Jack spun around and bolted up the stairs. He stopped outside Benny's door. "Meet me below your window in one hour," he said grimly.

"Jack!" Benny said. "If we're wrong, or we get caught by Mr. Stanford, we could be expelled."

"This is the surest way I know to get to Greyson," Jack said with a wry grin. "Even if we get caught, he always handles these post-lights-out escapes personally. If you don't want to come, I understand. But frankly I'm falling apart at the bare thought that Murray might be alive and need me. I don't know if I can hold up if I have to do this by myself."

"All right, then. But we'll meet under your window. You've hurt your leg with all that running, and you may need help getting down."

"I knew I'd picked a trooper." Jack clapped Benny on the back. "One hour. Pray hard, Ben."

*****

Benny hardly listened as Joseph gave a devotional that didn't make much sense. He said something about punishment following disobedience. Jason squirmed uncomfortably and kept looking at Benny as if he knew something was up. Benny lay quietly for half an hour after lights-out, thinking the time would never pass. He could hear both Joseph and Jason snoring as he crept out of his bed to the window. He slipped out of his pajamas; glad no one had seemed to notice that he had kept his clothes on underneath. Benny had complained loudly of stuffiness and had opened the window before devotions, rubbing some soap on the frame and making sure it would open and close quietly. He had one leg out the window when a hand fell on his shoulder. Benny almost screamed.

"You're not getting kicked out before me, Ben," Jason hissed.

"Jason, I'm helping Jack. I can't talk now. Go back to bed."

"Not a chance. Tell me what's up."

"Jack needs to see Mr. Greyson. Mr. Stanford wouldn't let him out of the dorm."

"Well, this is the way to get to see him. I always knew Jack was a smart guy. Okay, Ben, but you better let me in on the secret before too long."

"As soon as I can," Benny agreed. Jason helped him out the window and held his arms so he could drop safely to the ground. Benny heard the window slide closed. He figured Jason would wait up for him to come back and want to help him get back in. He wasn't sure if he'd need that. Surely they'd get caught, but he didn't try to tell Jason not to do it. Quickly he slipped around the side of the building and found the spot where he knew Jack's window must be. He was not too surprised to see Lee helping Jack down. Benny caught him and they waved to the tousled red head and disappeared into the bushes.

*****

"Greyson's house is back behind the admin building," Jack explained. "I hope his wife doesn't have a heart attack." They came to the small, neat building and

Jack threw a few small pebbles up against the bedroom window. Mr. Greyson's face appeared at the glass and he looked curiously at the two boys, pointed toward the back of the house, then disappeared.

"Notice how nothing ever surprises him?" Jack said wonderingly. They went around to the back porch as Mr. Greyson quietly closed the door and motioned them to sit on the steps. He set a lamp down and sat beside them.

"Murray Jacobs is alive, Mr. Greyson," Jack blurted out. "I have a message from him right here." He held out the paper to the headmaster. Mr. Greyson took it from him and held it under the lamp.

"Hmm. This is Hebrew for Rabbi," he said. "Williams, where did this come from?"

"Some fisherman from a houseboat left it with the kitchen staff, sir," Jack explained. "I know it's from Murray. We used Hebrew as a sort of secret code. I never learnt much, but I can read this." He translated it for Mr. Greyson. The headmaster glanced at Benny.

"And you dragged Carlisle along for exactly what reason?"

"He's my friend, sir, and I figured I'd need help to find Murray."

"Find Murray? You mean you want to go search for him now? Are you mad?"

"Sir, you'd be lecturing us right now about the rules, except you believe he's alive too," Jack said. "Ben says this mark here is a bloodstain, and I agree. Murray's someplace, hurt, unable to get home or here. We haven't got any time to wait."

Mr. Greyson rubbed his face and stared into the lamp. "You don't know where to look."

"Yes, I think I do, sir. I'm looking for a foreign fisherman with a houseboat, who's closer to the school than to Murray's home. He's probably illiterate, or Murray'd have had a real pen and paper to write on or someone would have written for him. And sir ... I think he's in some kind of danger, because he wouldn't write in Hebrew if he weren't afraid. Not when it's so important for me to understand and find him."

"Do you really think you can find him?" Mr. Greyson.

"I've got to try. Murray means the world to me, and his folks were so heartsick at the memorial service."

"All right," Mr. Greyson sighed. "I'll wake the stableman, Ryan, and he'll hitch up a cart for you. I'll tell him he must go along with you as well. No arguments. Ride along the shoreline and find your foreign fisherman. If you find Jacobs, I know a doctor -- Doctor Sawyer on March Street in Ridgeville -- who can be trusted. God speed you, boys. Be careful."

Benny hardly remembered any details of that long night searching for a houseboat that might hold Murray Jacobs. They went from boat to boat tied up at rickety docks and got some people furiously angry. Jack's face got paler and paler, and Benny knew his leg pained him after the jolting cart ride and the jumping from rocking boats to docks and the endless walking. Finally, in the chilly gray dawn, they approached a boat as a gaunt, unshaven dark man came out onto the deck and filled a pipe. Benny remembered the evil boat captain Jeremy had threatened to sell him to when they had crossed the Mississippi River years before. But this boat seemed well-kept and the man looked merely curious, not angry, as they approached. Jack was so exhausted Benny spoke up for him.

"Excuse me, sir," Benny began. "We're looking for a boy, a student from the boarding school upriver."

"No English," the man said with a shake of his head.

"I got this note," Jack said hoarsely, holding it out. The man glanced at it without touching it. He nodded, raised his voice just a little and said something they did not understand. After a moment a woman came out of the cabin. She looked at the two boys.

"Jack?" she said uncertainly.

"Yes, ma'am," Jack said, a little brightness coming back into his dull, weary eyes.

"Who is other?"

"A good friend." She still seemed unsure.

"He is very afraid. You come alone."

Jack shrugged to Benny and followed the woman on board. Benny waited impatiently. At last Jack came out.

"Ben, it's really Murray. I told him you were all right. Come on."

*****

The two boys nearly filled the tiny room where Murray Jacobs lay on a disorderly pile of bedding. He looked terrible, his face covered with bruises, one arm crudely splinted, his body twisted beneath the threadbare covers.

"Hallo, Ben," Murray whispered. "Thanks for propping up this mewling baby. I can't believe you found me, Jack. You're a mess."

"So are you, Rabbi," Jack said fondly. "I told Greyson we'd find you. He knows a doctor not far from here who can take care of you. We'll -- "

"They'll kill me if they find me, Jack," Murray said, groaning.

"What are you talking about?" Jack demanded. "Who would want to kill you?"

"The Enders," Murray said. "I broke them up last year. Nobody was supposed to know, but they found out somehow. My parents and I took that dull tour down the Missouri and a storm kicked up. Someone pushed me off the boat. I don't know how I stayed alive. Baba *Nanooshka* and her husband caught me in their net after I'd been in the water twelve hours."

"God have mercy," Jack breathed. "The Enders? They were all expelled or heavily disciplined. And anyway, it was just a secret club of some sort. Why would they kill anybody?"

"You don't know anything about it. It was too big of a scandal to let it out. Mr. Greyson thought the school would be closed down if anybody knew the kinds of things going on under his nose. But somebody's told what I had to do with breaking them up. They threatened to kill me, and you see they meant it."

"What were they doing -- the Enders?" Jack asked.

"It was gambling, and blackmailing students and faculty, and extorting from those they couldn't make pay any other way. Remember that rash of sports injuries? They caused a lot of them. Trevor Lang -- Jack -- I think they killed him. That carriage going into the ravine wasn't an accident. I'd been spying on them for months, trying to get proof, putting pieces together. I waited too long. But we did get them at last."

"I can't believe it," Jack murmured.

"That's why the school has so few seniors?" Benny asked. "They were involved in this -- this Enders group?"

Murray nodded. "I can't let them find me. I can't go back. But I -- I think they're trying to start up again. They'll try to get young boys, newbies who want to belong to something, and rich ones so they can get up a kitty to resume operations."

"Jack! Murray! Jason and I were asked to join a group called the Omega Society," Benny said. "I wonder if they could be the guys you're talking about?"

"Did they talk about doing charity work? Did they want to play cards right off the bat?" Murray asked feverishly.

Benny nodded. Murray fell back, despair in his face. "It's them. That's how they began before. But they haven't done anything wrong yet, I'll wager, so there'll be nothing that can be done. You see, Jack? I can't let them find me. What can we do?"

"We can take care of you," Jack said to Murray. "Mr. Greyson says we can trust this doctor in Ridgeville. We have to get you to where you can have better care. We brought a cart from school. Ben and I will go fetch it, and we'll get you out of here."

"All right," Murray said wearily. "They tried to take care of me, but I think I'm growing worse. I know my arm isn't set properly. Have your way with me, Johnny boy. But don't let them find me. Please."

## Chapter Fifteen – An Ultimatum

Mr. Greyson was waiting anxiously for Jack and Benny when they returned at midday. "I've made excuses for you both being out," he said. "I'm afraid Mr. Stanford was skeptical, but I can't help that. Church services and lunch are past. Come in and my wife will give you something."

Mrs. Greyson prepared them leftovers from a delicious roast beef dinner. Benny and Jack had had nothing to eat since supper the day before except some hard rolls and bitter coffee on the fishing boat. They devoured the meal and Mr. Greyson waited until they finished before demanding to hear their story. Benny took up the narrative when Jack became too weary to go on.

"The doctor said Murray would have died if we hadn't brought him in," Benny said. "He was bleeding slowly inside, and his arm was so badly crushed it could have developed gangrene."

"Tell him about the Omega Society," Jack urged. Benny related what had passed when Joseph had invited Jason and himself to the meeting by the lake.

"That seems so vague and harmless," Mr. Greyson said helplessly. "The card-playing of course isn't permitted, dorm or no dorm." He caught Benny's guilty look. "Benjamin, I can tell you've been punishing yourself for participating in their misdeeds. Sometime perhaps you'll ask Dr. Carlisle why it is that gambling is so attractive, and he'll explain it. I know it is, but I can't explain the attraction."

"I wanted to impress them, sir," Benny sighed. "They wanted to impress us with their rich clothes and their upper-classman superiority. I wanted to take them down a peg. It was pride. And pride is a sin. Everybody likes to sin, sir. Even those of us who ought to know better."

"Well said, my boy. Now, back to the subject at hand. Does Murray know who pushed him?"

"No, sir," Jack admitted. "He didn't see anybody. Just felt a shove."

"I can't act on such a little bit of information. The whole old scandal might come out if I accused anyone without more proof. The school was nearly destroyed last year. We had to dismiss faculty, staff, students--" Mr. Greyson looked sick with worry. "You two had better be very careful. Especially Benjamin, since they've touched him for membership and he refused them. Alert Owens without revealing anything that could endanger Murray, and stay on your guard.

"Benjamin, I think you're in the most danger. You've got an ability they want badly, but you made it clear you didn't like the sound of their secret society. You now know the truth about the Enders, and you know that Murray's alive and where he is. I'm going to get with Jack and put some fellows we know we can trust to watching you -- fellows who can protect you. You won't know who they are, but be assured I won't leave you to the wolves as I did Murray. God forgive me. I just didn't believe the hydra was still so very much alive."

*****

Benny went back to his dorm room. Joseph and Jason were not there. He collapsed into his bunk and slept for four hours. When he awoke Jason sat in a chair next to his bed, impatiently waiting for him to awaken.

"Joey-boy's out with his slimy buddies," Jason explained. "So hurry up and spill it."

"I don't know how much I can really tell you, Jason," Benny said wearily. "Something horrible is going on, and I think it's got to do with that Omega Society. We could be in big trouble for refusing to join." Benny got up and looked out into the hall. He closed the door and came close to Jason. "Murray Jacobs is alive, Jason. We found him last night. He's badly hurt, and he's sure somebody tried to kill him. We need to watch out for ourselves, and help Mr. Greyson find a way to catch whoever did it. Don't tell anyone about Murray or any of this. Promise me, Jason."

"I promise. How can I help?"

"We can keep an eye on the fellows we met who are involved in the society. We've got to try to keep them from hurting anyone else or causing more trouble."

"What kind of trouble?"

"Gambling, Murray said, among other things. It's not just card playing for fun like they wanted us to think. They may have killed a fellow last year because he wouldn't go along with them. Watch yourself, Jason."

"You bet I will. And I'll watch you too. You're the card-shark. They aren't just going to leave you alone."

"Don't remind me. I never should have picked up those cards."

*****

It was hard to go back to classes Monday as if everything were normal. Benny knew it must be doubly hard for Jack. He couldn't go visit Murray or get any news about his condition until Mr. Greyson could arrange to leave campus and go to his doctor friend later in the week. But Benny could tell Jack was so much happier just knowing Murray was alive. Mr. Greyson had sent a message to Murray's parents, urging them not to let anyone know the truth. Benny could feel the tension rising in Jason, who was not used to waiting for something to happen.

Benny enjoyed all his classes. Mr. Cartier did indeed make history interesting, though Benny already like the subject. He told them he was born in France and had traveled all over Europe until his French father had died. His mother had brought him back to the States after that, but he had seen and studied first-hand a great many of the things he taught them about -- the Parthenon in Greece, the Coliseum in Rome, the Rhine River in Germany.

Mr. Stanford's Biological Science class was pretty dry. Benny got the impression that he had already taken a dislike to Benny, maybe because of the knife, and because he and Jack had disappeared from the dorm and weren't being punished for it. He wondered if Mr. Stanford thought Benny would be a chronic troublemaker.

Mr. Stratford's Latin class was going to be hard, Benny realized. The man just knew so much, and he expected the boys to be as fascinated with languages as he was. Benny thought he would have a hard time just catching on to all the forms of the verb to be. *"Sum, es, est, summus, estis, sunt, eram, eras, erat, eramis, eratis, erant, ero, eris, erit, erimis, eritis, erunt,"* they all chanted together, though it was hardly smooth or in unison.

Benny enjoyed Mr. Talbot's class the most. The grammar wasn't much fun, but Mr. Talbot drew a two-headed dragon on the chalkboard and told them it was the 'Fused Sentence' and made them laugh. Somehow it was easy to think of things to write about for the essays. Mr. Talbot assigned an essay for the class to write about an event that changed the life of someone the student knew. Benny wrote about the night the cougar had attacked Jeremy, and all that had come of it. A two-page essay turned into a ten-page manuscript. He also mentioned that he had the cougar's skin as a reminder of how God can bring good out of evil.

*****

On Tuesday Mr. Stanford's apartment was broken into. Everyone was shocked, because there had been no theft on the campus for a long time, and for someone to rob a faculty member and dorm parent's quarters was extraordinary. Every person on campus was interviewed and the police investigated. All they could tell was that someone strong using a very sharp tool had gone through the place in a big hurry, gouging holes in drawers and cupboards, ripping pillows and upholstery to shreds, strewing torn clothing everywhere.

*****

Mr. Talbot was delighted with the essay Benny had written, and asked if Benny would do an oral excerpt from it in class and bring in the cougar skin to show everyone. But when Benny went into his footlocker to take out the skin before class, he could not find it. He looked carefully through all his things, and made Jason turn his out too. Then he remembered what Jack has said about Joseph being jealous about the skin. When Joseph came back from the washroom, Benny asked to look through his things.

"What makes you think I'd want a smelly old dead cat?" sneered Joseph. "No, you can't go rummaging through my stuff."

Benny reported the missing skin to the monitor on duty. The monitor promised to tell Mr. Stanford and said that a search would be made of the entire dorm while everyone was in class. But at the end of the day no sign of the skin had been found. Benny was heartbroken. Next to his knife, he couldn't imagine losing something he treasured more. It was a tie to Doc Daniel and Jeremy, a tangible reminder of an event both terrible and wonderful.

*****

That night Benny took one more look through his footlocker. Suddenly he noticed a slip of paper tucked into his winter boots. He pulled it out and opened it.

"The box is the key. Use it to unlock the door to the cat." At the end was a symbol Benny recognized as the Greek letter Omega. Jason and Joseph were both in the room when Benny found the note. Joseph watched every move Benny made when he found the note, though he tried clumsily not to show it. Jason read the note over Benny's shoulder. Like lightning, Jason leaped across the room and slammed Joseph down on the floor. He grabbed his throat and Joseph squawked. He was a much bigger boy than Jason, but he was not at all strong and could not get the furious boy off of him.

"You're the one who stole it!" Jason snarled. "I knew it all the time. We want it back right now!"

"Make him get off of me, or you'll be sorry!" Joseph squealed to Benny.

"Let him up, Jason," Benny ordered. "Joseph, I guess you don't want to be expelled, do you? I just want my cougar skin back. I don't want any trouble."

"You can't prove I had anything to do with that note or your -- cougar skin," Joseph said with an oath. "That's not my writing. One of the searchers could have put that in there. But the truth is, I don't have the blasted thing. I don't even know for sure where it is. You're just going to have to do what they say, or you'll start getting the pretty kitty back a piece a day. That I can tell you. You can tell me now what's in the box. Then they'll let you know what they want next."

"Ben, there's no way you're going to give in to them," insisted Jason.

"All right," Joseph spat. "What if something happened to your loudmouthed interfering little friend here? Don't you touch me again," he shrilled as Jason lurched toward him. "Something could just as well happen to Carlisle too. You have no idea what you're up against here. Don't treat us lightly. Murray Jacobs learned."

Benny paled at the careless way Joseph spoke about Murray. Could he actually have been the one who had pushed Murray off the tour boat? Benny was angry enough to let Jason do his worst, and saw that Jason would have been glad to clean up the floor with Joseph. But Benny looked at Joseph again, and saw something under the threat. Joseph was trembling and sweating.

"Tell me what's in the box," he demanded.

Benny and Jason looked at each other.

"I'm not bluffing! The kitty-cat won't make a nice patchwork. What's in the box?"

"If somebody wants to know, he can ask me himself," Benny said sharply. "Go deliver that message, Joseph. And maybe it's you who'll be sorry before this is over. Be sure and tell them that, too."

"Ben, I'm gonna make him sorry right now," Jason snarled.

"Wait, Jason," Benny said coldly. "Look at him. He's scared to death. Of them, not of us. We don't have to do anything to Joseph. They'll get tired of using him, and take care of him themselves. That's how the kind of people you hang around with take care of their friends, Joseph. You're a fool to think you have any power. I hope God shows you how wrong you are. And I hope it's not too late when He does."

Joseph made no pretense of leading devotions that night. He jumped into bed and turned his face to the wall. Benny and Jason read the Bible and prayed together on their own.

*****

The next day Benny went straight to Mr. Greyson, showed him the note and told him what Joseph had said.

"They broke into Mr. Stanford's apartment because they thought the box was there," Benny explained. "Maybe Joseph told them after Jack took me to Mr. Stanford. I'll do whatever you say, Mr. Greyson."

"I'm not Solomon, Benjamin," Mr. Greyson said helplessly. "Until I know who 'they' really are, how can I act? By the way, they didn't find the case. Mr. Stanford told me he carries it about with him, and locks it in his office at night. I called Drake in and gave him the third degree about that tool shed by the lake. He explained that the shed was set up with that secret room because the former grounds man used to keep some of his more valuable equipment hidden to protect it from thieves. Drake said he had never used it, and didn't know the boys had discovered it. He promised to clean out their things and make sure they couldn't get back in. He was very innocent and apologetic. Benjamin, he could be innocent. I just don't have any proof against anyone."

"Then I'll get them to meet me," Benny said firmly. "It's the only way to learn anything."

"I'm moving Joseph out of your room," Mr. Greyson said. "He needs to be disciplined anyway, and you shouldn't have to put up with such a situation. Then I can put someone in there that might be a help to you, not a danger. I'll try to find out who wrote this note. They'll agree to meet with you, I am certain, and when you go I'll make sure you're guarded by fellows who know how to get about without being noticed."

"Maybe you should make Jason one of them. He's lived in a tough city neighborhood and in the woods. He's a fine hunter and tracker. And I know he'll do his best to take care of me."

Mr. Greyson rose and opened his safe. He handed Benny the knife. "They'll want to see it for themselves. You may have to make arrangements at the last minute, and they won't be satisfied with an empty box. Keep it on your person at all times. Protect yourself with it if need be. I wish I thought I was doing the right thing," he said. "This could be very dangerous, Carlisle."

Benny didn't want to think about that. "How's Murray, sir?"

"Poor lad. That arm's useless to him. How he wept when the doctor told him. But otherwise he's doing well. His mother's let on that she's taking a trip to visit family back East, and the doctor's going to transfer Jacobs to a little cabin up by the lakeshore, location known to no one but mother and dad and doctor. He'll do better in his mother's care, since the doctor's done all he can for now. This thing must be made right, Carlisle, with all that boy's sacrificed. We must make it come right. But I don't want to sacrifice you too."

"God doesn't want the wicked to prosper, sir," Benny replied. "Christians are always at war with evil. And sometimes in a war there are casualties. Like the Bible says, 'Fear not those who can kill the body, but after that have no power. Rather fear Him who is able to cast body and soul into Hell.' But it's easy to quote verses. I won't tell you I'm not scared."

*****

Benny stopped by Mr. Stanford's apartment after he had stashed his knife in a place he thought would be safe. Benny had an idea that the person who was so interested in the case and the knife might make a move more quickly if he knew Benny had them back in his possession. Mr. Greyson had been reluctant to allow him to try the plan he had formed, but couldn't come up with another way. Benny wanted to make what he was going to do next as public as he could, and he hoped the right person would be watching.

It was just half an hour until classes were to begin, and many boys and teachers were moving throughout the first floor dormitory hall. The Science Master had been staying with Mr. Cartier in his apartment while repairs were made. Just now Drake was in the doorway, putting on the last coat of paint. Mr. Stanford expected to be able to move back in the following day. Mr. Stanford stood in the hall supervising Drake's painting. Mr. Cartier and Mr. Talbot stood with him.

"Carlisle," Mr. Stanford said sharply. "Looking on your handiwork, eh?"

"Sir?" Benny said.

"Don't think I don't know you had some hand in this," he snapped. Benny hadn't planned to get attention like this, and he flushed with anger. But he saw that everyone was watching and listening. Even Drake stopped painting and stared at the teacher. "You and your contraband," Stanford blustered. "I can't prove you did this, but at least someone who was after that -- that *object* did!"

Benny saw Drake's eyebrows go up as he went back to painting. "Mr. Stanford, I'm sorry about what happened," he said. "I'd like my case back. Mr. Greyson said I could ask you for it."

"What's all this flap about, Mr. Stanford?" Mr. Talbot inquired. "Are you implying that Carlisle could create such a swath of destruction?"

"Surely not," Mr. Cartier looked Benny over critically. "I was telling Stratford that I saw a drunken sailor stave in the hull of a frigate with a handspike and the marks looked like those in your room. I doubt this young man has that kind of strength, or a tool to do the work."

"You'd be surprised at what he has," muttered Mr. Stanford. "Why am I to just surrender the thing to you on your say-so, young sir?"

"Here's a note from Mr. Greyson, sir," Benny said. Mr. Stanford's eyes bugged out when he read it. "But -- but -- but --" he spluttered. Mr. Talbot took the note and read it aloud.

"'Dear Mr. Stanford. Please give Benjamin Carlisle back his black dragon case. John Greyson, Headmaster.' Short and to the point, I'd say. What's all the fuss about?"

"Here! Take it and welcome!" exclaimed Mr. Stanford. He opened his briefcase and thrust the box at Benny. Then he swung around and stalked away. Benny slipped the case into his jacket pocket.

"Has Stanford gone mad?" Mr. Talbot inquired. "What is so special about that box, lad?"

"Yes, I'd like to know too," Mr. Cartier said.

Benny didn't know what to say. He didn't know who to trust anymore. Everyone seemed to want to know what was in the box. Jason and Jack both stood nearby, wondering what Benny would do. The person who wanted the worst to know -- who would violently tear apart anything in his way to find out -- was probably listening right now, and once he knew, Benny was afraid of what might happen. Then he remembered that the box was empty. Quickly he undid the catch and opened the case.

"Yes, Stanford has gone mad," Mr. Cartier assured Mr. Talbot. "He was livid with rage over having to return an empty box. May I, Benjamin?" He took the case and looked it over carefully. His dark fingers traced along the velvet liner and he shot a searching glance at Benny. Then he handed it back.

"They call those puzzle-boxes, don't they? Well, Stanford's the puzzle, if you ask me," Mr. Cartier smiled. "Classes, gentlemen. The excitement, such as it was, is over."

*****

On the way to class Benny told Jason and Jack about his plan to provoke a meeting with the person who had stolen his cougar skin. Jack immediately refused to allow Benny to go. He vowed he'd make a row and spoil the whole plan. Then Benny told him about Murray's arm.

"Do you want them to be able to keep on doing things like that?" Benny demanded. "We've got to stop them, Jack. We've got to take it one step at a time, and this is the only step we have to take."

"I'll shake the truth out of that dog Banks."

"Joseph might not know who's behind this. But it puzzles me why they would want to know what's in that box so badly. They're taking a big risk to get it. I wonder what their game is?"

*****

Benny wore his knife in his ankle sheath from then on, keeping it hidden under his uniform trousers. He kept the case in his jacket pocket or under his pillow. After classes that day Jason and Benny met Tom Wilkes, their new "mummy," a broad-shouldered, friendly giant who showed up as Joseph sullenly cleared the last of his things out of 204.

"'Lo, Banks," Tom said genially.

"Say -- you graduated already, didn't you?" Joseph demanded.

"So I did." Tom's smile faded. "Guess I must be back for a refresher course, then. Ta-ta, Banks." As Joseph struggled out the door under his load Tom suddenly reached out a long, muscular leg and tripped him. Joseph's dainties flew halfway down the hall. Tom lounged in the doorway and watched Joseph wordlessly pick each item up. Joseph's face was scarlet but he still said nothing.

"Your body's leavin' this room, Joey," Tom said in a cold, hard voice. "Let your mind and your sick little soul leave it too, and let these fellows be. I won't speak to you about it again. I'll just pick your arms and legs off." Joseph stumbled away as fast as his burden would let him.

Tom entered with only a fringed deerskin bag slung on his shoulder. "Yep, these are all my worldly goods," he grinned at Benny and Jason. "I come from Kansas City.

On the frontier you can't carry much about you, so I didn't get in the habit. But I do have this, Carlisle, and I'd like to compare usefulness with you sometime." Tom showed them a gigantic curved hunting knife with a deer antler handle. Jason's eyes bugged out. Tom let him hold the knife and Jason commented that he could now die happy. Benny brought out his knife and Tom whistled at the ankle sheath.

"Handy," he said admiringly. "Pretty little thing. I like mine better, 'course, but I can see the advantages. I hope neither of us has to test 'em out. Since Banks already noticed it, I'll tell you straight off. I graduated from Brigham two years ago. I'm actually a cadet at West Point, but I was home on special leave and came here at Greyson's request to play bodyguard. He's my uncle, so he trusts me, and I hope you will, too. And no, he probably doesn't know about the knife. I've got some rules of my own, and God can judge me for 'em, but nobody's takin' my knife and puttin' it in a safe." Jason and Benny were both delighted with their new roommate. Tom told them about life in the wilds of Kansas and at West Point.

They swapped hunting and trapping stories. Jason admired the scar Tom had gotten releasing a wolverine from one of his traps, and Tom laughed till he cried when he heard from Benny just how many fellows twice his size Jason had knocked over. Tom answered Benny's unspoken question by freely admitting he had been chosen as a bodyguard as much as a spiritual leader for the two boys.

"The Lord's given me a strong body and a really frightening lack of common caution," Tom said without pride. "I'm glad to have a chance to use them for Him. I'll have ten good fellows to back you up. And I know I can count on Owens here to be one of 'em," he added when Jason looked as if he feared he might be left out. Jason brightened at once.

Jack felt better at once when he was introduced to the boys' new mummy. "Say, Gimp!" Tom rumbled when Jack came to call. "Good thing you're in on this too. We'll compass these fellows about like Elisha’s chariots and horsemen of fire if God gives us strength, won’t we?”

“That we will, Tom,” Jack grinned. “Omega Society beware. Your days are numbered.”

## Chapter Sixteen– The Cartier Factor

"Just a moment, Carlisle." Mr. Cartier stopped him one day as Benny left the classroom building on his way to lunch. "Would you mind sharing some sandwiches with me in my office so we could talk a little?"

Benny looked at Mr. Cartier uneasily. "Is anything wrong with my work, sir?" he asked.

Mr. Cartier laughed. "Come along, my boy. I've told Talbot not to expect you at the dining hall. We teachers are supposed to get to know the students a bit. Don't fret about your grades. It's nothing like that."

Benny entered Mr. Cartier's office and sat in the chair in front of his desk. Mr. Cartier brought out a basket with thick ham sandwiches and pulled a pot of hot chocolate off a little spirit lamp to fill the two mugs on his desk. Mr. Cartier prayed for the food, then waved at Benny to take a sandwich.

"We get all kinds of boys here at Brigham," Mr. Cartier said, "but you're not the common sort." He stood up and stretched. He didn't sit back down. Benny suddenly saw the man's muscles tense. Benny got up, too. Mr. Cartier moved to the edge of his desk. Benny braced himself. When Mr. Cartier suddenly shot around the desk to try to grab him, Benny ducked underneath his sinewy arms and rolled past Mr. Cartier's desk.

The history teacher almost lost his balance but he whirled around quickly and shot out a hand to try to grab Benny again. Benny dodged at the last second, then grabbed Mr. Cartier's arm as it passed his throat, turned sharply, and pulled the man up and over his shoulder. The teacher sailed through the air and, amazingly, tucked and rolled and came up on his feet, breathless and laughing.

"Who taught you to do that?" he demanded. "It was perfectly wonderful!"

"My -- my stepfather," Benny said. He was breathing hard himself, partly from the exertion and partly from fear.

"Your stepfather? He must have grown up in a rough neighborhood like mine in Paris," Mr. Cartier said. "I am so sorry, Carlisle. I've frightened you out of ten years' growth, haven't I? I wanted to see if you would use that knife."

"Knife, sir?"

"I saw the impress of a knife in your mysterious black case. Now I've noted you have an ankle sheath under your trousers."

"I can use it, sir, but I won't if I don't have to." Benny edged toward the door. Mr. Cartier sat back down at his desk.

"I'll never get you to eat with me now. Please believe me. I just wanted to make sure there was no danger of your losing your temper around the other fellows. Sit down, Benjamin. I swear I'm done attacking you. Seems as if I shouldn't succeed in getting near you if I wanted to hurt you. Here. Eat. I found a little French bakery and the bread is the best in the country." He took a big bite of his sandwich. Benny returned to his seat. He was hungry, and it was too late to make it to the dining hall.

"I-I have permission from Mr. Greyson, sir, to carry my knife."

"Greyson doesn't give that kind of permission, my boy." Mr. Cartier laughed.

"You can ask him about it, sir."

"I'm asking you, son."

"Sir, I'll go with you to Mr. Greyson if you want."

"All right, all right, I'm convinced. I thought Greyson really didn't know about it, and for some stupid reason I like to handle problems myself before I run to him. You probably learned to use the knife from the same clever fellow who taught you *Jujutsu*, eh?"

"My dad knows a lot about a lot of things," Benny hedged.

"And so do you, but you're not going to tell me any of them, are you?" Mr. Cartier said. "Would Mr. Greyson tell me if I asked him? Probably not. It's probably none of my business. Perhaps he's looking for suspects because that scandal he tried to hush up last year isn't quite gone away?

"I didn't have any fellowship to Oxford, you know. I quit last year because of that mess. I thought Greyson handled it outrageously. He begged me to come back. I said I would if there weren't any more coverups. I don't like lying to people about a school I used to be proud of."

Benny wondered if he could really trust Mr. Cartier. He realized that if he was the person who was using the boys in the Omega Society, he had now found out the truth about the knife case. But if he wasn't, he was a smart and strong friend who might be a big help in time of need. Benny wished he knew the truth. Then he saw something that made him start in fear. Mr. Cartier wore a handsome silver ring with a black onyx stone. In the center of the stone was a silver character. It was the Greek letter Omega. They finished their lunch and Mr. Cartier let Benny go without asking any more questions.

*****

Benny had thought that it would be easy to arrange a meeting with the mysterious leader of the Omegans. But he never saw Joseph around campus or in his new room when he went to look for him. He wondered if Joseph was really afraid of him. Benny fretted about his cougar skin, but he realized that more important things were at stake. He would just have to wait and see what this person would do next.

Benny had tried to hide the ankle sheath more carefully, but he made it obvious that he was carrying the case around with him. He took a hint from Mr. Cartier and brushed up the velvet lining so the imprint of the knife no longer showed. Mr. Stratford admired it profusely when Benny showed it to him. Benny noticed that he understood the mechanism and opened it without being shown the secret.

Mr. Stratford seemed disappointed to find the case empty but didn't ask any questions. Benny thought that could mean three things. One, perhaps he was just interested in the box itself and didn't really care what might have been in it. Two, Mr. Cartier might have told him about the knife already so he didn't need to ask. Three, maybe he was the one who desperately wanted to know the box's contents but knew he would have to be more clever than he had been to find out. Benny believed Mr. Cartier was strong enough to tear holes in wood like someone had done in Mr. Stanford's rooms. He wasn't at all sure Mr. Stratford could. But he could have gotten someone else to do it.

*****

The weather suddenly turned significantly colder. Everyone got out mufflers and heavy uniform coats, and you could scarcely tell one bundled-up student from the other. Benny knew that Tom's Guardian Angels, as the young man jokingly called them, were shadowing him, and he was sure someone from the Omega Society must be keeping a close watch on him. But over the next few days Benny became convinced that something very peculiar was happening.

"Hey, Ben, what were you doin' out by the ball field yesterday?" Jason asked one evening. "It's nice of you to come and watch us practice, but I thought you didn't care for it. And with that cold you shouldn't be hanging around outside."

"I wasn't there," Benny said, puzzled. "I spent the afternoon in the library. And I don't have a cold."

"I saw you there," Jason insisted. "You had on that hat with the cougar teeth hatband. An' you were coughin' up a storm. You left before I could talk to you, though."

"Jason, I didn't even bring that hat with me," Benny frowned. "What are you talking about?"

"What are you talking about?" Jason echoed. "I guess I did see you at the rugby field wearin' that hat today."

"I guess you didn't."

*****

Another time Tom came into their room flushed and angry. "Now look here, Ben," he said sharply. "My guys will do their best, but I'd swear you've split in two. Weren't you just up walking past the classroom building?"

"I've been here for the last hour, Tom," Benny said. "Someone saw me up at the classroom building? How can that be?"

"Mac Simmons was up there and saw you, and heard that awful bark you've got. You should get nurse to give you something for it."

"Tom, I wasn't there and I don't have a cold."

*****

Benny began to look out for this person who was being mistaken for him. One day he started to leave for morning classes and realized he had forgotten a book. He turned back to the dorm and ducked in the end stairwell and up the stairs.

Benny was surprised to see Drake just coming out of Jack Williams' room. He hadn't known anything in there needed repair. Then a deep, raspy cough made him glance toward his own room. To his amazement he saw someone coming out -- someone the same size and build as Benny, and wearing the hat with the cougar teeth. His back was to Benny. He saw Drake take in the figure emerging from Room 204. Drake stopped in the doorway and stared. The person didn't seem to notice him.

Benny was sure Drake hadn't seen him in the stairwell. Drake apparently thought Benny was coming out of his room. Drake had seemed astonished. Had he hidden in Jack's room -- or possibly searched it? Had he watched out the window and seen Benny leave a few minutes before? Would he have gone into Benny's room if the double hadn't shocked him? Drake looked around. He still didn't see Benny, but he was obviously shaken. He cautiously followed the double and disappeared after him down the center staircase.

Benny ran into Jack's room and peeked out the window. The person who looked so much like him -- his walk, his size, and his whole posture were eerily like Benny's -- trudged up the hill toward the classroom building, but on a side path, not up the main sidewalk. Benny saw Drake come out of the dorm and stand in the middle of the sidewalk, scratching his head.

*****

Finally Benny got the message from the leader of the Omegans. He found it slipped into one of his books when he picked them up from the shelves outside the dining room after lunch. The paper held a crude map directing him to the side of campus Drake had warned Benny and Jason contained bogs and briars. It had only one word, "Midnight," printed on it. He and Jason had passed along the old bridle path that led to the spot marked with the Greek letter Omega.

"Don't go to your room tonight," Mr. Greyson ordered. "We don't want you to have any trouble getting out. Mr. Stanford isn't in on the plan, and we can cover for you by putting you in the dispensary with a bad chest cold. You've been coughing all week, so no one will be surprised."

"Why does everyone think I have a cold?" Benny demanded. "Mr. Greyson, is there something I should know about?"

"Just check into the dispensary, Ben, and get to your meeting," Mr. Greyson said. "Let us do some of the worrying. Remember that there are all sorts of Guardian Angels."

*****

Benny hated wasting the evening in the dispensary. Mr. Greyson had written a note for the nurse and told him that he must pretend to have a cold, so he had coughed himself hoarse. The nurse, however, seemed skeptical.

"You've no fever," she scowled. "You throat's just a little red, and your chest is perfectly clear. Are you sure you're not funning Mr. Greyson, Mister Carlisle?"

Benny shook his head, not daring to talk. He wished he knew why this cold business was so important. That night he was surprised to find his door closely guarded. How was he going to get out? Benny searched the room for something that would help him escape. He found a spare nurse's cloak and cap in the closet. The nurse's office connected to Benny's sickroom by a door behind her desk. She sat there doing paperwork for a long time. Benny slipped into his clothes, then jammed the nurse's cap on his head, covering as much of the rest of himself as he could with the cloak. Finally the nurse got up and went to use the bathroom. Benny quickly tiptoed into her office and out through into the hall. He hurried around to the sickroom's outer door and past the guard.

"Good-night, then, nurse," the guard called out. Benny waved a gloved hand and ran out the door. He shed the cap and cloak in the bushes.

The night was very cold and clear, and he huddled against the buildings as he hurried across the grounds toward the meeting place. Passing in the shadows by his dormitory, Benny stopped dead to see a figure climbing out of the window of his room. The person was dressed in a school greatcoat, a scarf Benny's mother had made him, and the brown felt hat with the cougar teeth hatband. He coughed, a very genuine, deep, croupy sound.

Benny saw Jason and Tom both peeking out the window as the stranger disappeared into the shrubbery. Benny started after him, but then he saw another figure follow his double into the darkness. Benny caught a glimpse of his face. It was Dereck Sheraton, the boy who claimed to be president of the Omega Society. Obviously he thought he was following Benny. So Benny followed him instead, still wondering who the stranger in his clothes could be.

Just past the open area around the dorms was a grove of evergreen trees. Benny's double slipped into it. Dereck followed. Benny skirted around and entered from another side. He heard scuffling and coughing a moment later, then a kind of strangled bleating sound of pain and terror. Benny was filled with dread. His double had been attacked, perhaps hurt, by Dereck. Benny quickly moved toward the sound.

He stopped just short of the spot where the noise had come from. To his amazement, Benny found Dereck bound to a tree and gagged. Benny came up to him and the boy snorted and scuffled, terror in his wide eyes. Benny left Dereck just as he was and went on toward the lake.

Benny spotted his double as he broke out of the trees and crept along a ditch beside the ball field. He almost shouted a warning as someone rose up out of the ditch, but the double was very well able to take care of himself. In a moment the attacker had vanished from sight and the double was on the move again. Benny resumed following, only glancing at the unconscious Scotty Sullivan sprawled in the ditch as he passed.

*****

Benny followed the stranger to the clearing by the lake. Both of them hung back in the woods. Presently someone hissed, "Carlisle?"

"Here," Benny heard the double's hoarse, raspy voice say. Benny marveled that his voice did sound a lot like his own when he had a cold. The other Benny stepped out into the open. Benny couldn't tell exactly where the other speaker was. He moved cautiously around to the left side of his double.

"I assume you were smart enough to bring whatever's supposed to be in that case," the voice said. Benny realized the person was moving noiselessly through the trees. The direction of his voice had changed. Benny's double noticed it too, and turned warily, apparently searching for his unseen interrogator.

"What do you want it for, anyway?" Benny's double asked, coughing.

"I want it so you know that I can control you," the voice replied, moving again. "I can make you do anything I want."

"So why sick your thugs on me?" Benny's double asked, blowing his nose loudly.

"Yes, I know you dispatched your escorts. That was very handily done. It was a final test, and I'm very satisfied with your scores."

Benny slipped farther into the woods. The voice seemed closer to him now. He could not place it, though it seemed a little familiar. It was deep and a little hoarse. "You are a fellow of so many valuable talents. We could make it worth your while to join us. Tell me what you kept in the box. I think I already know, but I want to be sure."

Benny thought that it couldn't be Mr. Cartier, because he already knew about the knife. But then he realized that he hadn't actually shown it to Mr. Cartier. Maybe he had just been bluffing, and still wasn't sure. Or was it Mr. Stratford? As a librarian he'd have contact with every student. Then Benny remembered that Mr. Talbot had been just as curious as Mr. Cartier to know what the box held. Benny hadn't even considered him before.

"We weren't fooled by that visit to the dispensary. You were seen going to your room afterward," the voice taunted.

"Clever." The double bent over with a coughing fit and held out the knife case. Mr. Greyson had insisted on taking the case before Benny had gone to the infirmary. "Guess I know when I'm licked," he gasped, as if he couldn't get his breath. "Here, take it."

"In good time. I suppose your guardian angels are waiting to pounce on me as soon as I show myself," the voice mocked.

"They're not here," the double said with a wheezy laugh. He sat down on the ground and put the box in front of him. "I told Greyson the meeting would be tomorrow night, not tonight. I got to thinking about things, and I thought maybe I could do business with you. So it's just you and me." Benny realized that the woods had been too quiet. They really were alone.

"How did you learn to play cards like that? From your jailbird stepfather? Yes, I know about him. I could ruin your school record, and his medical career, if I let that slip. All my boys have a secret that only I know. That is why they serve me so willingly."

"Like the murder of Trevor Lang?" Benny's double asked.

"I did that myself," the voice said with a chuckle. "He was dead when he was placed in the buggy. He defied me, and I couldn't have that."

"I guess Murray Jacobs was one of your boys, too," Benny's double suggested.

The voice swore bitterly. "That stinking Jew-boy! He exposed us! He discovered almost everyone. I had to start all over again. So I made him pay. I did that myself, too. You see how frank I'm being with you, Carlisle. It's because I think you'll be more useful to me than the other fellows. I thought you would be difficult, but I'm glad you're being so reasonable. You'll be my lieutenant -- my right-hand man. Am I right that what you have in the case will be useful to me as well?"

"You'll have to judge that for yourself," the double laughed. "Come on and take a look."

Benny saw a flash of something metal catching the moonlight. Then it vanished. The leader of the Omegans was carrying a gun. He could easily shoot Benny's double if he realized he was being tricked. Whoever this person was, he was risking his life to take Benny's place. Benny's eyes scanned the brush, but he could not see the hidden speaker anywhere. Benny heard a movement off to his right. He reached down and drew his knife. The outline of a tall man separated itself from the trees. The double slowly rose to his feet. Suddenly a smaller, bundled-up figure crashed out of the brush.

"He's got a gun!" a voice shouted. The newcomer hurtled himself at the tall stranger.

"I don't know who you are," snarled the voice of the Omegan leader, "But you were a fool to come here alone." A shot shattered the silence as the two rolled into the underbrush. The double had started to spring forward but he halted at the sound of the shot. Benny sped toward the sound of the struggle in the brush. He got a clear sight of the two struggling men just as the tall one pushed the smaller one backward.

The bigger man pulled a second gun from his coat. Benny's knife hit the man in the shoulder before the gun could fire. The stranger and the tall man went down on the ground in a heap. They wrestled violently for a few moments, but Benny saw that their struggles gradually slowed. The tall man teetered on his knees and fell over on his side, clutching his shoulder. The man fighting him struggled out from under him and staggered up. Benny's double burst in on the scene. To his horror, Benny saw that he clutched his arm. He had been wounded by the first gunshot. His hat had fallen, and his muffler slipped to the ground.

"Dad!" Benny ran forward and threw himself on Jeremy, who had shaved his beard and made himself up to look remarkably like Benny.

"Oh, ow!" Jeremy moaned. "Ben, what on earth are you doing here? They were supposed to lock you up in the infirmary."

"Dad, are you all right?"

"I don't know," Jeremy said, and coughed several times in rapid succession. "Ow." He shrugged out of his coat and examined his upper arm. He reeled and Benny steadied him. "You know," he said, "Looking at my own blood is still the worst thing. It's just a nick, I think. Now who is this?" He asked as the small man moved toward them.

"Jacques Cartier, at your service," Mr. Cartier said gallantly. "This is your most interesting stepfather, eh, Carlisle? I am honored to meet you. It still seems as if there are two Benjamins. You do indeed know a lot about a lot of things, as Benjamin told me. I had no idea you were not Benjamin until his knife came flying from somewhere else."

"Is that what happened to him?" Jeremy chuckled. "That's my boy."

Benny, Mr. Cartier, and Jeremy warily approached the fallen man. Drake lay on his side, huddled in a ball of pain. Jeremy whistled and pulled the knife free. Drake cried out and cursed. Jeremy picked up his pistols and flung them into the bushes.

"You hit him right where it would hurt the most but do the least damage, Ben," Jeremy smiled. "Good job."

"Good thing I wasn't locked up in the infirmary," Benny grunted.

*"Merci, M'sieur Cartier. Merci.* And thanks, son. But I am so very glad it wasn't you here taking the shot."

"I did not know all that was to take place here, but I wanted to be sure Benjamin had some protection," Mr. Cartier explained. "I see that I misjudged Greyson. I really thought he would use Benjamin as bait to save his precious school. But perhaps you were not so wise in making yourself the target, *M'sieur le Docteur* Carlisle?"

"Gun. I didn't think he'd bring a gun," Jeremy said dazedly.

"There really are people coming, right?" Benny asked. "Dad, that may be a nick, but it's bleeding an awful lot." He tried to make a bandage with his handkerchief.

"I see you don't feel sorry for him," Jeremy laughed. Then he sat down heavily on the ground. "Yes, Greyson and the police will be here momentarily. I was hoping to get a confession out of him about Trevor Lang, and I did. I already know he pushed Murray Jacobs off the boat."

"How could you know?" Drake gritted. He tried to sit up but couldn't get his balance. "So you're Doctor Carlisle. Your disguise was very good. But you would not have known about Murray Jacobs if you had not tricked me into admitting I killed him."

"As far as Murray is concerned," Jeremy said coldly, "It's easy to prove you did it."

Drake cursed. "You are very confident."

"I visited Murray Jacobs' parents," Jeremy said. "We talked about suspects but couldn't pin anyone down. Then Mrs. Jacobs mentioned that they had waited till the last minute to inform the school, hoping against hope that Murray would be found alive and they could report some good news, and still so busy searching that they didn't have time to send word to the school sooner. She said Mr. Greyson actually had to be called out of the meeting hall to receive the message.

"When I got back together with Mr. Greyson and we went over every detail of everything we knew, Jack

Williams told us that business about you knowing Murray wasn't coming -- believing him dead when his own parents were still searching. I thought that was very significant."

Drake swore again. At that moment a crowd of people poured into the clearing. Mr. Greyson led the police up to them.

"We heard a shot," Mr. Greyson said. "Doctor Carlisle. Are you all right? Benjamin! What are you doing here?"

"Using my knife on something bigger than a lizard, Mr. Greyson," Benny said sheepishly.

"And Cartier," Greyson said, shaking his head. "I might have known you'd take matters into your own hands."

"It seems I was not really needed," Mr. Cartier admitted. "I suppose I should have come to you, *M'sieur* Greyson. I should have trusted you."

"I'd never knowingly sacrifice one of my boys," Mr. Greyson said. "Every day I pray that God will forgive me for what happened to Trevor Lang and Murray Jacobs. Perhaps we can work together to be sure we can both be proud of Brigham once again, Mr. Cartier?"

"Well, Mr. Greyson, I think you've got enough evidence to take care of Drake," Jeremy said grimly. "I already explained to Ben how we knew he was responsible for what happened to Murray Jacobs. He's also the one who tore up Mr. Stanford's room. He was trying to plant the handspike he used in Ben's room the other day when he thought Ben had already left for class. He was very surprised to see Ben come out of his room twice that day."

Benny gasped, remembering the day he saw his double in the dormitory. "He was so surprised he left the handspike in Jack and Lee's room. The monitor had already inspected, and testified that it wasn't there before. Ben and I both saw him come out of Jack's room." He winked at Benny.

"The handspike had chips of paint from Mr. Stafford's room on it. He burgled it when Ben's knife was supposed to be there but wasn't. We knew all that, but it wasn't enough to get him hanged, which is what I aimed to do. So I had to get him to tell me about Trevor Lang."

"But you already knew I'd killed Murray Jacobs-" Drake seemed to falter for the first time. "Why did you need to know about Lang?"

"Didn't you know, Drake?" Mr. Greyson smiled. "Murray Jacobs is alive."

Drake started. "Impossible. Impossible."

"You picked the wrong young man when you decided to ask Benjamin Carlisle to join your club," Mr. Greyson laughed. "He helped to find Murray and save his life. He baited you until you couldn't avoid revealing yourself. And he subdued you right handily. I guess he would have been a great asset to your side, Drake. But I'm glad he chose to remain on ours."

Jeremy rubbed his wounded arm, then put his hand on Benny's shoulder. "Mr. Greyson, I hope you don't mind if I bring my son back a little later?"

"Drake shot him, Mr. Greyson," Mr. Cartier protested. "The wound should be looked at."

"It's all right," Jeremy said. Benny felt him leaning rather heavily on his arm, though.

"Are you sure you're quite all right, Doctor Carlisle?" Mr. Greyson asked.

Jeremy picked up Benny's felt hat and clapped it on the boy's head. "Ow. I'll be fine. Ben, walk this way with me."

Benny picked up his knife case. Jeremy led Benny away from the group toward the path where Drake had come out of the woods. Benny gave a cry of joy and picked up his cougar skin. Jeremy motioned to him, and they walked on.

*****

They didn't talk for a few minutes. It was impossible to guess Jeremy's thoughts. The heavy makeup that made him look so much like Benny was an unreadable mask close up.

"Dad, I'm so glad you were here," Benny said. "I wanted to write and tell you so many times. I wish I had."

"I wish you had, too, Ben," Jeremy folded Benny into his arms and sighed. "Ow. I'd've had more time to get here, and I might have come up with a better plan. But that's part of growing up, trying to make decisions on your own. I'm glad you told Mr. Greyson everything. He wrote me right away when Murray was found. He didn't want you to go to the meeting, but he knew it was necessary for someone to go to try to get some proof.

"I suggested that if you had a double, it would accomplish two things -- it would confuse the Omegans and keep them from finding out that you were communicating regularly with Mr. Greyson, and tonight it would shift the danger away from you and onto me."

"But how could he have let you come alone? Dad, you couldn't be so sure something wouldn't go wrong."

"Sometimes my spirit of adventure still outruns my good sense. I told Mr. Greyson I was sure I could get a confession if I just had a few minutes alone. I just didn't figure he'd have a gun. It's good Mr. Cartier took some initiative."

"If I hadn't followed you --" Benny didn't finish. He hugged Jeremy very tightly.

"Ow. Never mind. It's all right. I promise next time I come to your rescue I'll think about the possibility of guns."

"I kept trying to talk to Joseph Banks to arrange the meeting," Benny said. "What happened to him?"

"Joseph was compromised. He was of no further use to Drake. We found him in his room two days ago -- Drake had poisoned him with a box of candy. We got it out of him, and he's going to be all right."

*****

The next day Jeremy was back to his normal self. He used the false beard he had worn when he first came up with his "new face," and he was preparing to go home. Benny learned that Tom and Jason hadn't known Jeremy was there, doubling for Benny, until his dad had walked into the dorm room the night of the meeting. Jason nearly spoiled the whole thing by shouting for the whole dorm to hear. But they fell in line quickly with the plan.

Jeremy had actually been there a little over a week, and had caused much confusion among the Guardian Angels.

Murray was brought to the school by his parents for a brief visit with Jack. Murray was anxious to return to classes, and Jack was thrilled when Jeremy agreed that Murray would be ready in another week or two, or as soon as his parents could bear to part with him.

Benny went with Jeremy so he could take his leave of Mr. Greyson. The headmaster shook hands heartily with Jeremy. "What about those teachers who had some kind of jewelry with the Omega on it?" Benny asked Mr. Greyson. "I thought maybe everybody was in on the plan."

Mr. Greyson shook his head. "Remember that Drake told you he served on the barque *Omega*?" Benny had forgotten. "He was captain, though, not mate. It was a pirate ship, though he escaped and made the crew take the fall for him. I just received a letter about that this morning. If we'd known -- But at any rate, last Christmas the lot of us received gifts with the Omega symbol on them, given anonymously, from 'A Friend of the School.' I have a penknife. Perhaps he wanted to create confusion about the Omegans and who was behind them.

"How can I ever thank you for what you've done, Doctor Carlisle?" Mr. Greyson said. "When I told Benjamin I'd like to meet you, I had no idea the event would be so life-changing. You and your son have simply put everything right for us."

"Believe me, sir, the Lord ordered all the circumstances," Jeremy said. "I hope it's really over now."

"I believe it is, finally," Mr. Greyson said. "I apologize again for the danger your son was put in, and you." Neither of them could help laughing when they heard how Benny had escaped from the infirmary. "He may not be yours by blood, but a lot of your cunning seems to have rubbed off on him. Thank you again for bringing us light in this dark business."

"God brings things to light in His time, Mr. Greyson," Jeremy said. "We just wait and trust him, even when things seem such a mess they'll never come right.

Isn't that so, Ben?" He gave Benny a rough hug. "I'll tell your mother I found you well and happy and that your school is a very exciting place, shall I?"

"Does she know why you really came, Dad?"

"Mr. Greyson wrote me on plain stationary, no school letterhead. I let your grandfather know what was passing as soon as I heard," Jeremy replied. "He wrote back immediately and asked me to come and help him look into some matters of his investments and a trust he had set up for you. Your mother saw that letter and no other. My business with your grandfather took about two hours."

"I don't think we should ever tell her," Benny said.

"She won't hear it from me. I think we can trust your grandfather and Mr. Greyson to keep it quiet. Mr. Greyson, I'll take my leave, now. I want to thank you for taking such good care of my son. And I'm also glad to learn he seems to be able to take care of himself if the need arises."

## Chapter Seventeen – A World of Silence and a Willing Apprentice

"It feels funny to be home," Benny said as he and Jason got out of his grandfather's carriage. Trevor had brought them home from boarding school for Easter Recess.

"I know. That blizzard kept us at school all Christmas vacation. I'm sure glad we got home for Easter," Jason said. He looked around Schuylerville's main street. Jason's father was to meet them at Benny's house, which also housed Jeremy's doctor office. Sure enough, Carl Owens came out the front door just as Trevor and the coachman were beginning to take down the luggage.

"Howdy, howdy, howdy," Jason's father greeted them. "Well, this is what I call timing. The Carlisles have both their kids arriving at the same time."

"What?" Benny asked. "What do you mean, Mr. Owens?"

"I mean your mother's having her baby, Ben," laughed Mr. Owens. "And I mean right now."

"Now?" Benny gasped.

"Yep. Now. Oh, I wouldn't necessarily be in a real big hurry to go inside, Ben." Mr. Owens grabbed Benny's arm as he started to run up the steps. "It's a beautiful spring day. And it's a lot quieter out here than it is in there."

Benny heard a faint wailing sound. "What's wrong?" he asked. "Is that mother?"

"Yep. Been doin' a bit of yellin'," Mr. Owens said. "Now, don't fret. It's not like when Jason's ma had Pip. She's doin' fine. But they always yell a bit. Baby's almost here. Ah-hah!"

The window of Benny's parents' bedroom flew up and Jeremy stuck his head out. "Hello, and welcome, boys!" he shouted. Then he disappeared. A moment later he was back and held out a small bundle. Benny could only see a red, wrinkled face and some dark hair sticking straight up above it. "Look, Ben. It's your sister. She almost beat you home. We've named her Sarah Grace. How d'you like her?"

"Mother was right. It is a girl," Benny said. "Want to come see, Jason?"

"Naw. Remember I already saw eight get born at my house," Jason sniffed. "C'mon, pa, can we go home? I'm hungry."

Benny ran inside and upstairs to his parents' room. Sally Grimsby, the midwife, passed him going out, carrying a basin. "Welcome home, Benny," she smiled. "Now you let your mama rest. Help take care of your sister, all right?"

"I will, Mrs. Grimsby." Benny went into the bedroom. His mother lay on the bed. She smiled and held out her arms to him.

"Hello, darling. I'm sorry I can't get up," she said. Benny hugged and kissed her fiercely. "Well, I missed you too." She laughed.

Jeremy went out with a big bundle of linens. "Be right back," he said. Benny bent over the little cradle where Sarah Grace lay, squinting up at him. She flinched and waved her fists.

"Did I look like that when I was born?" Benny asked.

"Exactly like that," Benny's mother replied. "Pick her up, darling, and hold her. Just be careful to support her head."

Sarah started and made a little squeaking sound as Benny lifted her up. She pushed her face against Benny's jacket front.

"She's hungry," Benny's mother said fondly. "I'll take her. You go down and have some lunch with your dad. Oh, Benny, we're so glad to have you home."

Benny kissed his mother on the cheek and deposited Sarah in her arms. Downstairs Sally Grimsby was leaving with the bundle of linens in a big basket.

"Thanks for taking care of those, Sally," Jeremy sighed. "And thanks for all your help."

"Anytime, Doc," Sally said. "I fixed some sandwiches earlier for you menfolk. Thought maybe Jason and his father might stay, so there's lots."

*****

"We forgot Trevor and James," Jeremy exclaimed. Benny and Jeremy hurried out and found the two men sitting patiently on the steps with Benny's bags beside them.

"Trevor! James! Good to see you both," Jeremy said as he shook hands with them. "Come in and get something to eat before you go back." Jeremy grabbed one of Benny's cases.

"Congratulations, Doctor Carlisle," Trevor said. "Mr. Richardson will be delighted to hear he has a granddaughter to spoil."

"You tell him he's welcome to come and spoil her anytime," laughed Jeremy. They brought Benny's things into the hallway and Trevor and James joined them for lunch.

"I nearly fell over the first time Mr. Richardson made me dine with him," Trevor admitted. "It wasn't even thought of while madam was still alive. But I suppose he was lonely. It still feels strange to eat with him. With you it isn't so very odd, Dr. Carlisle. You have such a way of putting a fellow at ease."

After Trevor and James had left for the return trip to Detroit, Benny and Jeremy went up to check on the womenfolk. They were both asleep, Sarah nestled in Benny's mother's arms. Jeremy took the baby and put her into the cradle. She squeaked, squirmed, and went back to sleep.

"Someone's knocking on the door," Benny said. "I'll get it."

*****

Rose Mitchell had gone back down the front steps and was twisting herself around the porch steps railing. "Hey, Benny, welcome home," she said.

"Hello, Rose," Benny said, hiding the wash of memory that swept over him. He thought of the time he had taught school for his mother. Rose's twin sister Violet had made Benny angry when she had asked about Benny's plans. She suggested that he might be afraid of what God would do to him in the future and bitter about the troubles in his past. Benny had not seen either of them since that day.

"So how's boarding school?" Rose demanded. She continued to jump and dance and spin around, as if she couldn't be still. "Gosh, wasn't the winter just awful? Jason Owens come back with you? Isn't it neat to ride in your grandfather's big fancy carriage all the way from Detroit? Is the doctor home?"

"Which question do you want me to answer first?" Benny laughed.

"Oh, well, I guess the one about the doctor. Oh. Here he is," she said as Jeremy came out on the porch. Rose pranced up and down the walk. "Hey, Doctor Carlisle. Ain't it good to have Benny home? When's that baby comin'? Wouldja like some peach preserves? Pa wants t'know do ya got any more a' that liniment?"

"Rose! Does anyone ever get to answer any of your questions?" Jeremy asked. "The baby's here. She's a girl, Sarah Grace. Why did you need to see me, Rose?"

"Oh, Violet's sick again," Rose sighed. She ran along the picket fence a few feet. "Can I see the baby? Did that big tall fellah come with ya, Benny? Is --"

"Violet's sick?" Benny asked.

"Violet's been sick with one thing or another all winter," Jeremy nodded. "Poor little thing. She's gotten awfully run-down. Now, Rose, why didn't you tell us that right off? Your ma wouldn't send you over here if she didn't think it was important for me to get the message quickly."

Rose stopped spinning. "Yeah, well, she did say hurry, an' Violet's got a fever, an she's got some kinda rash, an'--"

"Fever? Rash? Ben, hitch up the buggy, and do it as quick as you can. Rose, no, you can't help. Stay right out here by the front steps." Jeremy disappeared into the house. Benny ran to the stable and got Black Switch ready. Jeremy came along a moment later with his bag. He helped Benny finish harnessing the black stallion. They brought the buggy out front to where Rose stood, silent and wide-eyed.

"Ben, Rose didn't touch you, did she? Did she come any closer than she was when I came out?"

"No -- I don't think so --" Benny faltered. "Dad, what's wrong?"

"I ain't dirty," Rose insisted. "An' I wouldn't touch a boy if ya was ta pay me a million dollars. I been down here the whole time."

"Come on, Rose. Ben, stay back from Rose." Jeremy pushed Rose up onto the seat. "Ben, try not to go into the room with your mother and Sarah. I might not be back for a while. If you need help, call Mrs. Grimsby."

"Dad, please, can't you tell me what's the matter?"

"I'll tell you as soon as I know for sure," Jeremy said. He chucked the reigns and Black Switch trotted off. Benny stood there watching them go. Then he hurried into the house.

*****

He looked in at the doorway to his parents' bedroom. His mother and Sarah slept on. Benny went downstairs and cleaned up the kitchen. He took his things up to his room and unpacked. Still Jeremy did not return. Finally Sally Grimsby arrived about two hours after Jeremy had gone, carrying a big iron pot.

"Mrs. Grimsby!" Benny exclaimed. "Am I glad to see you!"

"How's mama and baby?" Sally asked. She did not seem to notice that Benny was upset.

"They're fine. They've been asleep pretty much since you left. My Dad --"

"I'll fix your mother a pot of soup," Sally said briskly. "Maybe you're hungry too." She bustled off to the kitchen. Benny followed.

"Mrs. Grimsby, my dad went to see Violet Mitchell. She --"

“I got a message from your dad,” Sally said. She put the soup pot down on the stove and blew up the fire. “That’s why I’m here. Violet has the Scarlet Fever. It’s real serious, and it’s real, real catching. He’s got to stay away from here so you-all don’t catch it, especially your ma and the baby. Mitchells are quarantined. Thank the Lord they ain’t been around nobody else. Doc’ll stay with them till the danger’s past. You been in the room with them?”

“No -- I -- just looked in the door.”

“Good.” Sally pulled a bottle out of her apron pocket. “Doc didn’t think you’d been infected, but he wanted to make sure. You go draw a bath and put this stuff in the water. It don’t smell good, but it should kill the germs and make you safe to be with your ma and the little one.”

“Sally, my dad’s going to be okay, isn’t he?”

“I should think so. He’s a good, strong fellow. He don’t catch too much of what he doctors folks for.”

“Then -- then what about Violet?”

“As weak and sickly as she is ... well, I don’t know if she’ll make it. I just don’t know.”

*****

Benny played with Sarah, learned to change diapers, and did all he could to make his mother more comfortable as the days passed. Sally Grimsby and the other ladies in the town came by frequently to make sure they were fed and to help with the housework. Everyone was impressed by how much Benny did to help take care of the baby and keep the house in order. Benny found that he could walk down to the stone wall that separated Jason Owens’ farm from the Mitchells’, and Jeremy would come out to where they could shout at each other.

“Some holiday you’re having, Ben,” Jeremy said sadly.

“Babies sure are a lot of work, but it’s all right,” Benny smiled. “How’s Violet?”

“Her fever’s finally broken,” Jeremy said. He sat down on a big stone in the field. “Thank the Lord no one else seems to be getting sick. Violet’s so weak, though. She just doesn’t seem to care if she gets better. We all pet her, and talk to her, but she doesn't seem to pay any attention. We're getting ready for a big washday and everyone and everything here's going to be cleaner than it ever was. Me included. I should be home tomorrow. I'm sure the danger's past."

"And Trevor and James are coming for us the day after tomorrow," Benny said ruefully. "Take care, Dad. And take care of Violet."

*****

As Benny walked home, he saw that a peddler had come into town and set up a display right near his house. Benny stopped and looked at the things he had to sell. The man had some housewares and a few clothes. Then Benny noticed two gold chains with little flower pendants. One was painted to look like a rose. One was made like a violet. Benny bought them both, then hurried back to the Mitchell farm. He put the necklaces on the rock where Jeremy had sat and went back across the fence.

"Dad!" He shouted. "Dad!"

Jeremy came out of the house. "What's the matter?" he demanded. "Something wrong at home?"

"No. Everything's fine. Dad, look on the rock."

Jeremy picked up the two necklaces. "Well, these are very nice," he grinned. "Rose will be thrilled. I believe she asks more questions about you than anything else. And I think this might even perk Violet up."

*****

Benny and Jason got back to school and were soon busy with classes and sports and chores. Then a letter came for Jason from home.

"Ben, I'm gonna have to leave school," Jason said.

"What? What happened?"

"My dad got gored by our bull Nosy. Your dad thinks maybe he'll be -- crippled. They need me to help at home. Dad can't work anymore. The other boys are too little to do all the farm work, an' we never got enough money from that, anyway. I gotta go home, an' look for some work, an'..." Jason shrugged.

“Jason, I’ll miss you. I hope your dad will be okay.” Benny tried not to think selfishly. He knew how disappointed Jason must be not to be able to finish school. “Maybe Mr. Greyson could let you take some books home and you could keep studying on your own. Talk to him and see.”

Jason brightened. “There’s an idea,” he grinned. “Thanks, Ben. Boy, I’m gonna miss you, too. I’ll even miss this place. It sorta grows on ya, doesn’t it?”

*****

Before Benny knew it Jason had gone. Jack Williams and Murray Jacobs both tried to fill the gap. Benny spent a lot of time with them anyway. Murray was still very clumsy learning to use his left hand, and Benny and Jack took turns writing his essays and assignments for him and helping him handle the things that had once been so simple with two hands. Benny learned that when Murray and his family had become Christians, the rabbi at their synagogue had held a funeral for them. The rest of their relatives considered them to be dead.

Benny went to the post office one day and found a strange envelope addressed to him. The paper was plain and rather coarse. There was no return address. Benny opened it and was shocked to find that it was from Violet Mitchell.

*Dear Benjamin,*

*I’m sure it will surprise you to hear from me,* Violet wrote. *Folks call me the little invalid. Your dear father worries about my health, but I feel fine. Perhaps your mother has told you I no longer go to school.*

Benny hadn’t known that. He wondered why, since he had thought Violet had said she wanted to be a teacher. He had been standing in the post office reading the letter, but he roused himself and went outside to sit on a bench along the walkway. Then he read the next sentence.

*It seemed pointless, you know, since I cannot hear the lessons.* Benny read the words three times. *It was a long time before anyone really understood that I've become deaf. I kept telling them I couldn't hear but they thought I just wasn't paying attention, or was still sick or tired. The truth is, I can hear nothing at all. What a terrible, silent world I live in now. No one can speak to me. My family never learned to read or write, except Rose a little, and we cannot seem to understand each other. They have just come to let me alone.*

*Your parents have been so kind and other folks have tried to help, but everyone has his own life and responsibilities and it is very hard to sit with me and write notes back and forth for every little thing, I know. Rose gets so frustrated because she must bear the brunt of communicating with me. She has been so good to me, though, and laughs and says I'll make her literate yet.*

*Oh, dear, look how long my letter has become, and I haven't even come to the point yet. I never had a chance to thank you for the lovely necklace you sent when I was sick. Rose thanks you too. We both treasure them and always wear them. Your father says they are handy because he never confuses us anymore. As if he could when I am such a thin, pale ghost and Rose is bursting with health. She hugs me tightly and rubs her plump little cheek against mine and says 'Here, Vi, I am rubbing some of my konstytooshun (so she spells it) into you so you can get strong.'*

*May I take the liberty of writing to you now and then, Benjamin, and may I hope that you will answer if you are not too busy with your studies and friends at school? It was Jason Owens who urged me to write to you. He comes over sometimes and he flies into a rage at my family when they treat me as if I were not here. What a bluff, good fellow he is. He cheers me each time he comes.*

*Do you remember when I asked you if you were bitter because of all God had brought into your life, and if you were afraid to plan for the future? How sorry I was to have made you angry. How little I understood just how thoroughly God can turn our lives upside down. I am sure you have borne your troubles better than I have borne mine, but I have never had any before, and I never imagined life could be so very hard, or the future so very frightening.*

*Please pray for me, Benjamin, that I might perhaps learn to bear this burden more cheerfully. I cannot hear my sister's voice. The bird songs are only silence. The wind moves the leaves without making a sound. I could even wish to hear the rain leaking through our porch roof in a storm. This silence is so hateful to me. It has blighted my life.*

Benny sat on the bench in shock for a long time. He wondered why his parents had not told him about Violet's deafness. Maybe they had thought he didn't care. He thought about the letters he had written lately, full of news about his own doings. He hardly even asked any questions about home. Was his mother getting enough rest with the baby to take care of on top of everything else she had to do? Was Jeremy able to get along without his favorite nurse, as he had often called Benny's mother? How were they managing now that he wasn't helping with the chores and Black Switch?

How was Jason bearing up under the burdens of caring for the farm and working at all his odd jobs? How was Carl Owens recovering from his terrible injury? How could everyone but himself, Benny, take the time to minister to Violet and he not even ask about her? Suddenly Benny laughed at himself. He felt like Rose, asking a million questions and not stopping to get the answers to any of them.

"Hallo, Carlisle. What's so funny?" Murray Jacobs flopped down on the bench beside Benny. "A moment ago you looked so glum, and now you're laughing like an idiot. Explain yourself at once."

"Oh, Murray," Ben sighed. "I got this letter from a girl I know back home ..."

"A girl? A girl?" Murray crowed. "Carlisle, I never would have dreamed. What? Don't tell me she's thrown you off? Absence makes the heart go wander. Then what's to laugh about, says I? You should weep, weep your heart out, star-crossed lover."

"Murray, shut up and listen," Benny ordered. He told Murray about Violet and her deafness. Murray sobered at once.

"I can understand a little what the girl must be going through," Murray nodded. "This arm of mine still gets me down at times. Suppose we all write to her? That'd cheer her up, don't you think? I know mail cheers me up."

"That'd be great, Murray," Benny exclaimed. "I'm sure Jack would be glad to do it."

"Sure, Jackie boy'll go along. He's a soft-hearted old slob. Is she pretty? Never mind. Doesn't matter. Violet, sweet Violet. Yessir, Ben my lad, don't you fret. Send word to Miss Violet that the Brigham School Glee Club is at her service and she will soon be flooded with correspondence."

Benny laughed and went home to write his letter at once. Jack and Murray were very vague about what they had actually written to Violet, but insisted that they had adopted a most cheerful tone and Violet had better be cheered up or else. Benny hoped Violet wouldn't mind hearing from strangers. And he hoped Murray wouldn't be too silly.

*****

Benny found that his mother and Jeremy were delighted to receive his new breed of letters. His mother confessed that she had worried he was growing self-centered, but had been afraid to say anything. Benny did mention Violet, but did not share all her heartache with his mother. Either she already knew, or Violet would not want her to know, that she was so depressed.

In a few weeks another letter came from Violet. This time it came on fine, fragrant, pale cream stationery decorated with beautifully painted violets. It bore a gold seal and had Violet's return address printed on it. Benny tore the letter open carefully, hardly daring to damage the envelope.

*I shall forgive you for breaching a lady's confidence, Dear Benjamin, for I have never felt so happy and so fussed over. I have just finished answering my mail. I have received a total of two hundred and thirty-six letters, packages and telegrams from Brigham School, and I blame you for a permanent case of writer's cramp. How did you get every single boy at the school to write to me?*

*They are all such dears. I have got as little as a scribbled line and as much as ten pages from one boy called Murray Jacobs. I have got poetry, sweet little storybooks, real watercolor paintings, lace hankies, scarves -- more than I could ever wear -- rings, bracelets, perfume, postage stamps and this dear beautiful writing paper -- Oh, Benjamin, did any girl ever have so many boys asking for her hand in marriage and promising undying devotion? It is all so silly and so sweet.*

*Thank you! Thank you so much. I knew I did the right thing to write to you. I knew you would find a way to get me out of my dumps. I have told the boys I must share all this wealth with Rose, and some of the other girls here in town, for I would need a castle to hold all these gifts fit for a princess. I hope they do not mind. There is so much! But the best of all is that I feel in touch with people again. For that, to only say thank you is so poor. God was good to let us be friends.*

*In Christ, Violet Mitchell*

“Murray!” Benny looked up and saw the older boy peeking in the door of his room. Murray waved a scented letter at him. He sniffed it deeply and put a hand on his heart.

“Ah, Sweet Violet!” Murray sighed. “Ben, I want to thank you for introducing me to the girl of my dreams.”

“You got everybody to write to her? Everybody on the whole campus? Everybody?”

“Of course, but she loves only me,” Murray grinned. “Ben, remember what I said to you? I said let’s all write to her. And I meant all. She was pleased, wasn’t she?”

“Yes, she was pleased. She thinks I’m responsible for it all. I need to tell her it was you.”

“Look here, Ben, don’t do any such thing. Violet knows you. She doesn’t know me, and she probably never will know me. Let her shower you with gratitude. You’ve learned a valuable lesson out of all this -- the power of unselfishness. Enjoy its fruits. But we have started something that needs to be kept up. That’s an intelligent girl who’s locked in a wall of silence. Letters and reading could be the only things that keep her in this world. We must send her books and write her often.

“My uncle is a teacher of the deaf. There is a school for their instruction right here in Detroit. I wrote to him about Violet and he urged us not to abandon her. He said he was temporarily made deaf by an accident when he was a child. His hearing is almost back to normal now, but he never forgot that awful silence.”

“A deaf school?” Benny murmured. “How do they teach kids who are deaf?” Benny tried to imagine a class where the teacher had to write everything on the board, a room full of silence except for squeaking chalk and scribbling pens.

“There’s something called sign language -- it’s spelling and making words with your fingers,” Murray explained. “They also teach them to read lips, and to talk if they can. It’s still very hard for a deaf person to get on in a hearing world, but this school helps a lot of them.”

*****

Murray's uncle came to visit at the school and brought Benny a book about sign language. Benny painstakingly copied the drawings of the alphabet in letters to Violet and his mother and Jason. Violet happily reported that she was learning to finger spell, and that Rose had an absolute genius for it. Benny imagined anything involving motion would appeal to Rose. Benny's mother reported that Violet had begun to come out to church again, and that they were all trying to learn finger-spelling and to help Violet learn to read lips. Benny was afraid he'd just given everyone more work. Murray's uncle had suggested that Violet should enroll in the deaf school. Benny knew how poor Violet's family was. But he knew that would be the best thing for everyone.

*"You should be a writer, Benjamin,"* one of Violet's letters had urged him. Benny had fought with that idea for months. He had to choose a major area of study before he began his second year at Brigham, and the school year was almost over. He and Murray had swapped writing samples and Murray had praised and criticized his work. Mr. Talbot, the English Master, had also told him he had great talent. But Benny could not imagine what use a writer would be out in the western wilderness. He had always thought God would lead him to become something useful to the frontier to which he still wanted so badly to go.

"Someone's got to write all those wonderful adventures and terrible hardships and God-given victories down for the rest of us to read," Murray exclaimed. "You'd be a historian for generations to come. Of course writing's not like farming and logging and trail-blazing, lad. But it's necessary all the same. It both feeds the soul and preserves it for others to share. How could you have ministered to Violet if you hadn't had a turn for writing? God can use a writer, and so can the wild west, Ben."

*****

End-of-year ceremonies came all too quickly. Benny's grandfather brought his family and Jason out to

Detroit for the occasion, and Benny was very surprised to receive a prize for journalism, a very prestigious award seldom given to first-year students. It carried with it a significant cash award and a summer apprenticeship at an important Detroit newspaper.

"But I was going home for the summer," Benny said dazedly to his mother. "You need help with the baby, dad has no one to help with his calls, the chores are --"

"Darling, the school informed us that this apprenticeship was going to be offered to you," Benny's mother said. "We hated to keep it a secret from you, because we were afraid you had your heart set on coming home. But if all you're thinking of is the work we have to do, then don't worry. Grandfather Richardson has invited Sarah and I to stay here in Detroit with him for a bit. He insists that you can't properly spoil a granddaughter by mail. And we are going to get someone to look after the house and assist your dad while Sarah and I are here."

"Well ... if you're going to be here, that's wonderful ..."

"What's bothering you, Ben?" Jeremy asked.

"The -- the award I won. I was thinking ... It's enough so that we could go west right away, this year, isn't it?"

"Well, yes, I suppose it is," Jeremy agreed. "But who would take over my practice? Sarah is so small to make such a hard trip. Your mother's still getting her strength back. Grandfather Richardson -- We don't know if he'd ever see Sarah again if we went away now. You have this opportunity to work at the newspaper. If you want to be a writer, you shouldn't pass up the chance to learn the job. This is June already. It'd be a month before we could actually leave. The plains will be drying out and the animals might not have enough grass if we leave so late. No, Ben, I think the Lord is keeping us here another year, at least."

"Another year?" Benny felt like crying. "Why does it seem like the Lord doesn't want us to go, Dad?"

"Maybe we're not ready yet," Jeremy said. "I don't think we're sinning or holding back when we should be moving out. I believe the Lord has ordered all these things. If you're sure the Lord wants you to write about the west when you get there, then be as prepared as you can be. Learn all you can at the newspaper. Get another year of schooling. When we're ready, and God's ready, then it will be time to go."

"All right, then," Benny said, taking a deep breath. "I will get a salary with my job at the newspaper. I can save most all of it, and we can use that for our trip. So I was wondering if I could use my prize money to enroll Violet in the deaf school. I -- I already looked into the costs, and it would completely pay for her first year; books, tuition, room and board -- it's just enough."

"Why, Ben, I call that handsome," Jeremy said. "What a great thing that would be for Violet. Let's talk it over later with your mother and see what she says."

*****

Next came the very hard task of saying good-bye to Jack and Murray, who had finished their final year at Brigham. Jason had not seen them in three months, so he found himself saying hello and good-bye all at once. Jack was off to college in Ohio to study Chemistry. Murray was planning to attend City College in Detroit part time, and Benny learned that Murray already worked at the same newspaper where Benny would have his apprenticeship. Benny was delighted that he would not be losing all his friends at once. Murray promised to "show him the ropes" at the newspaper. Afterward Benny and his family and Jason went to Mr. Richardson's grand house for dinner.

"Say, Ben, I sure was wishin' we could be together this summer," Jason sighed as they sat on the front porch after dinner.

"I was, too, Jason," Benny said. "How is your father doing?"

"He's gettin' better real slowly. Walkin' with a cane, but still in a lot of pain. I wish he'd take it easy, but you know my dad. We're doin' a little better than we were. There ain't -- I mean isn't -- much in the way of work around Osage."

“Violet told me you’ve been a good friend to her,” Benny smiled.

“Ah, I run over there once in a while an’ squawk at her folks. ‘She’s deaf, but that doesn’t mean she’s stupid,’ I tell ‘em. They tiptoe around her like they’re afraid of her or they yell in her face as if she can hear ‘em if they just blow the doors off the house screamin’. It ain’t -- I mean isn’t -- good for her to be there.

“Rose has turned into a real peach, an’ helps her a bunch, but those dumb people don’t appreciate it. They get jealous of Rose ‘cause she can do the hand talk, which they’re too lazy to learn, or they wear her down messagin’ all kinds of stupid stuff to Violet that she already knows or doesn’t need to know. I wish I had a nickel for every time that mother of hers has said ‘Rose, tell Violet not to step on the chicks when she goes out in the yard, since she can’t hear them peepin’.’ As if Violet would! Both a’ them girls are too good an’ too smart for that family. Don’t you ever wish God would just go *Whoosh* an’ fix stuff?”

Benny suddenly realized what it would mean to Rose if Violet came away to school. Rose had begun to blossom. Violet had said in her letters that Rose could read and write very well now. She no longer scorned education as she had the first time Benny had met her. She had once hinted that since most of the care of Violet during her illness had fallen to Rose that she would like to be a nurse. Suddenly Benny gasped.

“Jason! The *Whoosh!* I think it’s going to happen!” Benny cried.

“What did that fellah say to the Apostle Paul? ‘Much learning doth make thee mad’? What are you talkin’ about, Ben?”

“I have to talk to my mother and dad,” Benny said. “Go tell my grandfather we’ll be right there.” They all had planned to go for a carriage ride after dinner, and Benny’s grandfather had appeared out at the street with Trevor and James and the coach. Benny tore off to find his parents, who were just coming downstairs with Sarah.

“Mother! Dad! Can I talk to you for a minute?” Benny pulled them aside before they could go out the front door. "This is really important. Mother, I told Dad I wanted to give my prize money to Violet so she could come to the deaf school. Did he tell you?"

"Well, yes, darling, but we haven't really had time to discuss it," Benny's mother said uncertainly.

"We have to do it, Mother. We have to. Violet's got to get out of that house and get back to school. Mother, she wants to be a teacher. She can't just sit at home and do nothing. Now, we also have to do something about Rose. She told Jason and Violet she'd like to be a nurse. What if she stayed with dad and helped him this summer? Dad could teach her all kinds of things, and she could earn money to go to nursing school. What do you think? Can we do it?"

"Oh, dear," Benny's mother said. "That's a lovely plan, darling, but we couldn't pay Rose enough to help her save for nursing school. And your prize money ... Shouldn't you put it into savings for college?"

"Violet needs it right now, Mother," Benny insisted. "And I can give part of what I earn at the newspaper to Rose so it wouldn't cost you as much. It would be perfect."

"Even if it meant less money saved for the trip west?" Jeremy said grimly. "We were just talking about how long we've been waiting."

"Well, I have been thinking about that, also." Grandfather Richardson came quietly up behind them. "I like your plan, Benjamin, but I suggest you change a few details. Your prize money and your job money go into a savings bank, and I pay for schooling and on-the-job-training for the Misses Mitchell. Now, now, no protests. I'm looking at throwing money out the window in bushel baskets because I can't think what to do with it all. Here's what we'll do. I was planning to hire a nanny for Abigail while she and Sarah are here. We shall invite Miss Violet to render us that service, and let her look at it as earning her own way to school.

"I shall furthermore engage Miss Rose to assist the good Doctor Carlisle and keep house for him, for which she shall be paid money for her nursing school whenever she goes. This way no one is just giving away money to anyone. We are investing in the future, as I invested in Benjamin and Jason. And I hope that Jason understands that at any future time when circumstances permit his return to school he may call upon me to renew my investment. Perhaps he may be too proud or embarrassed to ask me, Benjamin, but you will not let me be in ignorance if the time comes, eh? Now, come. We have a carriage waiting."

*****

So Jeremy and Jason returned to Osage. Benny later got a letter from Jeremy describing how he proposed the arrangement for Rose and Violet to the Mitchells.

"I had expected them to protest a little. Instead they seemed eager for the girls to be off at once. Their things were packed and Trevor and James and I transported them to the Carlisle house the same day. Grandfather Richardson's carriage was to depart for Detroit the next day.

"I thought it good to leave the girls the run of the house and let them say their good-byes gradually. Yet I could not help hovering about because I felt something was wrong. Rose dragged Violet through the surgery and my study. 'Look at the instruments. Look at the medical books, Vi,' she signed to her sister. It was good that she chattered, too, for I am not that adept at signs and my eavesdropping would have been in vain. 'Oh, isn't this heaven? I'll take such good care of the doctor, and think of all I can learn! Aren't you just happy enough to burst?'

"And, indeed, Violet seemed about to burst. But it was into tears that she burst, and shocked Rose very much by doing so. She sank down on the floor and wept like she would die. Rose was beside herself. Violet could not even attend to Rose's frantic signing to know what was wrong. Violet seemed to have lost the power to cry out loud, or perhaps she tried to keep quiet because she feared to let the rest of us know she was so troubled. She really frightened me when she did not seem to be recovering herself but went on making those awful, noiseless sobs. Finally I entered the room and took her up in my arms.

"'Rose,' I said, 'Ask Violet if she is ill. Violet,' I said desperately, turning her poor pale face up to look into mine and speaking as clearly as I could, 'Are you sick? Can I help you?'

"'No, no, dear, good Dr. Carlisle, I am not sick,' Violet insisted. 'I'm so sorry to be ungrateful. I am afraid. I am afraid of those gentlemen I must ride all the way to Detroit with alone. How will I speak to them? And when I come to Mr. Richardson's house, it will be the same thing. My family was not always kind to me, but I was used to them, and Rose helped me so much. Now I shall be alone. Look at how happy Rose is. She has her heart's desire. Do I not also? Then why am I so miserable?'

"I gave her some advice which seemed to do her good, Jeremy finished. "She and Rose went happily along after that, making plans for my housekeeping and her care of Sarah. I am sure she will do very well. They are sweet girls."

Benny had to rely on a letter from Rose to reveal what advice Jeremy had actually given her. Violet never mentioned it, but Rose's letter bubbled over with admiration for Jeremy.

"Dear Dr. Carlisle rocked Violet like a little child," Rose reported. "'Poor Violet,' he said. I began to sign for her, and Violet's eyes went back and forth between us like a tennis ball in a match. 'I think I understand. Remember my friend the Cougar Evangelist?' She shuddered because she had heard the story and we had both seen his face when he had to stay at our house, of course. 'He took away my pretty face that I was so proud of and left me as I am now. I had asked Christ to save me, and I knew he had. But it wasn't enough. Those scars were a wall between me and my plans to be a preacher and a doctor.

"'But God gave me a new face. Then I wasn't so afraid to go out among people and preach the Word and tend their ills. God has given you new ears, Violet. Your quick eyes and sharp little brain are learning to read lips, and the finger spelling helps you too. But you know these new ears aren't the same as the old ones. I know my new face isn't the same as the old one. I dread meeting new people because I'm not sure my new face will work with them. But there are so many kind and good and wonderful people in this world who will be patient with your new ears. You will find that it will not be so terrifying after all. Our lives change over and over, Violet. We must accept those changes, and let God keep teaching us and molding us until we are so like His Son that others can see no one else.'"

*****

The summer passed so quickly. Benny was assigned to work with Murray, and he realized that running a newspaper had very little to do with writing and a great deal to do with fixing presses and cutting sheets and tying bundles. Benny complained to Murray that he didn't think he was learning much about journalism. Murray laughed and asked him how he was going to write out west if he didn't start his own print shop and newspaper, and how would he do that if he didn't know everything about presses and cutters and type and all the rest? Benny admitted he was right.

Sarah was delighted with her new nanny. Violet became acquainted with Murray's uncle and some of the other people at the deaf school. Everyone became at least a little more proficient at sign language and Murray's uncle worked with Violet on lip-reading. Benny's mother returned home with Sarah after a month and a half, unable to stay away from Jeremy any longer. Benny's grandfather became very attached to Violet, and she claimed that he had such perfect speech it was easier to read his lips than anyone's. Several people acquainted with Murray's uncle asked Violet to care for their deaf children from time to time.

*****

Before Benny knew it, it was time to return to Brigham. Violet went off to board at the deaf school, and Benny's grandfather declared himself desolate. So he wrote to Benny's mother and told her about a nursing school in Detroit and begged her to send Rose to stay with him and go there to study. Benny's mother readily agreed, and explained that a young man had come to stay with them. He was a medical student whose father was an old friend of Doc Daniel's. Benny did not learn until much later the odd circumstances under which young Louis DeBarr had come to be under Jeremy's wing. His mother finally wrote Benny and explained.

> *I had sewing circle, and your dad had a town board meeting, so we were not at home when Louis arrived. We returned and found an envelope stuck in the door and a note with it. Louis introduced himself in the note and apologized for being delayed. Doctor Connors had sent a letter telling us to expect him, but we had thought he would arrive a day or two earlier. He said he regretted not finding us in, but hoped he might come by in the morning to make our acquaintance and begin his duties.*
>
> *Your dad was quite annoyed. 'Two days late,' he fumed. 'Not getting off to a good start. And he doesn't even say where he's staying. I'd go and get him and bring him here if I knew. Well, we'll have to make our acquaintance on the run, because tomorrow is a very full day.'*
>
> *I picked up the envelope which your dad had dropped when he began to read the note. I opened it and was shocked to find two thousand dollars cash in it. There was also a letter from Louis's father, Mr. Raymond DeBarr. Mr. DeBarr seems a most blunt and blustery sort of man.*
>
> *'Louis shall get no more of my money thrown his way,' said the elder DeBarr. 'If he is a help to you, and does his work well, I shall be surprised but pleased. If not, cut him loose. The money is yours in any case. By no means should you return it to Louis if he changes his mind again and wants another occupation. Tell him he may go anywhere or do anything he chooses so long as it does not involve putting his hand in my pocket ever again. I am through*

*with the lazy, indecisive rascal and you are free to tell him so. Sincerely, Raymond DeBarr.'*

*'What has Daniel got me into?' your dad said. 'He said this fellow had set his course and seemed sincere, and I should give him plenty to do and a fair chance. Are these two men talking about the same fellow?'*

*'We must give him a chance, dear,' I said to your dad. 'Two thousand dollars is such a lot of money. At least we may meet him and see what he is like.'*

*"Your dad grumbled and said all right. The next morning I came out to gather the eggs and there was this tall, thin young man with red hair. His clothes seemed very wrinkled. He was trying to smooth them as I came across him and he seemed very flustered.*

*"'How do you do, ma'am. I'm Louis DeBarr,' he said. I made him welcome and took him into the house to the kitchen where your dad was finishing breakfast. The dear doctor barely let me make introductions.*

*'Well, it's good you're here early,' your dad said. 'Stayed at the hotel, did you? They serve a nice breakfast there. Can my wife get you anything?'*

*"Louis looked at the plate of eggs and hotcakes your dad was devouring and licked his lips. I brought him a cup of coffee and he thanked me and refused anything else. I wondered as I filled his cup why his collar was so damp. He jumped up as soon as your dad did.*

*'All right -- Louis, is it? -- We're off. Good-bye, my love,' your dad said, and they were out the door. I barely managed to push a basket of bread and ham and two apples into your dad's hands as he ran out. Louis was rather clumsy about helping to hitch up the buggy, and I could see your dad trying to be patient as I went back*

*to my egg-gathering -- you know how the hens always invade the stables to hide their nests.*

*"Finally they were off, except that as they left you dad complained that he would have to speak to John, the boy who cares for Switch and the buggy now, and remind him to be more careful sweeping out the seats and floor. Indeed, I noticed a good deal of straw in the buggy, but I would have sworn it was not there before Louis got in.*

*"They came home after dark, and your dad praised Louis for his attentiveness and his knowledge. I hurried to get supper on the table, knowing that the evening office visits would start in only half an hour and would go on until ten at night. Your dad ran upstairs to put on a fresh shirt.*

*'Say, Louis, we forgot to fetch your horse and your bags from the hotel,' he called down the stairs. 'I doubt if anything I have will fit you. Perhaps you can take Switch and ride over there.'*

*'I -- I left nothing at the hotel, sir,' Louis quavered. I suddenly noticed he was trembling and very white. 'Louis, sit down before you fall,' I urged. 'What is wrong?'*

*"Your dad came quickly back down the stairs as Louis dropped into a hall chair. 'What do you mean? Where are your bags -- your clothes? And your horse -- didn't you ride into town?'*

*'Sir,' he answered, the words dragged out of him with seemingly great unwillingness, ... 'Three days ago I was attacked and robbed as I passed through a lonely wood. Three men stole my horse and everything I carried -- my bags, my purse -- That envelope from my father they somehow missed. I opened the envelope, thinking to use some of the money to get on my way, but then I found the letter my father wrote you.*

*'I realized how great a fool I had been and how right my father was to cast me off. But I made a resolve then to get here and to prove myself by going through with my training and working as hard and faithfully as I could. I also told myself I would never touch another cent of my father's money, and especially not that which was intended for you. I walked all the rest of the way. I slept in the woods, drank from streams and ate berries and nuts if I could find them.*

*"'Last night when I arrived and found no one here I hid out in your stable and slept on your horse's straw. He very kindly pretended not to mind. I washed at the pump before anyone arose and was waiting for your wife when she came out. I did not want to knock too early.'*

*'You've walked for three days, slept on the ground, and lived on berries?' your dad exclaimed. 'Why didn't you tell us as soon as you got here this morning? We were so busy we didn't even stop for lunch.' You must be exhausted and starving.'*

*'I couldn't, sir,' Louis said. 'I couldn't fail again. I had to keep going, and help you. I've been weak and selfish too long. But I am ... I am so tired. '*

*Oh, my, what a flurry of activity followed. Your dad drew a hot bath and made Louis soak in it. His clothes were full of rips and straw and burrs and we ended up throwing them away. I was so glad I had brought home some of the shirts and trousers we had finished in sewing circle. It did not take long to fit something to Louis. Your dad told him to eat dinner and go straight to bed. The poor boy did, and slept the clock round. He was mortified when he arose and realized what had happened.*

*Your dad just laughed at him and said he guessed he would keep him on all the same. He has been such a help to your dad, and has proved himself over and over. Just recently your dad wrote to his father. Mr. DeBarr did not believe any of the glowing praise your dad heaped on Louis when he thanked him for sending the boy to him. He came straightaway and stayed in the hotel three days. He accompanied them on rounds, watched the evening surgeries, saw everything Louis did. He never said a word until he announced he was ready to leave.*

*'Louis, I have only one question for you,' Mr. Debarr said as he sat at dinner with us that last evening. 'I must have said the same words that you found in Dr. Carlisle's letter or worse to you a hundred times. Why did they work this time?'*

*'I can answer that, Mr. DeBarr,' your dad replied. 'Louis probably doesn't know himself yet. But it's only this: Every man has a bottom -- a place where he has nothing left but himself and his God. Louis stood on that road with nothing but that envelope and what was in it. He knew that he could not go home because you said so in your letter. He knew that if he took any of the money he was a thief because you said it was mine. Some men turn away from God when they get to that place. Louis turned to God, and you see it's all come out well.'*

## Chapter Eighteen -- A Simple Christmas

Brigham School held each year a legendary Christmas party, the one occasion of the year when students were permitted to invite female visitors. Last year Benny had gone alone, but this year he invited both Violet and Rose. He had seen little of either girl during the fall. Studies kept them all busy. Benny waited for his grandfather's carriage impatiently with a group of other boys. When it finally arrived Benny hurried forward to help the sisters out.

He stopped dead when the girls emerged. They both wore long white knitted capes with angora fringe. His grandfather had given them both new gowns as Christmas gifts, similar yet subtly different. Rose's was shades of dark pink and blue, changing colors as she turned in the light. Violet's was dark purple and silver. Both had their hair up for the first time that Benny had seen, decorated with tiny white silk flowers, and they looked so elegant and grown up Benny could not speak. Violet especially had developed a grace and beauty he had never expected.

"Whoa, Carlisle!" exclaimed a boy. "Two dates? And stunners at that. You'd better share!"

All the boys made comments, some rude, some already vying for a place on the twins' dance cards. Violet and Rose were simply mobbed. Then Benny saw the look of distress on Violet's face. She could not tell what these boys pushing themselves in her face were saying. Benny quickly slipped between the two girls and gave each an arm.

"Away with you now, fellows," he said sharply. "These are ladies, and deserve to be treated as such. If you want a dance, you can approach quietly, one at a time, after we are safely inside. Out of the way."

Benny steered them past the disappointed rabble. Inside he took the girls to a quiet alcove.

"Rose, help me talk to Violet. I'm still not sure about my signing," Benny said. "Violet, I'm really sorry. I should have realized how hard it would be for you to be comfortable here with all these people who don't even know you're deaf. If you want me to take you home—"

"No, no, of course not," Violet said firmly. "At school they tell us we have to get out in the hearing world and learn to cope, so we don't just give up and hide. I just -- I just didn't know we'd create such a sensation." She and Rose both blushed. "You can help by capturing me for the whole evening and not leaving me at the mercy of strangers, Benjamin." She waggled her dance card at him invitingly.

Benny blushed too. "Alumni can come to the party, so Murray will be here," he replied. "He made me promise to save him a dance with you. And I don't think it would be fair. There are lots of fine fellows here, and you'll like them."

Benny tried to read Violet's expression. Was she just teasing, or shy, or did she really want to spend the whole evening with him? She looked so at ease now, so sure of herself, and so ready to have a good time he couldn't imagine she wanted to tie herself to him alone.

"So, here's where you've hidden," exclaimed Mr. Talbot, the English teacher. He bowed to Rose and Violet. Benny hastily made introductions. "Shame on you, Mr. Carlisle, hiding these lovely young ladies away. Mr. Carlisle has written about you both in essays for my class. Miss Violet, I believe you may take the credit for having made Mr. Carlisle a writer. I must have the honor of the first dance." He took Violet's hand and led her away. Benny and Rose both stared in shock.

"Well, Rose, will you dance with me?" Benny asked awkwardly. She smiled and took his hand. No sooner had they stepped out of the little room than a dozen boys crowded around them. Benny saw a similar crowd around Violet and poor Mr. Talbot. Both girls' dance cards filled up so rapidly Benny felt lucky to get one dance with each of them. Benny did notice that there were far fewer girls than boys at the dance. Some of the faculty members' wives danced with boys who seemed too determined to be wallflowers, but Benny found himself without a partner and forced to endure Murray's gushings or other boys' teasings a good part of the evening.

*****

Benny was surprised to find Rose a good deal more shy than Violet now. It occurred to him that she felt awkward in the company of these boys, many of whom came from wealthy or well-educated families. Rose's nursing school hadn't given her as much of the social training and polishing Violet got at the deaf school. Living with Grandfather Richardson had made her more at ease, but Benny realized that Rose's old gregarious nature was failing her now.

"I guess I asked the wrong person if she wanted to go home, Rose," Benny said when he saw Rose sitting waiting for her latest dance partner to bring her a plate from the loaded refreshment tables. "You don't look very happy. What's wrong?"

"Oh, Benny, I feel like a fish out of water," Rose almost cried. She pulled him down into a chair beside her. "I don't know what to say to these boys. They're all so smart, and so polite, and so used to all this. I really can't dance very well. They taught Violet at school, you know, and she and Mr. Richardson both tried to teach me, but I'm stepping on somebody's feet every minute. I wish I was back on the farm where I belong."

"You don't belong on the farm," Benny retorted. "You look just as beautiful as Violet, and all the fellows love you both."

"They don't even know whether it's me or Violet they're dancing with," Rose complained. "That is, till I trip over my skirt or spill punch in a fellow's lap. Then they know. I only came because Vi enjoyed dressing me up, and I thought she'd need my help, which she certainly does not. This really isn't any fun."

Rose's partner came back just then. Benny whisked away the plate he carried and sent him off to find someone else to wait on. Benny couldn't help noticing that he seemed relieved to do so. Poor Rose. He glanced over at Violet, swirling around with the look of a queen enjoying her court, and belonging in it, on her pretty face. He looked back at Rose and saw her watching her sister. There was no jealousy on Rose's face, only admiration, and a trace of tired impatience.

"Oh, I'm sorry, Benny," Rose exclaimed when Benny sat back down beside her. "I didn't mean to be ungrateful, and I certainly didn't mean you had to come and nurse me. It was so nice of you to invite us. The boys are all so sweet."

"It's all right, Rose. This party's a required event, and to be honest, it's not really my idea of a good time either. What would you be doing right now if you could?"

"You know that old oak tree in back of our house, just over the hill?" Rose sighed. "I used to get up into the crook of those big branches and look all around the county. At night I'd look up at the stars or around at the smoke coming out of everyone's chimneys. Winter or summer, that was my favorite spot to just sit and watch the world. I'd be there if I could."

"You have to come home to Osage for Christmas," Benny insisted. "I know you still have your exams to take, but we could go home a couple of days later than we planned and wait for you. My Grandfather's never celebrated Christmas with my family. He'd come if we all asked him. We can try out your oak tree, and see Jason, and visit Doc Daniel. Come on, Rose. Say you'll come. You want to see Sarah, don't you? And Dad misses you too. Please, Rose."

Rose looked shyly up at Benny. "You're trying too hard to be nice, Benny," she smiled. "Why put your whole vacation out of whack for me? Vi's been telling me how lovely Christmas will be with just the two of us and your Grandfather."

"I'll bet you'd rather be home," Benny said shrewdly. Rose stared at him.

"Do you -- Do you think our parents will -- Will they want to see us?"

Benny started. "Of course they'll want you," he said. "What makes you think they wouldn't want to see you?"

"They seemed glad to get rid of us," Rose shrugged. "Mama's got her prize pullets and Daddy's gunsmithing business has really caught on with the folks around Osage. They're so busy. Jason tells me so in his letters."

"Jason writes to you?" Jason didn't even write to Benny. Rose blushed as if she'd given away a secret.

"Not often," she admitted. "Just to be neighborly, to let us know how Mama and Daddy are doing. He -- he says they asked him to."

"Well, then, that means they miss you."

"That could just mean Jason's a big, fat liar who's trying to make me feel better," Rose laughed. "You're serious, aren't you? You'd take us home? Oh, how I'd like to, Benny. Let me talk it over with Vi. I wouldn't want to disappoint your Grandfather."

"I told you, he's coming with us too." Benny wished he were as confident of that as he sounded. He and Jason had spent last Christmas with his Grandfather when the blizzard had kept them in Detroit. His grandfather decorated the whole house with lavish, expensive gold and red and silver ribbons and balls, rented a horse and sleigh, took them to a skating rink -- every day was a costly celebration in itself. He wasn't sure if Grandfather Richardson would be content with the Carlisle family's simple celebration. And Benny felt sure Jeremy would not want his Grandfather to go wild spending money on them and making their Christmas over in his image. But he'd deal with those problems later.

"Come with me, Rose," Benny urged, pulling her up. "There's a place I want to show you. It's not your old oak tree, but I think you'll like it."

*****

He got their wraps and hurried Rose over to the library. Students who brought visitors to the party often took them on a tour of the campus, so the main buildings were open. Benny whisked Rose back into the stacks and up a spiral staircase until they found themselves in a small, circular room with windows all around.

"We call this the crow's nest," Benny explained. "You can see most of Detroit from here. There's my dorm, there's Violet's school, there's Grandfather's house, there's --"

Rose planted a kiss on Benny's cheek. He stopped and stared at her. They both looked away suddenly.

"We should get back to the party," Benny said quickly. "I didn't think -- I'm sorry, Rose. I shouldn't have taken you out alone."

"I'm glad you did," Rose replied. "Thank you for making this a lovely evening, Benny. Merry Christmas."

*****

When they returned to the hall where the party was being held, Violet came up to them.

"Where have you been?" her eyes flashed with anger. "I saw you talking and talking, and then you ran off. A fine host you are, Benjamin Richardson. You were next on my dance card, and I sat and waited for you. I thought you said you wouldn't enjoy yourself, Rose. You seemed happy enough monopolizing Benjamin."

"But Violet -- I --" Rose flushed, scowled, and turned away. Violet held out her hand.

"Well? Aren't we going to dance?" Violet asked. Benny glanced at Rose's retreating figure. "Or would you rather stay with my sister?"

Benny took her hand and led her out onto the floor. Violet chatted about how nice everyone had been to her, how little problem her deafness had given her, and how happy she was that Benny had invited her.

"Your Grandfather has planned so many nice things for Rose and I to do," Violet sighed. "This will be such a wonderful Christmas."

"Violet, I asked Rose if she'd like to come home to Osage for Christmas," Benny said uneasily. "You'd be welcome too. And I'll ask Grandfather if he'll --"

"Osage?" Violet echoed. "But why would we want to go there? I mean, it'd be nice to see your family and say hello to Jason, but we'd miss all the fun here. There are so many things to do in Detroit, especially this time of year. Why, we've got tickets to see the Nutcracker Ballet on Christmas Eve. Benjamin, you're not serious, are you?"

"Rose seemed to want to go home very much," Benny said uncertainly.

"Rose is not going to ruin everything for me!" Violet snapped. "She knows I can't do without her. She's just being selfish. And so are you, Benjamin. Do you know what Christmas was like at our house, even before I got sick? For the first time in my life, I'm looking forward to it. How could you even think I'd want to go back to Osage?"

"I think you'd better ask yourself who's really being selfish, Violet," Benny said coldly as the dance ended. He released Violet's hand and walked away.

*****

Benny was free to leave the campus as soon as the Christmas party was over. He brought his bags out to his grandfather's carriage and they rode home together. The atmosphere in the carriage was thick with tension. Rose knew very well what Violet had said about going home. She sat in miserable silence. Benny was partly angry, partly confused.

His grandfather had made plans for a splendid, busy Christmas for the two girls. Was it selfish of Violet to be disappointed that it might not happen? Perhaps Rose would enjoy herself if she stayed, and perhaps Violet hadn't really become as independent as she had seemed tonight.

Benny thought about the first time he had realized that his grandfather could give him, and indeed was eager to give him, literally anything in the world he wanted. He knew there had been times they had needed money badly even when his father was alive. He could hardly forget the real want he and his mother had gone through and their struggles just to get to Missouri. How different their lives might have been if his father's parents had been a part of his life from the beginning.

He remembered what Jason had said to Benny after his first taste of Grandfather Richardson's hospitality. "I could get completely ruined by all this, Ben," Jason had sighed. "And would I love it."

His grandfather met them at the door, smiling. Violet and Rose both kissed him, and Violet gushed about what a wonderful time they'd had and how much she was looking forward to their planned celebrations. Rose murmured her thanks to Benny, looked up at him with eyes that wrenched at his heart, and went upstairs with her sister.

"This evening didn't quite go as you thought it might, eh, Grandson?" his grandfather asked pointedly. "Your wallflower Violet became belle of the ball, and Rose was the shrinking violet of the evening. I hope Rose wasn't really unhappy."

"Grandfather, I need to talk to you," Benny said. His grandfather led the way into his handsome study and they sat down by the fire on the big leather chairs. Benny told him everything Rose and Violet had said.

"This is my fault, Benjamin," his grandfather said sadly. "I am the one who's been selfish. When I first became a Christian, I wanted to spend every cent I had making you comfortable and happy. I told your mother I wanted to take you both back with me. Your grandmother would have made things difficult, of course, but I believed she would come around, and even become saved herself, in time. I never dreamed she would die six months later, still unrepentant.

"Your mother was opposed to my plan from the start. I thought she was only afraid of your grandmother. I told her I would set the two of you up in your own house. You needed never have seen your grandmother unless you chose. I would have bought your mother any house she chose. I would have given her anything she asked for, and I told her so. All I wanted was for you and her to be near me and for her to let me provide for you both.

"'You have suffered so much, my dear Abigail,'" I said to her. 'I am certain my son never in all his dreams of serving God intended for you to go on struggling. You are destitute. He left me because I opposed his service to God. But now I believe as you do, and I know that God has given me riches to spend helping His people. Who better to help than my own son's wife and child, whom I have neglected all these years because of my stubborn pride?"

"'Dear Father Richardson,' your mother said to me, 'I thank you for your generous offer. The hardships we have endured and are still enduring are the refiner's fire we must go through if we are to be fit for God's kingdom. My brother offered me a permanent home on his farm where I would have been comfortable and useful to Caroline and Tom. I have never been more convinced since I met your son that I will soon come to God's place for me. I will stay here until He moves me by forces I cannot resist. My resolve is as firm as prison walls.'

"You see, Benjamin, your mother knew even at that time that she would marry your Doctor Dad. How clearly she saw that only God could have brought the two of them together. No man would have ordered such outrageous events as those surrounding the meeting and courtship of your mother and Jeremy Carlisle. What a gift of God your mother is to him, and he to her. They have both known that refining fire, and it is hard for me to imagine that they would have need of more refining. Yet the Lord's ways are not my ways.

"Then I offered to set her up right there -- to build a house for her if need be, to give her servants instead of having her labor at farm work, to pay for your education -- my plans changed quickly enough, and yet they did not change at all, really. She pointed that out to me, that I was still taking you both out of the Lord's hands and trying to shield you from His gracious will.

"She did tell me that I might help a little from time to time, if you really had needs that could not be met any other way. I put money in an account which she might draw upon at her discretion, for you or for herself, or for whatever needs she saw and wanted to meet. From that fund came some of the money to repair Mrs. Salter's home and shop. She took from it for the church repairs and Doctor Shepherd's home, what your friends at the Mercantile could not, in all their gratitude and graciousness, afford to give. She always gave me a thorough accounting, though I never asked for it.

"The one thing I did without her permission, and which she still does not know of, was that I investigated the whole legal proceedings against our Jeremy. I thought his trial had been handled in cavalier fashion and his sentence was unjustly harsh. I read the fine statement Doctor Connors had made at his sentencing and thought that the judge had too little regarded it. So I set in motion certain legal proceedings which eventually brought about the reduction in his sentence and his release.

"Some would say I spent recklessly. I meant to ensure a quick resolution, and I succeeded. I certainly paid no bribes, nor was anything in the least shady or underhanded. Understand that your dad does not know of this either. I think he suspects Daniel Connors of doing it, but I fear even that extraordinary man's connections and resources would have failed him. I believed that God had given me all that money. I was not permitted any significant means of using it to help you or your mother directly. So I turned in a direction no one had forbidden me to go and spent to my heart's content. I considered it money well-spent.

"Dear me, I have said things I never intended to say, and have neglected the thing that started us talking. Since I have had you here, Benjamin, and since Jason and Violet and Rose have been in my care as well, I have forgotten your mother's fears of the destructive power of money. You have resisted my efforts to spoil you, as have Jason and Rose. I fear I have spoiled Violet, though. What can we do to begin to repair the damages? I will be guided by your advice, since it seems my only solution to life's problems is to throw money at them, and that cannot be the right thing to do here."

Benny swallowed hard. He had not expected his grandfather to let him make this decision. He was sure he knew the right thing to do, but it was going to be very hard to accept all the consequences that would surely come. He was afraid nobody was going to have as happy a Christmas as they might have had if he suggested what he believed had to be done.

"You and Violet and Rose should all come to Osage with me, Grandfather," Benny replied. "We should leave as soon as Rose's exams are over. Violet and Rose need to make some things right with their parents and be with them for Christmas. And you shouldn't take very much money with you. Stay with us, and let us show you how we celebrate Christmas. Maybe we shouldn't even have Trevor and James come with us, but I'll let you decide that. All of us have gotten to love things too much. Let's see if we can do without some of them, and remember the Lord and all He gave up for us to come to Earth and be born."

"It shall be just as you say, Benjamin," his grandfather nodded. "I shall arrange public conveyances to take us to Osage. Trevor and James may spend Christmas with their families. Violet and Rose shall be with theirs, and I with mine. We shall see if I can spend one Christmas without spending, eh? Do not fear, my dear grandson. I see your heart clearly, and I shall do my best to prevent you from having to bear all the burden of this change in our plans. We cannot deceive Violet about how it came about, I am sure, yet if the Lord is gracious to us we can still give her a Christmas to treasure, minus some of the earthly treasure."

## Chapter Nineteen --Bad Things, Blessings and Peace to All

Benny had helped his grandfather shop for some ordinary, warm travel clothing. Rose was forced to oversee the packing of Violet's things herself. Violet refused to acknowledge that she was really going until Grandfather Richardson took her gently but firmly by the arm and handed her down the steps and into the hired coach.

They had lost time waiting for Rose's exams to end. Rose's happy face when she announced that she had made top honors in all her classes made that easy enough to bear. Grandfather Richardson deliberately planned their travel arrangements to be as ordinary as possible, so they lost another two days over the more direct route the private carriage could have taken. Benny and Rose and Grandfather Richardson enjoyed the trip, though, playing travel games, pointing out the sights, and studying the amazing variety of people they saw as they traveled. Grandfather Richardson vowed he would travel like this from now on, wondering why he had shut himself off from so many interesting experiences.

Violet had scarcely spoken the whole trip. Grandfather Richardson had tried gentlemanliness, pleading, even a touch of bribery. They had passed through a town where signs proclaimed a local production of the Christmas Story was to be staged. He had offered to take them to see it, since they had to wait a few hours to make their next connection.

"I have missed a world-famous ballet's performance of the Nutcracker," Violet said. "Why would you think I would care to see a rustic nativity play?"

*****

Grandfather Richardson's resolve had faded faster and faster as the roads and the weather became worse, delay after delay set them back, and the modes of transport grew rougher. The last leg of their journey the only available coach broke down. They had to hire a farmer to take them on to Osage in his hay wagon. At dusk two days before Christmas the man dumped their baggage in the snow outside Benny's house and drove off without so much as a "Merry Christmas."

"This has been just the loveliest holiday I have ever had," Violet exclaimed sarcastically, hiking up her soaked skirts and grabbing a bag. "I can't wait for Christmas day. Surely something even more horrible can still happen."

Benny and Rose each took Grandfather Richardson by and arm. He hardly seemed able to walk. They were both afraid he was actually ill. They left the rest of the bags where they sat and followed Violet up the slushy front walk.

The front door burst open and out came Jeremy and Benny's mother. "Welcome! Welcome! Merry Christmas!" They shouted. Their happy faces sobered when they saw the bedraggled, weary group, and especially Violet's rigid stance apart from the others.

*****

Fifteen minutes later all the travelers were wrapped in heated blankets and sipping hot chocolate in front of the big front room fireplace. Jeremy had applied some of his special liniment to Grandfather Richardson's aching bones and Benny's mother had brought hot apple turnovers in for them.

"Madam, as delicious as I am sure this is," chattered Grandfather Richardson, hugging his pie to him, "right now I prefer to enjoy its warmth. Later I shall savor its goodness to my insides."

"Say, if you want warmth, here's a little heater for you!" Jeremy snatched up baby Sarah, who had been resting in Benny's arms, and arranged her in Grandfather

Richardson's lap. Benny's grandfather put his long, thin finger into the baby's firm grasp and smiled.

"Well, my Lord," Jeremy smiled, using his pet name that Benny's grandfather hated, "I guess you've learned why God gave you money. He knows you're not up to the kind of travel regular folks make do with. It's possible to get too carried away with trying to shed your materialism, you know."

Benny had explained all the circumstances of their change in Christmas plans in a letter sent home right after his talk with his grandfather. He had told his parents nothing about his grandfather's part in Jeremy's early release from prison, for he felt sure his grandfather would not wish it. Yet it was a knowledge he would always treasure.

"There are so many lessons to be learned," sighed Benny's grandfather. "Lessons God wants me to learn, I'm sure. I've hidden from them all my life. But perhaps I may indeed be trying too hard to learn them all at once, Doctor Carlisle."

"Take God's lessons as He sends them, my Lord," Jeremy advised. "They come fast enough and hard enough as it is, without us trying to hurry them along. I won't say we're not glad you came to share our home and our celebration, though. Nothing can ever make me say that. However you got here, we're so glad you came."

"So very, very glad," Benny's mother said. She kissed Grandfather Richardson's cheek. "Merry Christmas, dear Father-in-Law. God bless you for taking care of our boy."

"We've neglected the Misses Mitchell," Jeremy said. "Welcome to you too. Your parents were here earlier, and waited until it was time to milk the cows. We weren't sure how late you might be, so we suggested they might as well let you sleep here and come for you in the morning. I hope that was all right. We'll gladly take you over tonight if that's what you want. The roads are fair over that way. I'm sure we could get through."

"No!" Violet exploded. She had seated herself on the hearth and had been staring pointedly into the fire, withdrawn from the whole group since their arrival. "We'll stay here tonight, of course." Her eyes swept the room in panic. Then she blushed and looked back into the fire.

"You can't drive over to our farm in the dark with all this snow, Dr. Carlisle," Rose said quietly. "Don't even think of it. Thank you so much for your kind offer."

They feasted on warmed chicken and dumplings, Benny's favorite meal. He was sure by the quantity of the food that his mother had planned a big reunion dinner with the Mitchells and their daughters, but that had been spoiled by their coach mishap and late arrival. Benny wondered how that reunion would go when it finally came.

He tried to guess whether the Mitchells had come because they felt forced to collect their daughters, or if they had really been disappointed not to be able to take them home tonight. He was afraid to ask. Rose hoped so much for a warm welcome from her folks. He wasn't sure what Violet hoped for. She didn't act like she even wanted to see her parents. It was as if she wished they didn't exist.

*****

Benny rose early the next morning. He took up his old chore of feeding Black Switch and mucking out his stall. Carefully he gathered the two or three tiny eggs one of his mother's persistent chickens had hidden in the hay of the stallion's stall. More snow had fallen during the night, leaving a few inches' fresh coating on the roads. What if the Mitchells didn't come? Today was Christmas Eve. Benny knew Rose didn't want to spend another minute at their house. He determined to get her over to the Mitchell farm if he had to carry her in his arms the whole way. She was going to be the easy one to handle compared to Violet.

Benny came around to the front of the house with a snow shovel just as Rose came out the front door. She wore that rose-colored cloak his mother had made her to take to nursing school and a furry white hat that tied under her chin. She smiled at Benny, but he could tell she hadn't slept much.

“Violet really lit into me after we went to bed last night,” Rose sighed as she cradled the tiny warm eggs Benny handed her and sat on the porch step. Benny dropped the shovel and took a seat beside her. “I was ready to go out and sleep in the stable with dear old Black Switch. She said she hoped I was happy about all the trouble I had caused. I was to blame because you missed part of your holiday. All the things that went wrong on the trip were my fault. Your grandfather will probably get pneumonia because of me. I made our parents come all the way over here and wait for hours for nothing yesterday. She had a terrific earache from riding in that open wagon. Her boots were ruined. Her travel case was ruined. Her hair was ruined. And it was all my fault.”

“And then she rolled over and slept like a baby, I suppose,” Benny grunted.

“Exactly,” Rose laughed. “I stayed awake worrying if she was right.”

“If anybody’s to blame, it’s me,” Benny insisted. “This whole thing was my idea. I sure didn’t think things would go this badly.”

“It hasn’t been that bad, dear old Benny. It’s Vi who’s bad. We’ve all petted her like a princess and she thinks she ought to get to keep her castle always. We all share the blame for not making her suffer through her hard times. We’ve tried to spare her God’s will. We haven’t let her struggle.

“She’d tear my hair out if she heard me say this, but she’s had things so easy. Since her illness someone’s always been there to pick her up, and cheer her up, and kiss her skinned knees -- I’ve done it, you’ve done it, your mother and father have done it -- believe it or not our parents have done it, or tried to the best they knew how. All the boys at your school did it. We’ve half-killed her with kindness. This trip she found out again that life can be hard. And she hates it bitterly. She doesn’t know what to do now that her silken pillow’s been pulled out from under her and there’s no more saucer of cream. So she’s stuck out her claws.”

“She’d better pull them in quick,” Benny grumbled. “I’m sick of them.”

"I'm going to get some sugar for Black Switch," Rose said. "I'll take these dear little eggs into the kitchen and go see him. No, don't come please. I was hoping for a little quiet crying time when I came out, and I think I still need it, even though you've made me feel much better." She kissed him on the cheek again, just as she had in the library cupola. Then she was gone.

*****

Benny grabbed the shovel and attacked the new snow with fierce determination. Jeremy came out just as he finished the front walk and had started a path to the stable.

"You don't know how glad I am to have you home, my boy," Jeremy exclaimed. He hugged Benny and lifted him up off the ground. "Whew! That's getting too hard! Maybe it's been too long since I broke up rocks. Think I should volunteer just to get back in shape?"

"How's grandfather?" Benny asked.

"He'll be fine. I checked in on him a couple of times during the night. His breathing's good, he hasn't any cough or congestion, and no fever. He was just bone weary. You should have suggested a compromise on the roughing it, laddie."

"I should have done a lot of things differently," Benny sighed. "I tried to do something I thought would be best for everybody, and now everybody's miserable."

"Everybody's not miserable. Violet's miserable," Jeremy shrugged. "M'lord will recover. Rose will rebound once she's sure her parents still love her. And they do. Trust me on that. It would have broken your heart to see how disappointed they were when they left yesterday. It was all I could do to persuade them not to try to come back. Really, their roads were not good yesterday. I hope they can make it today without killing themselves. They love Violet, too. It's up to her to mend all the fences she's broken down."

"Rose said we made things too easy for her," Benny said.

"Rose is a very wise little woman," Jeremy smiled. "No doubt our good intentions were somewhat misguided. But the blame for Violet's present state of mind lies with Violet. And once Violet's all right again, perhaps Benjamin Richardson Carlisle will be better too. Let the shoveling go. I don't have to go out today unless there's an emergency. It's starting to snow again anyway. Your mother's got some of that absolutely wonderful German bread Mrs. Salter taught her to make. We've got ham and eggs and coffee and more stuff than an army could eat."

When they came into the kitchen, Benny saw that Rose must have had a very quick cry, because she was helping his mother fix breakfast. Sarah made delightful noises from her much larger cradle to Grandfather Richardson, who sat beside her in a wrapper warming his toes on the fender.

"Good morning, darling," Benny's mother called over the pop of frying ham and the clatter of skillets. "Violet said she's not feeling too well this morning. Rose is going to take a tray up--"

Benny took the tray Rose had prepared. "Let me do that, Rose," he offered. If Violet was going to stick her claws in somebody, there wasn't any need for it to be Rose again, he reasoned. Benny went up the stairs to the room the two girls had shared and knocked on the door. Then he chided himself. Violet probably couldn't hear him knocking. Should he just go in? Suddenly the door opened and Violet, her nightcap disheveled and her face gray, looked out.

"Rose? Oh! Benjamin!" she darted back into the room and dove under the covers. Benny chuckled about girls' modesty. Violet wore a thick fleecy nightgown that covered her from neck to ankle. It must have been her bare feet she was embarrassed about.

"Here's your breakfast, Violet," Benny said. He carried the tray to the bedside table. Violet stared at him, only her eyes visible. "Are you really sick, or are you just going to try to hide from life?"

"You don't understand what it's like," Violet pouted.

"I watched my father die in the middle of a street in Philadelphia when I was ten years old!" Benny shouted. "I crouched under a rock ledge in the pouring rain in a mudslide and wondered if my mother was lying there dead beside me. I had a bank robber stick a knife in my throat and say he was going to kill me. My best friend got chewed up by a cougar trying to save my life. How dare you tell me I don't understand what it's like to have bad things happen to me?"

Benny took Violet's plate, opened the window, and threw the food out. "If you want breakfast, you come down and eat it like the rest of us, with the rest of us. Nobody's going to baby you anymore, Violet. Not if I can help it. And if you say anything else to Rose about how anything you don't like is her fault, I'll do worse than toss your breakfast on the ground. You get dressed, you come downstairs, and you join my family and your sister. Your parents will be here soon. They love you and they missed you. May the Lord God of Heaven help you if you say one more word about missing the ballet."

*****

Benny stormed out with the tray, slamming the bedroom door. He stomped down the stairs and into the kitchen. Everyone sat at the table staring at him. Benny realized they must have heard his whole speech. Probably the rest of the town could have, too, if they'd had their windows open.

"Dad, I feel better already," Benny announced. He set Violet's place setting on the table and put away the tray.

"Uh ... I'm glad, Ben," Jeremy said cautiously.

"Will – Will Violet be joining us for breakfast?" His mother asked timidly.

"We'll wait five minutes. Then we'll start without her." Benny took out the pocket watch with the picture of his father inside. His grandfather had given it to him for Christmas the year before. They sat in silence while Benny watched the hands move slowly.

Four minutes later Violet rushed into the kitchen and slipped into the seat beside Rose. "I'm sorry," she said. "I'm sorry for everything. I'm so very sorry." She looked into each person's eyes, leaving Benny until last.

She looked at him the longest. Benny did not smile. He closed up his watch and put it in his pocket.

Jeremy prayed for the food. Benny ate heartily. He noticed that Violet ate almost nothing. She did not participate in the lively conversation around her. Benny stared at her until she looked up at him. He gave her a warning frown. Her face grew even paler and she grabbed more food to put on her plate.

"This is so good, Mrs. Carlisle," she exclaimed. "It's so kind of you to open your home to us. Rose, I'll help Mrs. Carlisle clean up after breakfast. Mr. Richardson, I do hope you didn't take a chill. Sarah has grown so much!"

Benny almost laughed out loud. He kept a straight face, though. Violet was trying. He gave her credit for that. She was a perfect angel all morning. She washed dishes, fussed over Benny's grandfather, changed Sarah, and shooed Rose away when she went up to tidy their room.

"Let me do that, Rose," Violet said. "You look so tired. Go and rest on the couch until Mother and Father come."

When the Mitchells arrived, Rose flew into their arms. They all cried. Mrs. Mitchell looked at Violet, who stood hesitating. Then she slowly signed, "I love you."

There was more crying after that. The Mitchells stayed for dinner and then took their girls home. After they had gone Benny's mother took him aside.

"You were very hard on Violet, darling," she said.

"Sometime God handles us with gentleness. Sometimes He's hard on us. We'd tried gentleness with Violet, and look how well that worked. So I decided to try something else."

*****

Benny went out with his dad, Sarah bundled up on the sled, to find a tree, a custom they had started when they had lived with Mrs. Salter. They came back with a handsome specimen, and Grandfather Richardson produced some family heirloom ornaments which had miraculously not been broken on the trip. They had to wait for the branches to settle before decorating it, but he also put four mysterious packages under the tree. They had already exchanged with Violet and Rose, and their gifts were set under the tree with the family presents.

That evening they sang Christmas carols, read the passages from Matthew and Luke about Jesus' birth, and prayed together. His mother brought hot apple cider with cinnamon and doughnuts to the fireside.

"Never have I had such a wonderful Christmas," Benny's grandfather sighed. "I always kept busy. I suppose I was afraid if I stopped I'd hear that Christ was the only thing that was really important. Today I haven't done a thing, and I know what the angels meant when they said 'Peace on Earth.' I have stopped and listened to God say, 'Here is My Son.'"

"And the best part is, it's not even Christmas day yet, Grandfather," Benny laughed.

## OTHER BOOKS AND PRODUCTS FROM FINDLEY FAMILY VIDEO PUBLICATIONS

All our books (including Historical Fiction, SciFi, contemporary relationships short stories, and an Archaeological Mystery serial) are linked on our website, Findley Family Video Publications, https://findleyfamilyvideopublications.com/

Our blog, *Elk Jerky for the Soul,* includes posts on current issues, excerpts from our fiction and nonfiction works, Bible teaching, travel and everyday observations, and more.

Visit our YouTube Channel https://www.youtube.com/channel/UCGhwNpU115ARMwgYwTIJBrA/featured. Book trailers, video excerpts, project teasers, and more.

Science, History, Literature, and biblical worldview studies are the focus of our book and video projects.

**Historical Fiction**

by Michael J. Findley
The Ephron the Hittite Series (Including boxed set of all titles)
*Ephron Son of Zohar*
*Tawananna Daughter of Zohar*
*Heth Son of Canaan Son of Ham, Noah*
*Shelometh Daughter of Yovov Wife of Ephron*
*Zita Son of Ephron and Shelometh*

Adult Romantic Suspense

by Mary C. Findley
*The Baron's Ring* (Book 1 in the Men of the Realmlands series)
*The Captain's Blade* (Book 2 in the Men of the Realmlands series)
*Send a White Rose*
*Chasing the Texas Wind*
*Carrie's Hired Hand* (novella)

**Young Adult Historical Adventure**

by Mary C. Findley
*Hope and the Knight of the Black Lion* (plus illustrated version)

the Benny and the Bank Robber Series
*Benny and the Bank Robber* (Plus homeschool editions for student and teacher with review and vocabulary)
*Doctor Dad*
*The Oregon Sentinel*
*Lines in Pleasant Places*

**Science Fiction**

by Michael J. Findley
*The Empire Saga* (all six of the following books in one volume)

*City on a Hill* (Novelette)
*Sojourner* (Short Story)
*Nehemiah LLC* (Full novel also available as standalone ebook, paperback, and hardcover versions)
*Empire One: Humiliation*
*Empire Two: Repentance*
*Empire Three: Sanctification*

**Steampunk**

by Sophronia Belle Lyon (pen name for Mary C. Findley)
The Alexander Legacy Steampunk Literary Tribute Series
*Book One: A Dodge, a Twist, and a Tobacconist* (including illustrated version)
*Book Two: The Pinocchio Factor*
*Book Three: The Most Dangerous Game*
*Book Four: Beware the Bustle*

## Fantasy/Allegory

by Mary C. Findley

*(Allegorical clockwork novella inspired by Little Red Riding Hood)*
*The Acolyte's Education*

(a Paranormal Urban Fantasy serial)
*His Sign: The Wait Is Over*
*His Sign 2: The Ezra Solution*

## Contemporary Fiction

by Mary C. Findley

(Romantic Suspense Novella)
*Fall On Your Knees*

Relationships Short Stories
*Fifty Shades of Faithful*
*Fifty Shades of Faithful 2: In Living Color*

Serial Archaeological Mystery (including boxed set of all titles)
*The Great Thirst Part One: Prepared*
*The Great Thirst Part Two: Purified*
*The Great Thirst Part Three: Pursued*
*The Great Thirst Part Four: Persecuted*
*The Great Thirst Part Five: Persevering*
*The Great Thirst Part Six: Protected*
*The Great Thirst Part Seven: Prevailing*

Murder Mystery
*Mapped Out Murders*

## Nonfiction

by Mary C. Findley

*Write for the King of Glory, 2nd Edition* (updated, with tips on indie writing and publishing)

by Michael J. and Mary C. Findley

*The Good, the Bad, and the Ugly: A Readers' and Writers' Guide for Believers*

*Biblical Studies* (Teacher and student editions plus excerpts in OT and NT Manuscript History)

*Antidisestablishmentarianism* (illustrated and plain versions)

(serial versions, illustrated and plain)
*What Is an Establishment of Religion?*
*What Is Secular Humanism?*
*What Is Science?*
*What Are the Results of the Establishment of Secular Humanism?*

The Conflict of the Ages series (All have teacher and student editions plus one combined teacher edition for 1-3)

*I. The Scientific History of Origins*
*II. The Origin of Evil in the World that Was*
*III. They Deliberately Forgot: The Flood and the Ice Age*
*IV. Ice Age Civilizations*
*V. The Ancient World*

Short Recaps of longer nonfiction works
*Disestablish: An Overview from Creation to the Ice Age*
*Under the Sun: The Truth about History from the Beginning*

Christian Books in Multiple Genres. Join Christian Indie Author ~ Readers Group on Facebook.
https://www.facebook.com/groups/291215317668431/

www.ingramcontent.com/pod-product-compliance
Lightning Source LLC
LaVergne TN
LVHW050536160826
845677LV00011B/2056

*9798227187741*